Born in Northern Ireland in 1931, Bob Shaw is one of the best and most ingenious of British SF authors. Having worked as an engineer, in aircraft design and industrial PR and journalism, Shaw has been a full-time author since 1975, turning out highly professional, consistently entertaining work.

By the same author

BOB SHAW

# The Ceres Solution

**GRANADA**
London Toronto Sydney New York

Published by Granada Publishing Limited in 1983

ISBN 0 586 05652 1

First published in Great Britain by
Victor Gollancz Ltd 1981
Copyright © Bob Shaw 1981

Granada Publishing Limited
Frogmore, St Albans, Herts AL2 2NF
and
36 Golden Square, London W1R 4AH
515 Madison Avenue, New York, NY 10022, USA
117 York Street, Sydney, NSW 2000, Australia
60 International Blvd, Rexdale, Ontario, R9W 6J2, Canada
61 Beach Road, Auckland, New Zealand

Printed and bound in Great Britain by
Cox and Wyman Ltd, Reading
Set in Times

Granada ®
Granada Publishing ®

# Prologue

*Observe!*
*The whole universe lies before us – a billion galaxies frozen in flight.*
*The focus narrows.*
*Now we see a single galaxy, beautiful but unremarkable, a conglomerate of a billion burning orbs. Now we observe a single sun; now a planet; a continent; a sunlit hillside. A creature moves on that hillside – slowly, painfully, without grace.*
*He is a member of his planet's dominant species, but immature and sickly. Name: Denny Hargate. Age: twelve years. Illness: multiple peripheral neuritis. Prognosis: not good.*
*Is this, we may ask, a random sampling? What reason could there be for singling out this insignificant being whose world-line is destined to be so pitifully brief?*
*What reason indeed?*
*We must decide for ourselves . . .*

The handgrips of the duralloy crutches had become buttery with sweat.

Denny paused for a moment, wondering if it really had been a mistake for him to try reaching Cotter's Edge alone, and with his own silence the sloping meadow seemed to come to life. The rustling of the dry grasses, endlessly multiplied, gave him the sense of being adrift on a murmurous ocean. He closed his eyes, rejecting the surrounding multi-hued brilliance, and reviewed the morning's inconclusive skirmish with his mother.

Twice he had nailed her, with neat verbal sniper-shots which would have silenced anybody but his mother for days. During the night there had again been dreams of being able to walk and run, and he had allowed himself to be completely deceived by them, with the result that the awakening had been very bad. The illusions and memories had been persuasive, though, and when he rose and saw the brightness of the day he had made a genuine attempt to stand. Perhaps, on such a morning, the universe would have relented a little. He had commanded his thighs to stiffen and lock the knee joints into useful rigidity, but there had been an immediate sagging when he had attempted to move forward without the crutches. Obviously the universe was not going to play ball.

'How are you this morning, Denny?' his mother had said. Her voice, as always, had been light and casual, masking the fact that she was really asking if a miracle had occurred.

'Better than I would have thought possible,' he had replied, smiling and waited until a naïve hope appeared in her eyes. 'I do believe my dandruff is going to clear up altogether.'

Denny snorted with triumph as he recalled the way in which Kay Hargate had turned away from him, her face wan and introspective. Later, when he was preparing to go out, she had watched him struggling into his bomber jacket and had asked if he would not be wearing an overcoat. 'I'm going to wear my overcoat,' he had said, 'but I always find it's best to put it on last. Any other arrangement looks plain silly.' Again, she had reacted like someone struck in the face and he had wondered if it would mean an end to the hovering nearby, the continual solicitude and damned stupid questions, but the respite had lasted only a minute. She had even tried adjusting his collar as he headed for the door, and that had been the final annoyance which had decided him that he was going all the way out to Cotter's Edge, to visit the secret place.

As he stood swaying slightly in the centre of the pasture the decision began to appear childish. Getting out of the Greenways housing development and across the near-derelict interstate highway had been easy enough, but the strip of woodland for which he was aiming was more than a kilometre from the road and it was uphill most of the way. The effort needed for driving the crutches through the long grass had tired him out. Perspiring freely beneath his layers of clothing, Denny opened his eyes and fixed his gaze on the trees which plumed the crest ahead. They were etched in all the optimistic colours of April, picked out against a wind-busy sky in which there was a constant shifting of sunlight and rearrangement of white and blue, light grey and dark grey. It had been on a similar morning, two years earlier, that he had discovered the secret place and now he could feel it calling to him.

Denny tightened his lips and began moving forward again. Ten minutes later he was entering a stand of field maples. The ground here was covered with dry leaves and he found he could progress with comparative ease. He skirted a rocky outcrop which marked the crest of the ridge and began the gradual descent towards the concealed clearing which was his destination. The air already seemed alive, possessed of a tingling sense of imminence.

Denny had been in the literate stream at Carsewell Junior and some of the classic children's books he had read had acquainted him with the notion that there might be 'special places', secluded natural nooks which could be recognized only by young people and towards which they felt a strange attraction. He had never expected to find one in the real world, however, and might have doubted his instincts had not the other ten-year-olds in the party been similarly affected. The four of them, two boys and two girls, had sat in the brown silence of the clearing for the best part of an hour, experiencing a rapport which was profound, vaguely sexual and – as far as Denny was concerned – deeply thrilling. But later, when he had tried referring to the incident, the others had joshed him with unexpected fierceness. It was as though they had all taken part in something shameful, something which was best forgotten.

Social pressures exerted by his friends had prevented him returning to the clearing as often as he would have liked; then had come his illness and the drastic reduction of his mobility, but he had made a number of visits to the secret place and had always been rewarded, though not necessarily in ways he understood. There was a silence there that was somehow articulate, a solitude without loneliness. The outside world was reduced in importance until it was no more than a bright diorama, partially glimpsed through the screens of vegetation, and that was one of the secret place's principal charms. Denny liked the idea that life was merely a shadow-play, that he was not going to miss out on much.

He carefully negotiated an area where roots patterned the ground like upraised veins, ducked his head to enter the clearing proper, and came to a halt – numb with shock – as he saw the auburn-haired young woman who stood there. She spun to face him, apparently as surprised as he, and for a long ringing moment he was transfixed. The girl appeared to be about twenty, was dressed in a simple bottle-green jacket and knee-length skirt, and was flawlessly beautiful in a way that Denny had not known was possible for any human being. He experienced a pang of reverence, the only immediate reaction of which he was capable, then saw the change in her eyes as she assimilated the fact that he was crippled. The sequence was a familiar one to him – concern, pity, diplomatic cheeriness

– and he hated it all the more because she was unlike any girl he had ever seen and everything about their meeting should have been different.

'Hello,' she said in a low and unaccented voice. 'Lovely morning, isn't it?'

Denny turned his head, insolently, assessing the morning like a prospective buyer. 'It's all right.'

'You don't seem too sure about that.' She smiled a challenge, and merely looking at her filled Denny with a sense of loss. Life was not a shadow-play, after all.

'I have to go now,' he muttered, beginning his laborious turning manoeuvre.

The girl started forward. 'You don't have to leave on my account.'

Denny gave her what he hoped was an obscene leer. 'You don't know what I came here to do.'

Then he was fleeing, lurching away through the trees, gasping with the effort needed to move quickly and keep his balance on the uneven ground. *That was a good one*, he thought vindictively. *You don't know what I came here to do. Bet that shook her up a bit. When are they going to learn that I'm not a . . .?* The tip of his left crutch slid off the rounded surface of a root and skidded sideways before jamming beneath another. Pain encircled his ribcage. He teetered wildly, realized he was fighting a losing battle and went into a semi-controlled fall which stretched him face downwards on the blanket of dead leaves. The disturbed humus smelled of mushrooms.

'Please,' he whispered, 'don't let her know.'

He lay quite still and listened for any sound which could indicate that the girl had seen or heard his fall and was coming to investigate, but the woodland remained quiet. The silence seemed to intensify with each passing second, and for the first time since the start of the odd little encounter Denny found himself thinking rationally. Surprise and resentment over the girl's presence in his sanctum had diverted his thoughts from the question of why she had been there at all. He was certain she did not live in Carsewell, but even if she happened to be a visiting relative of the Reigh family, owners of most of the surrounding farmland, what had drawn her to that particular spot in the wood? Was it possible that although grown up she felt an affinity for the place? Perhaps she had been there as a child, and *he* was the intruder . . .

Denny gathered the crutches closer to him and raised himself up on them, thankful for the strength of his arms. He brushed some dried leaves off his clothing and looked in the direction of the clearing, his face warming with embarrassment as he recalled the way he had spoken to the girl. In addition to being rude he had been utterly stupid – she had been friendly, and by making the proper responses he could have extended, perhaps indefinitely, the privilege of looking at her. The sensible thing to do would be to go back and apologize, but that called for social graces he had not yet acquired. Besides, could any apology be adequate, and would she even be interested in hearing it?

He stood for a time, frowning, his body and the two duralloy supports in delicate equilibrium, then went slowly in the direction of the clearing. Doubts about what he was proposing to do caused him to move with unconscious stealth. He paused, disturbed by a sudden voyeuristic thrill, as he reached a vantage point from which he could see most of the secret place. There was the spring which in wet weather became the source of a noisy brook, there was the mossy limestone shelf which formed a natural armchair, there was the overturned stump whose roots were at exactly the right height to double as the control levers in a nuclear submarine or spaceship. And, in the centre of it all, there stood the girl, the incredibly beautiful girl.

Her arms were by her sides and her face was tilted up to the light, eyes closed as though in prayer. The vertical illumination emphasized her breasts, created a triangular shadow at the juncture of torso and thighs. Denny's cheeks and forehead tingled hotly as, without warning, the girl's sheer sexual allure began to flow over him. He held his breath, fascinated and at the same time wildly afraid, as the conviction stole over him that he was about to witness something secret and sacred, something he had no right to see and which was therefore totally irresistible.

The girl raised her right hand and traced a complex curve in the air. And vanished.

The disappearance was instantaneous, complete and magical. Denny, whose gaze had not wavered, gave a tremulous sigh. He waited in the same place for more than an hour, not daring to advance into the clearing, and only when the strain on his shoulders and legs became unbearable did he accept that he would not see the girl return. Not on that day, anyway, and perhaps never. He turned his back on the place and – with frequent stops for rest – made his way out of the wood and down the sloping pasture towards the buckled and weed-infested strip of the old interstate highway. His progress became slower and more painful as the minutes passed, and by the time he reached the Greenways security fence his narrow face was pale with exhaustion.

The gate opened in response to the coded signal broadcast by his identity disc. Denny passed through, grateful to be back on firm pavement, and turned left to go along the perimeter path to J Precinct. It would have been quicker to head straight through the shopping area, but his toes were now dragging noisily on the ground with each forward swing and he knew he would have attracted more attention than usual. When he turned the corner in J-12 he

11

saw that his mother was waiting at the door of their ground-level apartment. She was dressed for going out – it was the day of her smoke-sculpture class in the community centre – and he realized she had waited until he returned home. He squared his shoulders and did his best to approach her in his normal manner, but Kay Hargate was not deceived.

'Oh, *Denny!*' Her eyes, sombre with concern, traced a zigzag course down his body as she moved back to let him enter the apartment. 'Where have you *been*?'

'Just out. Nowhere special.' He tried unsuccessfully to take evasive action as she reached out and plucked something from his coat. It was a dead leaf, looking like a scrap of dark leather.

'Not Cotter's Edge,' she said. 'You haven't been away up there again.'

'If you say I haven't – then I haven't.' Denny lowered himself into an armchair and lay back, yielding to his fatigue. He closed his eyes and allowed himself to float in a sea of after-images.

'Is everything all right?' his mother asked, and a troubled quality in her voice told him she had once again performed her own kind of miracle, one which was almost as awe-inspiring as being able to vanish into nothingness. 'Did anything happen while you were out there?'

He briefly considered telling the truth, weighed up the consequences, then decided that life was difficult enough as it was. 'Happen?' He injected a note of mild surprise into his voice. 'What could have happened?'

# CHAPTER 1

Gretana ty Iltha had devised a technique for dealing with mirrors.

She knew the location of every reflective surface in her own home, in her friends' houses and in her place of work, and before glancing at them she invariably made certain preparations. First, and most importantly, she drew in her upper lip to help disguise the fact that it was easily as full as the lower. The mouth was a principal focal point in the Mollanian culture of perfection, and for that reason its proportions had to conform very closely to those of the Lucent Ideal. Gretana also made sure that she only saw herself in three-quarter profile, a flattering angle which minimized the excessive flare of her nostrils and the projection of her ears. Finally, she always widened her eyes as far as was possible without giving herself an expression of perpetual astonishment.

With all those precautions taken she could look into a mirror and see an image which, although far from beautiful, did not necessarily inspire a pang of pity or self-revulsion. Some of her other physical flaws – being a little below ideal height and having an unacceptable shade of pigment in her hair – were more intractable, but she had come to accept that nothing could be done about them. There had been times in her fourth and fifth decades, just at the beginning of womanhood, when she had briefly considered rebelling against her active upbringing. As a member of the passive classes she would have been free to increase her height by wearing built-up shoes and to modify her whole appearance through the use of cosmetics, but – and her commonsense had always asserted itself in good time – the sacrifices would have been too great. A counterfeit beauty, a spurious conformity to the Lucent Ideal, would have been poor compensation for loss of the right to serve.

Gretana reminded herself of that fact as she performed the unavoidable morning chore of actually facing the mirror in her sleeproom and arranging her hair.

She finished pinning her hair into place, then put on a white one-piece suit which was decorated at the collar and cuffs with tablets of green-veined gold imported from the tenth planet. The garment was one of her favourites and when she surveyed the overall effect, having first adopted her mirror-watching attitude and drawn herself up to her full height, she judged it quite passable. No man would give her a second glance, of course, but other women should appreciate the effort she had made.

She left the sleeproom and tuned the windows of the circular main lounge to a degree of transparency which admitted the full force of the morning light. The bright panorama which sprang into being clamoured at her senses. She paused momentarily to look at the view which might have been contrived as a sampler of contrasting geographical features. To her left the opposite slope of the valley, powdered with many shades of green, shelved down in a series of chalk-rimmed steps to the Karvinso River which opened to form a triple-fingered delta before disgorging into the salty waters of Karlth Bay. The cliffs forming the northern rim of the bay grew steeper as they receded into the distance, gradually merging with a mountain range which provided a hazy blue back-drop for a chain of hump-backed islands.

It was high summer on Mollan and even at that early hour the sky had a purple tint which presaged a day of continuous sunshine and warmth. Gretana gazed at the familiar scene for some time, eyes intent, wondering what was different or missing, and was on the point of turning away when there came a sudden insight into her own mood and its causes. Everything beyond her window was exactly as it had always been – the lack was in herself. There had been no pleasurable response.

Early morning had always been the best part of the day, a tranquil period – before there had been too many reminders of her problems – in which she felt uplifted by the mere sight of the white and pastel-coloured buildings of the city, random scatterings of flower petals, glimmering all through the middle distance, on the triangular islands of the delta and along the valley sides. She had been able to feel at one with family, community and race, reassured that all the centuries lying ahead of her would be good and meaningful. This morning, however, she had felt . . . *nothing*.

She went into the kitchen and prepared a breakfast of vegetable protein and fruit, the former in the shape of a savoury cake garnished with herbs. From the rear of the house she could glimpse among the trees the other dwellings of the Iltha family, including one which was being built for eventual occupation by her, as yet unborn, nephew or niece. Her father and mother were doing the work themselves, using a stalagmite technique in which mineral-laden water was directed along narrow channels to accrete very strong walls over a period of several centuries. By changing the mineral content of the water once or twice a decade it was possible to produce a structural material which was as beautifully striated as a gemstone, but the principal attraction of such a house was that it was extremely durable – some had been known to last a full Mollanian lifespan.

Annoyed at her apparent inability to keep her thoughts on a positive level, Gretana disposed of the remains of the breakfast, cleaned her teeth and decided to leave the house even though she was perhaps an hour earlier than usual for work. She went outside and looked all about her, breathing deeply. The air was warmer than she had expected, heavy with the smell of foliage and freshly cut grass. Trying to choose between going directly to the hostel or taking some time in the coolness of the mountains, she approached the nearest of the white-flowered shrubs in her garden and made a bird-like whistling sound. The flowers, deceived as always, chirped and twittered back at her.

Gretana made a sudden decision to visit the mountains.

Walking quickly to the path, which itself was a tributary to one of the larger paths winding through the Iltha estate, she turned right in the direction of the minor node used for local travel. In less than a minute she was within sight of the circular paved area, focal point of many paths, which marked the position of the node. Physical indicators of that kind were not necessary for recognition purposes – Mollanians could easily skry junctures in influence lines – but for aesthetic reasons it was the custom to have an elaborately tiled plaza at much-used nodal points.

It was early in the day for anyone to be up and about, and she was surprised on actually reaching the node to see two small boys standing near the mosaic star marking its centre. She recognized them both. One was Stedran tye Lthanne from the neighbouring family and the other was Clath tye Liv from a newer estate further up the hill. They smiled as she drew near and Gretana smiled in return.

'Fair seasons, boys,' she said. 'What brings you out so early? Can't you sleep?'

'We like being out early,' Stedran replied. He was standing with his hands behind his back and the face he turned up to hers was absurdly perfect.

'So do I.' The sheer beauty of the boy was painful to

16

Gretana, a reminder of all that was denied to her. 'It's the best time.'

Gripped by a sudden yearning to be alone on the cold high slopes of Mount Reckann, she advanced to the middle of the circular mosaic. She cleared her mind of all extraneous thoughts and images, and began to conjure on a mental screen the elements of her destination's spatial address. As the mountain was on the planet of Mollan, actually on the same continent as Gretana's home city of Karlth, the key equation was a relatively uncomplicated one – a modified quartic – and she was able to assemble it in a fraction of a second. At that point it was not sufficiently precise to effect a spatial transfer. Gretana raised her right hand and began to trace a curve in the air, a three-dimensional mnemonic containing the numeric coefficients of the transfer equation, and she began to feel a subtle and indescribable *loosening* – the sensation that always accompanied Mollanian internodal travel.

Her eyes were partially closed with the effort of concentration, but she was still in visual contact with her surroundings. All at once she became aware that Stedran was watching her intently, and that his smile had become a broad grin. He had brought an object from behind his back and was running his fingers over it. Gretana realized, too late, that it was a variable mathematical model of the type used in teaching children the techniques of internodal travel. The very presence of the model in her vicinity, plus the fact that it was acting as an enormously powerful amplifier for Stedran's thoughts, shattered her fragile mental imagery. She tried to withdraw from the transfer mode, to blank out her mind, but there was no time. The instantaneous leap took place.

Gretana cried aloud with shock as she found herself standing knee-deep in cold water.

Loose sand was shifting beneath her feet, making her

17

struggle to retain her balance while taking stock of her surroundings. She was in the sea, about forty paces from the water's edge. Scimitars of white beach curved away on each side, both surmounted by near-identical headlands upon which were perched domed belvederes built of pink stone. Gretana gasped as a swelling wave surged around her from behind, chilling the backs of her thighs, forcing her to take a step forward.

'The little *monster!*' She gave a shaky laugh which was inspired by a blend of anger and admiration for the expert way in which the child had shunted her to a destination of his own choosing. In all probability he had done so in full awareness that the target node was at that moment in tidal shallows. She shook her fist at the empty air, then came the realization that Stedran's prank had misfired.

Had the deserted bay been unfamiliar to Gretana she would have been forced to wade ashore and either arrange cursive transportation back to Karlth or obtain information about a suitable nodal point in the area which would enable her to transfer home. Either way a considerable time would have elapsed, but the boy could not have anticipated Gretana's knowing exactly where she was. Mollan had no moon and, as was the case with any planet where only the weak solar tides reigned, broad sandy beaches were comparatively rare. That had provided the first clue to her location, and the twin headlands with their distinctive gazebos had confirmed that she was in Ulver Bay, some six hundred miles to the north of Karlth. She had been there many times as a child and, furthermore, could remember the precise reciprocal address of the node upon which she had been standing a few seconds earlier. The mischievous youngsters, Stedran and Clath, had no way of knowing it, but they were due for a surprise.

18

Gretana cupped her left hand and scooped up some sea water. She then gathered her thoughts, half-closed her eyes and sculpted a unique quartic curvature in the air.

The transfer occurred.

So rapid had her recovery been that Stedran was still facing the circular mosaic when Gretana materialized at its central point. She darted forward with a mock-ferocious snarl and sent droplets of cold water spraying into his face. The reaction was not what she had expected. Stedran, his mouth contorted with fear, dropped his model – causing it to collapse into the neutral configuration – and at the same time sprang backwards so violently that he fell. Clath fled immediately, leaving his friend scrabbling frantically on the pavement. The white-rimmed terror in Stedran's eyes as he stared up at her swamped Gretana with remorse. She knelt and tried to help him to his feet, but he beat her hands away with a ferocity that took her by surprise.

'It's all right, Stedran,' she said, trying to soothe him. 'I was only . . .'

'Don't touch me!' He whimpered like a small animal, rolling away from her as he got to his feet.

Gretana shook her head and smiled a reassurance. 'I'm not going to hurt you.'

'You better not try!' The boy seemed to feel safer standing and as he recovered from shock his panic turned to anger. Watching the change take place in him, Gretana felt a cool premonition about what was coming next and did her best to forestall it by picking up the fallen model and offering it at arm's length.

'Here's your trainer, Stedran,' she said in a soft voice, despising herself for wheedling but unable to do otherwise. 'Don't you want it?'

'Not after you touched it.' Stedran's eyes widened with gratification as he saw the effect of his words. Still backing away from her he funnelled his hands around his mouth.

'Ugly,' he shouted. 'Ugly, ugly, UGLY!'

Gretana turned, throwing the model aside, and ran. She kept on running, plunging down the hillside through widening avenues, even when the sound of the boy's repetitive chant was lost behind her, even when salted froth had begun to gather in the back of her mouth. *Now you're being stupid!* The inner voice was angry, but coldly clinical. *You have a long time to go, Gretana ty Iltha. Are you planning to fly away like a scissor-wing each time some brat says aloud what everybody else is thinking? If that's the case, you're going to cover a lot of ground, Gretana ty Iltha. Better wear lightweight shoes in future. And an exercise mask . . .*

She came to a foot-slapping halt, suddenly aware of being near a populated area surrounding a fairly major node which had spatial links with several other cities. Some vehicular traffic was on the move in a freight arterial a short distance ahead of her, and many roofs of dwellings and commercial buildings were visible among the surrounding banks of white-flowered foliage. She could not see any people in the immediate vicinity, but it was possible that others had already observed her actions and had been amused or intrigued by them – it was rare for anyone to run without donning an exercise mask to protect the face in the event of a fall. Glancing selfconsciously from side to side, Gretana began walking in the direction of the hostel. The violent exercise had shed all the sea water from her clothing, but it would take some time before her breathing and complexion returned to normal, and she had no wish to arrive at work looking flustered. She decided to complete the whole journey at a gentle stroll, thinking cool and untroubled thoughts, regaining her composure.

*Lucent Ideal, Twelfth Rubric: Charm lies in the animation of the features, beauty in their immobility.*

In spite of her resolve and attempted concentration on

the Twelfth Rubric, she found herself reliving the point-less incident and wishing she had handled it differently, thus avoiding the pain and humiliation that was throbbing behind her eyes. There was no question as to why Stedran had wanted to hurt her – she had startled him, robbed him of his dignity – but how had he known what to say? A child barely out of his first decade could not have studied the Twenty Rubrics, a fact which seemed to indicate that there was nothing arbitrary about them. There had to be an ideal configuration of the features which was as right and universal as the sphericity of the planets, and any serious deviation from it was an affront to nature. Gretana unconsciously drew in her upper lip as she tried to remember the first occasion on which she had looked at herself in a mirror and had known . . .

Doctor Kallid was already waiting in the spacious atrium when Gretana entered. He was a blue-eyed man with ice-smooth blond hair and a casual mode of dress which belied his position of authority in the hostel. Gretana knew him to be entering his ninth century, but – largely because of his unfailing enthusiasm for his work – she tended to think of him as being only slightly older than herself.

'Fair seasons, Doctor,' she greeted him. 'Am I late?'

'According to yesterday's schedule, no – according to today's, a little.' Kallid made no move towards the inner geriatric wards, which Gretana had been expecting to tour for the first time as part of her training. 'Your programme has been altered, I'm afraid.'

'I wasn't notified.'

'Neither was I,' Kallid said, showing some annoyance. 'We're desperately short of staff here, and Vekrynn knows it, but he puts his own requirements first – and it isn't fair to you.'

'I still don't . . .' Gretana paused, frowning. 'Vekrynn? I know of only one man with that name.'

Kallid nodded, his face now carefully impassive. 'It's the same one – Vekrynn tye Orltha, doyen of the Warden class.'

'But what possible interest could Warden Vekrynn have in me?'

'It appears that he is short of staff, too. Very short.' The doctor spoke in a casual manner which made the content of his words all the more shocking. 'I think he wants you to go to Earth.'

# CHAPTER 2

*I'll never go to Earth.*

The thought sustained and comforted Gretana as she waited in Vekrynn's pearl-walled reception chamber, but it had the unfortunate effect of adding to her nervousness.

Warden Vekrynn's visits to Karlth were very short and took place only a few times a century. That fact, combined with his absolute pre-eminence in Mollanian society, meant that few citizens could aspire even to set eyes on him, and far less had any hope of meeting him in person. His presence, however brief, at one of the glittering parties on Silver Island or Mount Elux was enough to elevate the fortunate host and hostess to a new pinnacle of respect. As a natural consequence of her physical short-comings, Gretana was unable to attend any of the more prestigious social functions and, had she given the matter any thought, would have estimated her chances of ever being under the same roof as Vekrynn tye Orltha at less than one in a million.

Now she – of all people – was about to have a private

audience with him, and furthermore was planning to give a flat refusal to any request he might make of her. The knowledge of what she had to do made Gretana both queasy and restless. She roamed about the large apartment inspecting its sparse furniture and ornaments while she strove to prepare herself for what was to come. In retrospect, the morning's tour of the inner wards seemed a relatively minor incident and she longed to be back among the familiar surroundings and circumstances of the hostel.

She was returning to her chair for perhaps the tenth time when a courtesy bell chimed to announce that Warden Vekrynn was about to enter the room. Gretana whirled to face the door, standing as tall as possible while at the same time drawing in her upper lip, widening her eyes and turning her head a little to one side. Observing the little ritual, so essential to her self-esteem, added to the tensions that were racking her body and as the door opened she felt the blood tingle painfully away from her face.

Gretana's first impression of Vekrynn as he entered the reception chamber was that he resembled a magnificent statue cast in various shades of gold. The darkest metal of all was represented by the tanned skin of his face and hands, a yellow gold had been used for the thick cap of closely waved hair, and something close to platinum for his embroidered tunic and trousers. His eyes, which were deep-set and alert, were cabochons of brown quartz radially needled with gold. Gretana knew him to be of great age – he had held the Wardenship of Earth for some thousands of years – but nothing in his appearance or manner revealed the fact. There had been no vertical compression of the body due to the millennial action of gravity, nor did his expression betray any of the morbid languor which sometimes troubled the faces of very old actives. Indeed it was his expression which had the most

23

profound effect on Gretana, for his eyes regarded her with warmth and interest, and in doing so held perfectly steady. There had been no flicker to one side followed by that forced gleam of geniality which meant to disguise pity or repugnance. She felt a positive and vital response to his presence, a reaction which was enhanced through being completely unexpected. *I'll never go to Earth*, she reminded herself.

'Fair seasons, Gretana ty Iltha.' Vekrynn said in a resonant baritone, surprising her by using the commonplace form of greeting.

'Fair seasons, Warden.' She cleared her throat, resisting the temptation to try repeating the words more clearly.

'It was good of you to come to see me. Under normal circumstances I would have preferred to call at your home, but I am very short of time.'

'I understand.' Gretana had never heard anybody but the most pretentious of her acquaintances claim to be pressed for time, but in this case she accepted it as a statement of fact.

'If you would care to sit down we can talk in comfort,' Vekrynn said. 'I'd like you to relax because I can see that Doctor Kallid has already told you why you are here.'

'I'm sure he was only . . .'

'It's perfectly all right.' He silenced her by raising one hand. 'He has done that sort of thing before, and in a way I'm quite glad because the very fact that you came here at all tells me a lot about your character. You could have gone into hiding.' Vekrynn's smile was perfect, with a hint of ruefulness which suggested he was pleased to have met an intelligent person who could understand his problems.

Gretana was flattered and simultaneously made wary. 'I

couldn't go to Earth,' she said, more forcefully than she had intended and immediately felt embarrassed. 'I'm sorry, but I . . .'

'Your feelings are perfectly natural, perfectly understandable, and I appreciate your honesty.' Vekrynn again gestured towards a chair and this time waited until Gretana had sat down. 'Now you're asking yourself why, as you have made your position so clear, I want to prolong the discussion – especially as I have pretensions of being a very busy man with all the problems of the universe on his shoulders.'

Gretana eyed the Warden in silence and then, realizing she had made the mistake of facing him directly, turned her head a little. The move did nothing to lessen the sheer impact of his physical presence.

'All right, Gretana! I'm going to be totally honest and admit that I intend to persuade you, before you leave this room, to join my personal staff and work for me on Earth for a short period of, say, five or six decades. Do you think I'll succeed?'

'No.' She was persuaded to smile. 'I don't see how you could.'

'In that case you can be generous. You can afford to relax and hear what I have to say.' Vekrynn walked to one of the high windows and stood looking out, the intensified light glowing like a nimbus around his hair. 'How old are you, Gretana?'

'I'm in my sixth decade.'

'Your life has hardly started, and if I'm not mistaken that ring on your left hand is a life recorder. Why do you wear it?'

Gretana was taken aback. 'I . . . It's the way.'

'Oh, I know all actives use them. They are part of the activist philosophy, a means of preserving a coherent memory and a single identity throughout a greatly extended lifespan – but how many entries have you made in your recorder in the past year?'

'I don't know,' Gretana replied, trying to anticipate the point. 'Several.'

'Several! And no doubt you'll make several more next year, and in the following year, and in the year after that.'

'I expect so.'

'Why?' Vekrynn turned to look at her, his face hidden in a corona of reflected sunlight, and his voice was both sad and compassionate. 'Why will you do that, Gretana?'

'I don't understand.'

'It's so that you won't forget, so that you won't lose those years from your memory, from your *life*. Don't you see what that means? What you are saying is that you are not really alive.' Vekrynn took one step away from the window, changing the light patterns on the nacreous walls of the room. 'This is only your sixth decade – what's it going to be like in your sixth century? Will you be like all the others? Growing coral sculptures and tree sculptures for excitement, and filling your recorder with notes of their progress?'

Echoes of her own early thoughts brought a return of the smothering sensation Gretana had experienced.

'I'm offering you the gift of your own life,' Vekrynn said. 'Go to Earth for me and you'll have material for a thousand entries a year in your recorder, but you won't need to make them, because you can remember what happens to you when you're really alive.'

Gretana drew a quavering breath. 'I couldn't go to Earth.'

'Are you afraid?'

'Yes.'

'Good! I'd have no use for you if you didn't have sense enough to be afraid.' Vekrynn moved closer to her. 'Is it the people, or the presence of the . . .?'

'It's the people.' Gretana pressed the back of a hand to her lips. 'I couldn't face them.'

'Doctor Kallid says you could.'

Gretana strove to marshal her thoughts, to present an ordered and logical case which would bring the interview to a speedy conclusion. 'It isn't the physical aspect of the people,' she said quietly. 'I know I could become reconciled to the presence of disease and deformity, perhaps even death. It isn't even the fact that they only live for eleven or twelve decades . . .'

'Seven,' Vekrynn cut in.

'Seven?'

'The life expectancy of an individual living in one of the developed regions is a little over seven Earth decades. As the Earth year is slightly shorter than ours, that works out at almost exactly seven Mollanian decades.'

*They begin to die from the moment they're born*, Gretana thought, chilled and distracted. 'What I couldn't ever cope with is . . . I mean, supposing I actually saw someone being . . .'

'Killed?' Vekrynn placed a chair in front of Gretana and sat down, bringing his face almost on a level with hers. 'You won't see anything like that. Believe me, you won't. Any of my observers who finds himself in a zone which is threatened with war is immediately withdrawn from the planet.'

'That isn't what I meant.' The concept of mass slaughter was so far beyond her comprehension as to be irrelevant. 'I'm talking about murder.' Gretana felt she had defiled herself merely by uttering the word, and she was startled when Vekrynn began to laugh.

'My dear child, you really must forget any stories you have heard about the people of Earth being blood-soaked monsters.' He shook his head, obviously deeply amused. 'They are uniquely handicapped, but they come from the same human stock as ourselves. The planet is hideously over-populated, and it didn't get that way through the inhabitants going around killing each other. Some of our people have worked there for two or three centuries at a stretch without ever witnessing anything more violent than a lovers' quarrel.'

'But I've heard that . . .'

'Gretana!' Vekrynn leaned forward and gripped her shoulders. 'Are you trying to tell *me* about Earth?'

The realization that Warden Vekrynn was actually holding her, that he was looking into her face with a kind of humorous amiability and no trace of revulsion, obliterated Gretana's thoughts in a cascade of whirling emotional shards. The surge of pleasure, confusion, timidity and awe was so intense as to produce a moment of actual giddiness. She stared in Vekrynn's gold-needled eyes, breathless, floating, unable to speak as his psychic aura enveloped her. And it was almost as an act of self-preservation, an attempt to stave off the complete submergence of her own identity, that she began the silent avowal. *I'll never go to Earth. I'll never go to Earth*.

Vekrynn released her immediately, as though tele-pathically aware of her reaction. 'It occurs to me that I have gone about this thing in completely the wrong way,' he said, smiling apologetically. 'I've spent most of my life away from Mollan, you see, and the Wardenship is so much a part of me that I tend to forget how strange and perhaps disconcerting it must seem to a person who leads a normal existence here on the home world. For instance, I have blithely assumed that you – in spite of being so young – are familiar with the history of the Preserva-tionist movement and that you believe in its ideals.'

'I do, of course.' Gretana wondered uneasily if, in an abrupt change of tactics, Vekrynn had hinted that her refusal to work for him indicated disloyalty or lack of responsibility.

'I wasn't implying anything to the contrary,' Vekrynn said reassuringly. 'I was merely wondering if you appreciated the historical origins of Preservationism and how vital it is to the future of Mollan.'

Gretana's uneasiness increased. 'My parents included some politics when they were designing my tutorial programme, but . . .'

Vekrynn shook his head. 'Please don't use the word politics in this context – it implies there can be more than one approach to the central issue. Look, Gretana, will you allow me to make one imprint? It's a straightforward educational outline, very simple and guaranteed to be without hidden bias. Do you mind?'

'I don't mind.' Gretana inclined her head forward as Vekrynn reached into a pocket of his tunic and withdrew two small gold medallions linked by a short length of metallic braid. He laid the braid laterally on the crown of her head, working it down through the upswept hair, and positioned one golden disc above each ear. He moved a disc slightly to bring it into perfect alignment with its counterpart, and in that instant . . .

Just as the position of a single particle is governed by probability density in the form of an asymptotic curve racing to infinity, so may the position of a conglomerate of particles – a human body – be altered by conscious adjustment of probabilities. A gifted individual should be able to position himself at any location in the cosmos, but that would require assessment of infinite probabilities. There is, however, a way of bringing the number of possibilities within our mathematical scope.

The cosmos is permeated with influence lines which link star to star, galaxy to galaxy. Where two or more of these lines intersect they form nodes. Knowledge of the relationship between any two nodes enables us to make a conscious selection of probabilities, to exist at one point or the other.

There is no conclusive evidence that Mollan was the world upon which the human species originated, but the likelihood is high. In Mollan's distant past philosophical awareness rose to a pitch at which some individuals became capable of teleportation, probably from one local minor node to another at first. Expansion into space must have begun later and continued until the radial impetus failed, establishing the human species on a known total of 172 worlds.

The significant point is that there is not one example of a civilization having survived continuously since its establishment. Furthermore, *there is no example of a civilization which has survived as long as 20,000 years*.

The implications for our own culture are obvious.

We have extended our life expectancy from the six centuries which is normal for the species to an average of fifty centuries, we have complete control of our environment – but the message from the stars is that all we have attained will some day be lost to us. The indications are that there is a latent instability in all human civilizations which, sooner or later, destroys them.

But Preservationism is not a philosophy of despair.

It is our belief that we can and will break free of the cyclic pattern of history which has characterized all other human social organizations.

Many measures have been taken towards the attainment of the Preservationist goal – one of the most positive being the founding, at the beginning of the Third Epoch, of the Bureau of Wardens. It is the continuing task of the Bureau to gather sociological data on one hundred selected human civilizations; to centralize, organize and interpret that data; and to forge from it a practical philosophical tool for the use of the World Government in its guidance of our social evolution.

There can be no more worthwhile objective, no loftier ideal.

. . . the knowledge was born in Gretana's mind. Most of it had been familiar to Gretana from her general studies, but it had never occurred to her that the placid and mellow civilization of which she was a part could ever suffer a reverse, nor had she ever viewed the Bureau of Wardens as its cornerstone.

'Did you say that was without bias?' she murmured, hoping the query would not sound too bold, as Vekrynn removed the medallions and returned them to his pocket.

'*Hidden* bias. I'd say that for a recruitment imprint it's very restrained.' Vekrynn remained seated close to her, adding a distracting hint of intimacy to the exchange. 'It doesn't even refer to the fact that the social credit rating for an observer is at least four times what you're getting now.'

'I'm sorry – it doesn't make any difference to me,' Gretana said doggedly, wishing the Warden would move away and give her the chance to compose herself. 'I don't want . . . I *couldn't* go to a place like Earth.'

She forced her eyes to meet his, expecting to see the beginnings of anger or disappointment, but Vekrynn's expression was still amiable, sympathetic.

'Tell me, Gretana,' he said, 'do you know what the natives of Earth look like?'

'No.' She tilted her head thoughtfully. 'I presumed they were just like us.'

'Not quite – there has been a certain amount of divergence. Look here.' Vekrynn touched his wrist console and the solid image of a woman appeared in the room several

31

paces away from where they were seated. She was small and was wearing a crimson blouse and a knee-length grey skirt, garments which had a certain kind of style to them, but which appeared crude to Gretana because of the coarseness of the weave and the fact that the seams were easily visible. The woman's shoes, which were blatantly designed to add to her stature, drew a glance from Gretana, but it was the head and face which held her attention. They were incredibly narrow by Mollanian standards, creating a disproportion of the features which both repelled and fascinated Gretana. She stood up to get a better look at the simulated face and was almost overcome with a curious blend of pity for the woman's ugliness and relief that she herself, for all her physical imperfections, had been spared imprisonment behind such a countenance.

'I . . . I've never seen anything so . . .' Gretana checked herself, remembering the pain a single word had inflicted on her that morning. 'Is she normal?'

'On Earth she would be considered so, perhaps even beautiful. The Lucent Ideal is a parochial concept.' As Vekrynn made an adjustment on his console the image of the woman vanished and was replaced by a series of representations of women and men, each persisting for only a few seconds. The men were generally smaller than Gretana would have expected, and she was also struck by the great variety in colorations, bodily shapes and proportions, and the actual arrangements of features. Virtually the only thing the images had in common was the small narrow head which gave their eyes the appearance of being much too close together. Ugliness was the common denominator.

'Were a native of Earth to arrive here on Mollan he would see the people as being tall, large-headed and very much alike', Vekrynn commented. 'We would all be brothers and sisters in his eyes.'

'I must have misunderstood something,' Gretana said, unable to turn away from the constantly merging image. 'I don't know much about the work of the Bureau, but I thought observers had to live as part of the societies under study.'

'Oh, they do. In your case you would have to go to Earth and live in one of their communities as one of them, and it would be essential that you did so without being noticed. If they were to discover that visitors from another world were living among them the data would be invalidated.'

'But . . .' She gave Vekrynn a perplexed smile. 'How could they fail to notice us?'

'Surgery, of course.' Vekrynn leaned back in his chair and spoke in casual tones. 'It's a matter of cutting some sections out of the cranium and facial bones, then re-assembling the skull to Earth proportions. The brain has to be shrunk a little to suit the reduced volume of the cranium, but oddly enough that's one of the easiest parts of the operation. I'm told the surgeons simply spray it with chemicals.'

The idea of saws cutting into her head made Gretana feel that the floor was tilting under her. 'Warden, are you making fun of me?'

'No. What I'm describing is standard practice.'

'But nobody would . . .'

'The process is reversible, of course. The excised bone sections are preserved, and at the conclusion of an observer's tour of duty the skull is rebuilt. The whole process is quite rapid, it's painless, and the end result is always perfect.'

Gretana stared at the Warden in disbelief. 'Are you trying to tell me that all the people who work for you on Earth – perhaps hundreds of them – have voluntarily submitted . . .?'

'Gretana, you weren't giving me your full attention.' Vekrynn rose to his feet, majestic and radiant as he breasted a slanting prism of sunlight. 'I told you the end result is always perfect.'

'I must go now,' she said faintly. She tried to move past Vekrynn, but he put an arm around her shoulders and drew her to him with the ease of an adult constraining a small child. He turned her to face the centre of the room again and her resistance faded as she saw that the image at the focus of the hidden projector had steadied and changed.

It was now in the form of a Mollanian woman, possibly the most beautiful Gretana had ever seen. The woman had the same upswept hair-style as Gretana, but there all resemblance ended, because the simulated creature had a face which matched the Lucent Ideal so closely, so perfectly, that looking at her filled Gretana with joy shaded with an obscure anguish which had something to do with the realization that even fifty centuries was too brief a time for such loveliness to exist. She allowed the vision to fill her eyes, drawing in to herself every detail of the ideally proportioned features and then, incredibly, as her cognizance of the beautiful, blind, immobile face increased there came a stirring of something like familiarity. The woman's eyes could almost have been those of Gretana's mother, and there was something about the curve of the chin where it merged with neck . . .

'This is a simulation based on just one scan of your bone structure, but I can assure you of its accuracy,' Vekrynn said. 'That's how you would look after returning from Earth.'

There was a prolonged silence during which the air of the room seemed to pulse in time with Gretana's heart. Across a murmurous distance she heard herself say, 'Cosmetic surgery is illegal.'

34

'The Bureau is allowed certain indulgences,' Vekrynn said, beginning a lengthy reply which Gretana heard only in part. 'The law prevents the disguise of what are almost regarded as genetic defects . . . idea being to ensure that no partner in a marriage can be deceived, especially with regard to the probable appearance of future offspring . . . observers returning from Earth . . . special category . . . amassed social credits . . . with the proviso that sterilization is accepted . . . won't worry too much if the Bureau's surgeons "accidentallŷ" fail to restore an observer's exact former appearance . . . whole new life before you . . . my consort at Silver Island . . . future is yours . . . '

The words flitted through Gretana's consciousness like wind-blown leaves, making brief brittle contracts, tumbling on their way again without having left any real impression. There was room for nothing in her mind but the vision of the face that could be hers, the face that was so perfect, so still, so painfully beautiful.

# CHAPTER 3

The ground began to tremble as the huge nuclear-powered prime mover approached the Carsewell pick-up point.

It had left Montreal nine hours earlier, lightly loaded because not many people wanted to travel through the night, and for the greater part of the long haul southwards through the Champlain and Lake George Valleys its twin traction cables had been quite empty. Dawn had been breaking as it rumbled nonstop through the string of towns between Whitehall and Albany, and from that stage onwards transfer modules – many of them bound for New

York – had attached themselves to it with increasing frequency. By the time the engine reached Carsewell it was trailing upwards of eighty modules in a double row and the cables were full almost to the point of overcrowding.

The situation was made worse by the fact that a number of the module drivers, having successfully clamped on to the cables, were not closing up to the regulation separation of twenty metres. This was because the automatic points on the southern stretches of the line were badly in need of maintenance and had become tardy in operation, with the result that modules sometimes missed their turn-offs and were carried inexorably onwards to later exits.

Hargate kept those factors in mind as the massive grey hull of the 8.30 nuke rolled past the Carsewell pick-up station and it became increasingly apparent that there would be very little room left on the west cable. He and his wheelchair were in the baggage section at the rear of the module, and from that vantage point he could note the growing restlessness of the passengers as the seemingly endless succession of carriages rolled by.

'Move up closer,' one man shouted at the tense, hunch-shouldered figure of the driver. 'How d'you expect to grab on from here?'

'I don't know why we aren't on the east side,' a plump woman just in front of Hargate said resignedly. 'The east cable always got more room since the fire up at Cohoes. You'd think the driver would know *that* much, wouldn't you? That's not too much to expect even these days, for God's sake.'

She half-turned in the seat, seeking approval for her comments, and her expression changed as she got her first good look at Hargate. He smiled maliciously, knowing that the paralysis affecting the left side of his face would make him look deformed and idiotic. The woman's gaze wavered and she quickly turned away nudging the red-coated woman seated next to her by the window. There was a whispered exchange and Hargate watched intently, maintaining his smile in case he would need to use it against the second woman, but she did not look back. *Got one of them anyway*, he thought. *And I'll watch out for the other one.*

The lateral procession of modules came to a sudden end, giving way to multiple catenaries of unoccupied cable strung out on their support bogies, and a short distance away to the north the flashing red lights of the rear-frame came into view. A sputtering whine and a tang of ozone rose from the module's electric engine, positioned somewhere beneath Hargate's feet, but there was no accompanying movement of the vehicle. The driver appeared to be struggling with a floor-mounted lever.

'Go, go, *go!*' An elderly man halfway along the car rose up and shook his fist at the driver's back. 'Move it out, fella, or we're gonna be here till Christmas!' The module lurched forward, turning at the same time and causing the man's legs to buckle. He sat down suddenly, half-spilled into the aisle and had to drag himself back to an upright position, muttering disconsolately as he brushed grime from his hands.

*Serves the old puke right*, Hargate thought, deeply amused. The module converged on the main railway line and there was a forward surge as its magnetic clutch locked on to the moving cable. Points clacked noisily beneath the wheels. The vehicle gave a yawing shudder, creaked a little, then it was part of the train, settling down for the leisurely journey to Poughkeepsie. At a nominal forty kilometres an hour the trip was going to take almost three hours, and Hargate had plenty of time to ponder on why his quarterly visit to the Dutchess County neurology clinic had been brought forward by several weeks.

There were two possibilities, one of which he did not dare to think about. During his last visit he had received confirmation of something he had intuitively known for some time, that the polyneuritis had seriously affected his heart. The official verdict was that there were only three or four years left to him. It could be that Foerster wanted to see him because the prognosis had been drastically revised, but if that was the case – had the figures been pushed up or down? Was he not even going to make it to his mid-thirties, or had he a chance of reaching the grand old age of forty?

Abandoning speculation, he unlocked the wheels of his chair, moved a little closer to the window so that he could look out. The transporter module was a veteran of many passes through urban Bomber Alleys, with the result that its armoured glass was liberally flowered by impact of rocks and occasional sniper bullets. Hargate found a relatively clear area and began staring nostalgically at the slow-drifting scenery which reminded him of the country-side near his boyhood home in Carsewell.

Twenty years had gone by since the spring morning on which he had struggled all the way up to Cotter's Edge and there, in the secret place, had seen a beautiful girl who had scribed a sign in the air and had vanished. He knew that the event had happened, although he had never mentioned it to anyone. He had no trouble distinguishing between memories of dreams and memories of reality – his illness had not progressed as far as the Korsakoff syndrome – but the fact remained that his 'reality' did not totally correspond with that of other people. One element he knew to be factual would be classed by anybody else as fictional or illusionary, so where should he draw the line?

The generally accepted reality of 2024 A.D. was one which contained and also was bounded by things like energy crises, the third world war which seemed both inevitable and imminent, attritive strikes, terrorism, failing resources, social decay, famine, and advertising campaigns for children's knife-proof undergarments. Hargate's composite picture was like a grainy, black-and-white photograph, but with one particle of colour in it – a bright-hued fleck representing his memory of the lovely and mysterious girl who could cast spells and make herself disappear.

Hargate shook his head in annoyance as he realized the extent to which he was still allowing childhood memories to occupy his mind. He turned away from the window and concentrated his attention on the other passengers, passing the time by trying to make Holmesian deductions about their occupations and reasons for travelling. In particular he kept an eye on the plump woman and her red-coated companion in the seat immediately ahead, half-smiling every now and then in preparation for one of them turning to look at him. Getting up at 6.30 to catch the early train had cost him some sleep, and before long – encouraged by the muggy atmosphere and the swaying of the module – he was drifting into a light doze. The feeling was pleasant, and he surrendered to it for the rest of the journey to Poughkeepsie, occasionally rousing himself with an extra-loud snore and almost at once sinking back into unconsciousness.

The day was mild and sunny, but Hargate felt cold, irritable and generally ill at ease as a result of having slept on the train. Taking advantage of the fresh charge in the wheelchair's battery, he bowled his way out of the 10th Street station at an inconsiderate speed which led to several near-collisions with pedestrians. He turned south in the direction of the Dutchess County clinic.

He considered spending the extra time sunning himself in the plaza outside the clinic, but groups of employees were already drifting out to spend early lunch breaks in the open. Staying there would involve him in a series of mimed skirmishes with strangers who showed too much curiosity about his condition, and after the long train journey he was too tired to face the daily battle with the rest of the human race. He decided to go straight up to Doctor Foerster's office and see if Vince Debrou was on reception duty. Debrou, possible because of his work, was one of the few who knew how to respond to Hargate in a totally natural manner and Hargate liked talking to him. There was also the possibility that Debrou had obtained some new orders. He rolled into the shabby redbrick building and took an elevator to the ninth floor, scowling over an increase in the surcharge.

'Hi, Denny,' Debrou said, when he entered the outer office. 'Congratulations!'

Hargate, who had expected to find at least six other patients waiting in the reception area, glanced around the empty room in some surprise. 'Congratulations? Have I just got myself engaged or pregnant?'

'Come on, Denny, you know what I mean.' Debrou, who was a pale young man with a permanently corrugated forehead and weightlifter's shoulders, went on sorting through a pile of X-ray slides on his desk.

'I have no idea what you mean,' Hargate said, his impatience increasing the nasal quality of his voice, 'If I had any idea what you mean I would say so, but I have no idea what you mean and that's why I'm asking you to tell me what you mean.'

'I thought they . . .' Debrou paused, eyeing him intently. 'The doc's down in the canteen – how about a coffee while you're waiting?'

'What if I tell your boss you've been talking out of turn?'

Debrou shrugged. 'For starters – you lose out on the coffee.'

'Cream, but no sugar,' Hargate said resignedly. He nodded his thanks as Debrou handed him a plastic cup and, without needing to be asked, a square of absorbent tissue. Within the last year the polyneuritis had seriously affected his palate, a weakness which – as well as imparting the nasal timbre to his voice – caused him to regurgitate fluids through his nose during the act of swallowing. As a rule he only drank when alone, except when he was deliberately setting out to embarrass somebody, but his rapport with Debrou was something special. He drank the warmish coffee, snorting and dabbing his nostrils after each mouthful, and decided against pursuing the reasons for his visit. It was a minor mystery which would soon be resolved. He nodded in the direction of the small abstract sculpture which glowed on a shelf behind Debrou.

'I haven't heard much from you recently,' he said. 'Nothing doing?'

Debrou shook his head. 'A couple of people showed some interest last week. Leastways, they were interested till they heard the price. Nobody can afford handmade stuff these days, Denny,'

'Are you telling me?' His coffee finished, Hargate sat with the tissue pressed to his nose and stared moodily at the sculpture, a sample of his work which Debrou displayed for him on a purely unofficial basis for a commission on orders received. It was a symbol of the lasting effects – both mental and physical – that the strange fleeting encounter on Cotter's Edge had had on his life. For several months after that unique day, each time circumstances had seemed intolerable he had hidden in his room and tried to escape by tracing talismanic signs in the air.

Later he had discovered in himself a genuine talent for mathematics, and had been subtly astonished to find that – far from expunging the remnants of his belief – the new field of learning had shown him undreamt-of ways of correlating the Cotter's Edge experience with the mundane world. His attitudes, reactions and thoughts were both complex and vague, but they sprang from one clearcut, even simplistic, idea. The gesture which had preceded the girl's disappearance had been made up of curves, and curves were embodiments of algebraic formulae, therefore there could be a link between mathematics and 'magic'. After a brief and disappointing excursion into numerology, he had become fascinated with the construction of mathematical models, a pursuit which – purely as a by-product – had solved the problem of how to supplement his state disability allowance.

During that period, although illness had continued to make inroads into his system – eventually confining him to a wheelchair – he had retained virtually the full use of his arms and hands. Kay Hargate, ever on the look-out for a wink from divine providence, had persuaded herself that the remission could be permanent and had even managed, at times, to begin treating him as an independent adult. For more than ten years Hargate had known something akin to happiness, then his mother had died – swept away with frightening suddenness in a minor outbreak of food poisoning – and soon afterwards had come the first chest pains and black-outs, fresh intimations of his own mortality.

He had continued his solitary existence in the same ground-floor apartment in Greenways, reading a lot – usually mathematical treatises – and working whenever he felt strong enough. And in visions he returned again and again to Cotter's Edge, striding towards the maple-plumed ridge on legs that were limber and strong, breathing the bright air of an April morning and exulting in the certain knowledge that she was there, waiting for him, and that this time he would get it right . . .

'Hey, *Denny!*' Vince Debrou had half-risen from his chair in his efforts to interrupt Hargate's reverie. 'I said the doc's back early. Want me to tell him you're here?'

'No, let it be our special secret.' Hargate said, angry at himself for having wandered into dreamland.

'Funny man.' Debrou flipped an intercom tab and within thirty seconds Hargate was rolling into the high-windowed inner office. Doctor Foerster was a broad-faced, balding man of fifty with weathered skin and large, work-roughened hands which were clues to the fact that he was passionately fond of sailing. He welcomed Hargate with a handshake, returned to his desk and dropped into the chair with a near-destructive impact.

'I'm sorry about asking you to come in at the lunch hour,' he said, 'but I wanted some extra time with you and this was the only way I could get it.'

Hargate quelled a spasm of unease. 'I've got all day.'

'Yeah, but I'm not so fortunate.' Foerster picked a speck of lint from his grey tweed jacket and examined it carefully before dropping it on the floor. 'How are your arms, Denny?'

'Everything still works.'

'Put them straight out sideways.'

Hargate did as instructed, all the while trying to read Foerster's expression. 'Like this?'

'Now wiggle your fingers,' the doctor said, glancing down at his wristwatch.

In less than a minute Hargate's shoulder muscles were desperately tired, but he strove not to give any indication. 'Would you mind telling me what's . . .?'

'Just keep wiggling,' Foerster said, concentrating on his watch. 'You're doing very well.'

Deciding he was being treated as something less than

43

human, Hargate promptly lowered his arms and returned his hands to his lap. His fingers tingled painfully.

Foerster eyed him with evident surprise. 'Why did you stop?'

'I have no interest in man-powered flight,' Hargate said stonily, meeting the doctor's gaze. 'And I'm not auditioning for *Swan Lake.*'

Foerster's lips twitched. 'It says in your file that you're ill-adusted and inclined to be anti-social and uncooperative.'

'Is that another way of saying I'm not overawed by white coats and stethoscopes?'

'Probably,' Foerster said, smiling ruefully, 'I'm sorry about the drill-sergeant routine, but it was a quick way of making sure you were still capable of doing a day's work.'

'Why? Have you got me a job?'

Surprisingly, Foerster nodded. 'A spare place has become available in a Government research centre, and I'm pretty sure it's yours if you want it. There's just one drawback – at least, most people would call it a drawback.'

Hargate leaned forward, intrigued, sensing that the doctor had withheld something important. 'Which is . . . ?'

'It's in the space colony.'

'In the . . . ? Hargate blinked once, twice, thinking about the twilight sadness of his solitary apartment in which lately it had become impossible to refrain from counting off his diminishing store of minutes and seconds. 'So what's the drawback?'

The single Aristotle space habitat, completed in 2021, had been built in the form of a cone – a shape which provided environments with differing gravities.

Among those benefiting from the conical configuration

had been medical researchers, who were grateful for the opportunity to study the effect of low-gravity conditions on patients with certain types of cardiac trouble. They had been given their own facilities in the 0.3G and 0.5G bands on condition that all patients who were fit enough would accept jobs in the zero-gravity production areas.

That proviso, as far as Hargate was concerned, was a bonus rather than a penalty. Foerster had carefully avoided promising too much, but it seemed there was a strong likelihood that residence in the 0.3G suite would increase Hargate's life expectancy by at least a factor of three. The new prospect of an entire decade of life stretching out before him was a fantastic luxury, but it would have lost some of its savour had there been nothing to do other than take medical tests and in between times stare at blank walls. In weightless conditions, though, he would be almost as mobile as an able-bodied person, every bit as capable of earning a living, of paying his way. And he had a craving, more insistent than that of any drug addict, for the blessed knowledge that he was putting more into the system than he was taking out.

*Independence, here I come!* The thought ran through Hargate's mind like a fugue, partially inuring him to the final indignities that Earth had to offer. He had wheeled out on to the concrete apron forty minutes earlier, part of a mixed payload of passengers and cargo that the orbital flier was due to carry aloft. The hump-backed craft, with canopies and hatches upraised like wing casings, resembled a huge red-and-white insect which had been captured by ants. It lay brooding on its booster platform, every detail highlighted by the intense Florida sun, sweating oil and water and other fluids Hargate was unable to identify.

The men carrying out the loading operation were KSC ground crew, not airline staff, and Hargate sensed they had divided the payload into three categories, with a descending order of priority – equipment packages, people who could walk, and people who could not walk. As the sole representative of the third category, he had sat morosely, his lungs labouring with the hot and humid air of the Cape, while the equipment had been loaded and secured, while seats had been custom fitted in the remaining floor areas, and while the walking passengers had been shepherded up the long ramp and installed in their places.

Sensitive to the curious scrutinies of nearby workers, Hargate kept his eyes on the flat, steamy horizons of the Florida water-world and tried to think thoughts appropriate to his last minutes on Earth. The task proved to be beyond his capabilities. He was too hot and too tired, and – above all – he now had to acknowledge that he was deeply afraid of the journey that lay ahead. It had been easy to be nonchalant in Foerster's office and during the subsequent three weeks of preparation for the flight, but now the future and the present had somehow drawn together, and the reality of his situation was daunting, overwhelming. He, who had never flown in a plane, who could not even walk, was proposing to venture into the black, alien and hostile infinity which waited beyond the atmosphere. The notion was preposterous, something he had been tricked into, and nobody could really blame him if – even at this late stage – he were to let his common-sense reassert itself.

'Sorry about the delay, Mr Hargate.' The young supervisor who approached him was carrying a clipboard and had symmetrical sweat patches on his blue shirt, like the markings of a badger. 'I expect you're pretty tired waiting.'

'It's all right,' Hargate said, choosing a degree of sarcasm he knew would go unnoticed. 'I've been taking things easy.'

'That's just great.' The supervisor frowned as he inspected Hargate's wheelchair. 'What sort of batteries do you have in there?'

'I don't know. Battery-type batteries.'

'Did anybody fit you out with zero-G units, Mr Hargate? We don't want blobs of electrolyte floating around the cabin when you're in free fall.'

Hargate shook his head. 'These are my regulars.'

The supervisor's lips moved silently as he jotted something down on his board. 'They've gotta come out. I'll notify Aristotle and they'll have a new set ready when you get up there. Okay?'

Hargate, who had been praying that he would be allowed to drive his chair up the ramp, digested the knowledge that he would have to be carried on to the flier like a babe-in-arms. For an instant he was tempted to engage the chair's drive and flee in search of a hiding place, then it came to him that he would be doing the opposite of escaping. As long as he remained on Earth, within the grip of his home planet's gravity, other people would have to carry him – physically sometimes, metaphorically every minute of every day – until the end of his life.

'It won't take long to strip the batteries out,' the supervisor went on. 'In the meantime, we'll get you into the ship, Mr Hargate. One of the men will carry you – if you don't mind.'

'So be it,' Hargate said ungraciously. 'But just make sure the guy who carries me is straight – I don't want anybody having a free grope.'

# CHAPTER 4

Finally, it was time for the transfer to Earth.

High Instructor Tabalth walked with Gretana to the circular courtyard at the heart of the building which had been her home for almost fifty days. The noontime heat had collected there like an invisible fluid in a dish, imparting a drowsiness to the atmosphere, causing the blue patterns of the central mosaic to ripple slightly as though under a film of water. All sounds were strangely muted. Gretana could feel the multiplicity of major skord-lines converging at the spot, interfering with the normal properties of space and time.

'As you know,' Tabalth said, his eyes fixed on her face with an unfocused quality which suggested he was not really seeing her, 'we make the transfer to Earth in two stages. The first will take you to the Bureau's Field Station 23, which is the control point for our Earth programme.

'As is usual where the subject race has shown an interest in space exploration, the station is not located in the home system. It's only twenty light years away, however, on a planet of the G-type sun catalogued on Earth as 82 Eridani. We like 82 Eridani because it is part of a web of stable skord-lines giving us eight major nodes on Earth's principal land masses.'

Gretana delved into her newly-implanted memories and nodded confirmation that Tabalth's subject matter was familiar to her.

'I hope this is an auspicious day for you.' Tabalth said, sounding polite rather than sincere.

Gretana nodded. 'I have the fifth planet.'

Tabalth held still for a second, attuning himself, then

glanced towards the east to where the fifth planet, Nuce, was invisibly lifting above the horizon. 'You are fortunate.'

'I know.' Gretana spoke without much conviction, wondering how she would be able to regulate her daily life once she had left the comforting matrix of planetary influences which permeated the home system. 'The time is right.'

'In that case – fair seasons!' Tabalth stepped back, taking himself outside the perimeter of the radial mosaic design, and by implication urging Gretana to proceed to its centre.

'Fair seasons!' Not allowing herself to hesitate, she walked to the mid-point of the courtyard, already assembling Station 23's spatial address on an imagined screen. The key equation was more complex than those she had used all her adult life, but she held it easily enough. She raised her right hand and traced the appropriate three-dimensional mnemo-curve, specifying the target's unique relationship with her present location. Once again she felt the subtle and ineffable *loosening* that always preceded an internodal leap. She closed her eyes in the final transcendental instant of concentration and the bulk of the planet beneath her feet seemed to stir, just once, like some vast slumbering animal disturbed by a dream.

Gretana opened her eyes to a night-time world in which faint stars scarcely penetrated barriers of radiance thrown up by encirclements of floodlights and brilliantly illuminated buildings.

The air was cold and had a faintly acrid tang to it, and a peculiar sense of emptiness at the core of her being told Gretana she was on a world which shared its sun with no other planets. Never before having completed an interstellar transfer, she felt both awed and humbled by the magnitude of her achievement, by the powers of the

49

Mollanian mind-science she had always taken for granted. *I could have done something like this a long time ago*, she thought, her feelings now complicated by a kind of exultation, *and yet it never occurred to me. Nor to any of my friends. It's almost as if . . .*

'Gretana ty Iltha,' said a female voice, accurately beamed at her from an invisible source, 'come to the reception chamber indicated by the marker lights.'

Twin lines of tesserae began to pulse amber and white, stippling a pathway to one of the buildings on the perimeter of the circular plaza. She set out along it on legs which tried to buckle with each step, a tendency which was enhanced by her unfamiliarity with Terran footwear. Positive that she was being scrutinized, and wishing she could at least have had the reassurance of wearing her own best clothes, she reached the building and entered it by way of an automatic door.

The square, brightly-lit chamber within was larger than she had expected and contained more than twenty desks interspersed with machines whose functions were unguessable, but which appeared to be electronic in nature. Only a few of the desks were in use. Their occupants were bored-looking men wearing the blue overalls of the Bureau of Wardens, and none of them appeared even to notice Gretana's arrival. It was impossible for her to decide if the place's faint air of desolation sprang merely from the fact that it was understaffed at night, or if it had been permanently run down from a higher level of activity. Unsure of what to do next, she was glancing around in the hope of seeing the woman who had spoken to her at long range when a door slid open in the nearest interior wall.

The man who appeared in the opening was tall and strongly-built, but with a pug-nosed, large-chinned face whose proportions were so far from those of the Lucent

Ideal that he would almost certainly never be able to marry. For an instant Gretana reacted as her old self – with compassion compounded by a sense of reluctant kinship – then remembered that with her present surgically-altered features it was she who was the prime object of pity. The stranger, however, seemed in no way embarrassed or perturbed by her appearance or his own. He greeted her with a smile of surprising amiability and confidence.

'Fair seasons, Gretana,' he said, coming forward to give her – as only someone in his unusual occupation would have considered doing – a Terran-style handshake. 'I'm Ichmo tye Railt, your section coordinator. How do you feel?'

'I . . . How am I supposed to feel?'

'Isn't this your first time off-world? Beginners often get quite severe reactions – faintness, nausea, powerful urges to skord straight back home.' The coordinator mimed a hasty and ludicrously complicated mnemo-curve.

'I'm all right.' Gretana realized, with some surprise, that her legitimate awe over treading the surface of an alien world had been displaced by curiosity about how a man so unprepossessing as Ichmo could appear so relaxed and content with himself.

'Good for you,' Ichmo said. 'Your assessment gives you an A2 rating, and they seem to be getting rare these days. No doubt that's why the Warden said you were to be taken straight to his office.'

Gretana felt a cool nervous tremor, and her hands rose of their own accord to mask her face. 'Now? Am I going to see him right now?'

'Yes, but as a projection.' Ichmo opened a second door and ushered her into an area of faint purple lighting. 'The Warden hasn't been able to spend much time here in recent years. We're under increasing pressure from some

51

non-human sectors, particularly the Attatorians. Their sensory apparatus is totally different to our own, so they won't accept the Warden's electronic presence – they expect him to negotiate in person.'

'I see.' Trying to conceal her disappointment, Gretana paused at a three-dimensional star map which floated in the cavernous dimness. She was able, by drawing on newly-imprinted knowledge, to identify the central region containing the 172 planetary systems where human life was known to flourish. On all sides of it, in volumes of space that had various background tints, were the non-human empires.

'You can see the Warden's problem,' Ichmo said, pointing at a star which was surrounded by a pulsing bubble of green light. 'Here's Sol, with Earth, less than a hundred light years from the Attatorian boundary in an area that's always been a bit of a jumble anyway. The Attatorians and some others are claiming that – because of the unique conditions on Earth – it should be declared a free zone, with unlimited right of access for scientific observers.

'We reject that viewpoint, of course – especially as the whole Terran civilization is balanced on a knife-edge – but the Attatorians are pushing pretty hard, and the number of unauthorised atmospheric penetrations is going up every decade. You'll probably see evidence of that yourself when you go into the field. Are you nervous about it?'

'I'm afraid so,' Gretana said. *Everything would have been all right if only I could have seen Vekrynn . . .*

'In that case, you shouldn't spend too much time here.' Ichmo spoke with brusque sympathy. 'My advice is to hear what the Old Man has to say to you, then move straight on to Earth before the witchcraft wears off. I'll be waiting in my office.'

'Witchcraft?' Gretana was prepared to be offended on Vekrynn's behalf. 'I'm afraid I . . .'

'Don't take it the wrong way,' Ichmo said, smiling his homely smile. 'The Warden couldn't have achieved a tenth of what he has done without using his own kind of magic to make people believe what he wants them to believe. He's a monomaniac, you see, totally obsessed with the Wardenship of Earth, and the rest of us aren't used to dealing with that type of mentality – so he wins all the battles.'

Gretana, eager to add to her scanty store of knowledge about Vekrynn, was both intrigued and disturbed by the hint that the Warden had to face his share of problems like any other human being. 'But he's the doyen.'

'So was his father, which means Vekrynn was generally expected to accept an administrative post on the High Council. Instead of that, he used the family influence to get Earth added to the list of the Hundred Worlds, and he has kept it there ever since, in spite of all the opposition.'

'I didn't know that.'

'That's because Vekrynn programmes all our educational imprints in person, and he likes to engender positive attitudes.'

'But you don't.'

'Wrong! I simply prefer different methods.' Ichmo regarded her quizzically for a moment, then turned and with a wave of one hand conjured up from the dimness a simulation of Earth, minus its normal cloud cover, as viewed from a distance of several planetary diameters. 'There it is – the unlucky one – in all its seething short-lived misery. As you must know, the sole purpose of the Bureau of Wardens is to study the evolution of civilization on a nominal one hundred human worlds – the actual number is now somewhat less than a hundred – and to develop a science which will enable the Mollanian culture to survive for ever. The official term is "indefinitely", but it means for ever.'

Gretana nodded. 'Well?'

'We come to the delicate question of relative time scales. As a matter of policy, we have mostly chosen worlds which have had no success in extending life expectancy beyond the norm of six or seven centuries, the theory being that they conveniently telescope or condense all social and evolutionary processes and thus yield far more data. The theory isn't generally accepted, though. Some authorities take the view that the lifespan of the individual dictates virtually all of his attitudes and consequently has a profound effect on the development of his civilization. They claim that the data obtained from human cultures with unmodified lifespans are highly suspect, not at all applicable to Mollan. They also claim that all observations of a pitiful freak like Earth are of academic interest only. Putting it bluntly, they would like the Wardenship of Earth to be discontinued.'

'I had no idea,' Gretana breathed, her mental image of Vekrynn acquiring new dimensions of circumstance. 'How does the Warden feel?'

Ichmo snorted quietly. 'The Warden doesn't feel anything. He *knows* that Earth has given us a uniquely valuable opportunity to chart the entire course of a human civilization, from beginning to end, within one Mollanian lifetime.'

'Well, I accept his view.' Gretana eyed the coordinator significantly. 'Even if others don't.'

Ichmo rolled his eyes, looking humorously exasperated. 'He really converted you, didn't he?'

'Is that something to be ashamed of?' The words were out before Gretana made the guilty discovery that she was allowing her manner towards Ichmo to be influenced by his remarkable ugliness. She tightened her lips and re-solved to be more considerate.

'I'm a believer in loyalty,' Ichmo said in a gentle voice, going closer to the three-dimensional projection of Earth and pointing at the North Atlantic. 'When I joined Vekrynn only three ships had crossed this strip of water. That was five centuries ago.'

Gretana lowered her eyes. 'I'm sorry.'

Ichmo appeared not to hear her. 'Of course, Vekrynn has seen it all – ancient Mesopotamia and Egypt, the Phoenicians and Minoans, India, China, Maya. He has taken imprints from every agent's report in our data banks, and when I think about that I get afraid of him. It hurts me even to try visualizing what he knows about that sad, sick, doomed little civilization down there, and sometimes I wonder if they're worth all the work he has put in.'

Gretana recalled High Instructor Tabalth's words. 'Work on his Notebook?'

Ichmo surprised her with a bark of laughter. 'Never *ever* let the Warden hear you say that, young Gretana.'

'I didn't mean any . . .'

'*Analytical Notes on the Evolution of One Human Civilization*, by Warden Vekrynn tye Orltha, is a modest-sounding title for a book, but Vekrynn's entire life has gone into it. To date it contains almost one billion words, and a *Conclusion* of at least ten million words will be written when Earth has finally snuffed itself out.' Ichmo paused to see if the figures he was quoting were having the intended effect.

'Up-to-date copies are stored on five widely separated planets, so that not even a supernova could endanger its existence. We're talking about Vekrynn's memorial, young Gretana, his bid for immortality. So take my advice – don't refer to it as his Notebook.'

Gretana was dismayed by her gaffe. 'I didn't know what Tabalth was talking about.'

'Neither does he most of the time,' Ichmo said, 'but don't get involved with inter-departmental bickering at this time. Run along and hear what the Old Man has to say to you.'

Gretana nodded and went through a series of radiance screens into a large circular room with a domed blue ceiling. Its furnishings consisted of a desk, a conference table and high-backed chairs. Part of the wall was occupied by a holographic view of Station 23 which revealed to Gretana that the entire complex was huddled beneath a hemispherical energy lattice which contained an artificial atmosphere. Her sense of being in an outpost was suddenly intensified.

'Thank you for coming to see me, Gretana ty Iltha.' Vekrynn's image, abruptly appearing at the centre of the room, spoke with the special confidential warmth she had almost forgotten. The lifelike projection of his figure, the heroic statue cast in precious metals, had almost the same emotional impact as the actual man. It brought light to the room. Gretana checked herself in the act of beginning the reply which would have gone unheard.

'It is a matter of deepest personal regret to me that I cannot be there to give you a few words of encouragement at this important moment of your life. I want you to know, Gretana, that my thoughts are with you and that I have the utmost confidence in your ability to succeed in your work for the Bureau. And you will appreciate exactly what I mean when I assure you that *fair seasons* really are in store.' The golden image smiled directly at Gretana, aiming itself by means of discreet sensors, then dissolved into glittering particles which swarmed and faded.

Bemused by the brevity of the recording, Gretana stared at the vanishing motes of radiance while she considered the meaning of Vekrynn's final remark. With the unusual emphasis he had placed on two words he had been reiterating, as openly as was prudent for a public communication, all that he had secretly promised her on the afternoon of their first meeting. She was going to be fair, as fair as any Mollanian woman had ever been, and her season lay only a small number of decades away in the future. It was to be a long and idyllic season, richly rewarding, impossible to visualize in advance, but with one quintessential and dominant image – that of her and Vekrynn dancing in the spangled twilight of one of the eternal parties on Silver Island, in the Bay of Karlth, where as a small girl she had watched the distant glimmers from the shore and had dreamed a thousand hopeless dreams. That image was too romantic and too simple, a remnant of her childhood, but now – with her understanding of Vekrynn as a human being, not a symbol – she could begin to elaborate on it and bring it closer to reality. Vekrynn had problems; she, as one of the premier beauties of Mollanian society, was certain to acquire great influence, and those circumstances might one day forge a powerful and enduring link between them, a true partnership.

Against that kind of vision, her sojourn on Earth could be regarded as an irksome but mercifully brief preliminary . . .

## CHAPTER 5

Standing at the centre of the radial mosaic, at an invisible crossroads, Gretana composed an equation and knew its shape to be correct. She raised her right hand and traced a unique quintic curvature in the air, replacing the equation's generalities with the specific values of the target address. For a barely perceptible instant there was a sense of resistance, of vast inertias being overcome, then the continuum yielded to her will.

The transfer took place.

And she gave an involuntary moan of dismay.

In spite of all her training and preparation, the onslaught of the Earth's Moon upon her senses nearly brought Gretana to her knees. It glowered, loomed, dominated. She could feel it hanging nearby in space, only thirty diameters of the planet away, an enormous generator and reflector of chaotic third-order forces which stormed and sleeted through her being, obliterating her finer senses. Panic spumed behind her eyes.

*I'm blind*, she thought as she tried vainly to skry the major influence line connecting her present position to Station 23. *I'm trapped! I'll be here for ever!*

Gradually, however, and with agonizing slowness, she became aware that a tuning process was taking place in her mind. It was as though the roar of a giant waterfall was being faded into the background to enable her to pick out the sharper notes of individual rivulets. She waited, hardly breathing, for her sensory balance to be restored. The planet known as Mars was the first to exert an identifiable tug, then came the two giant worlds of the local system, closely followed by Venus and Mercury. At that point, having oriented herself in the matrix of planetary influences, Gretana opened her eyes.

She was standing in a quiet, tree-screened hollow. A spring murmured introspectively a few paces away from her to the right, and on the other side was a low shelf of mossy rock which formed a natural chair. Gretana nodded and, despite the slow-subsiding inner turmoil, almost smiled. The place had the feeling of *rightness* she always associated with a major permanent nodal point. It was as though Nature had been coaxed and guided by timeless forces into arranging the topography just so, into providing shelter and water and a place for the traveller to rest, as an affirmation of the Mollanian belief that life and matter were both synergistic and interactive. The fact that neither buildings nor ornamentation marked the spot was an indication that she had entered a blind world. She transferred the small suitcase, which had been provided by Ichmo, into her right hand and moved away through the copse in the direction of the nearby community of Carsewell.

Although Gretana's knowledge of the area was good, it had been derived from maps and texts, and she was unprepared for the vividness of the sunlit reality which greeted her as she emerged from the shade of the trees. The statistics on overcrowding, famine deaths and pollution levels had led her to expect uniform vistas of smoke-laden squalor, but here were untrodden pastures, and in the middle distance swathes of forest land gradually yielding to blue-green ranges of hills – all without any obtrusive signs of habitation. The air was clean and scented by grass and . . .

Gretana gasped as she saw jewel-like flecks of blue and yellow here and there in the sloping meadow that lay ahead, and it came to her that the wild flowers were *coloured*. She picked several tiny blossoms and stared at them, entranced, trying to reconcile their incredible glowing actuality with the bare fact – she now recalled it from the recent imprint on Terran ecosystems – that many plants here were attractive to minute winged creatures called insects.

*Why*, she wondered, *does Mollan import gold and pearls?*

Something far away emitted a mechanical wailing sound and, tentatively identifying it as a train, she was reminded

59

that she had hundreds of kilometres to travel to her assigned base area near Washington, D.C. It seemed prudent to cover as much of the distance as possible by daylight. She put the flowers into a pocket and walked briskly down the long slope, towards the unknown, rehearsing some of the salient facts of her new existence.

*This is May 10th, 2002 A.D. I am Greta Rushton, aged twenty-one, unmarried, American citizen, but grew up in Aberdeen, Scotland – which accounts for any atypical features of my accent or unfamiliarity with current American usage. My father was an oil company executive. Both he and my mother were killed in the Saudi Arabian revolution of 1997, but their overseas investments provide me with an adequate income which lets me indulge my interest in travel.*

She reached the bottom of the meadow, crossed a small bridge which spanned a drainage ditch, and found herself at the side of a blacktop highway which was showing signs of disuse. Some distance beyond it was the edge of the Greenways housing development, which was actually the westernmost offshoot of the small city of Carsewell, but she knew that entering it without a resident's identity disc would involve her in an exchange with security guards. It was, she felt, too soon for anything so taxing – her first conversations should be with disinterested parties.

She crossed the highway, walked a short distance to a link road and turned south on a two-lane orbital which curved away towards the city. Sensory overload, a continuous bombardment of new impressions, filled her with a bemused numbness, damping her reactions to the astounding fact that she, Gretana ty Iltha, was alone on the planet Earth – *Earth!* – and was committed to it for perhaps seven decades.

Her job, as outlined by Vekrynn, was simply to act as a human recording machine – reading, watching, listening without any conscious selection, receiving a general impression of how the populace in her assigned area reacted to the historical forces that shaped their everyday lives. She was also to return to Station 23 twice a year and make a 'cerebric deposition' – a near-instantaneous process, akin to an educational imprint in reverse – which would be processed and fed into the Bureau's data banks.

In some ways it was the least demanding job imaginable – except for the ambivalence of her feelings towards the Terrans. On the one hand there was a choking pity over the tragic brevity of their lives, on the other was the physical revulsion and fear inspired by beings who were condemned to wallow in sickness and death almost from the moment they were born, but who accepted their fate with such resignation.

It took her an hour to reach Carsewell's Warren Station. The Bureau's basic training enabled her to get through the procedure of buying a ticket and boarding the correct train, but all the while she was uncomfortably aware of something she had never experienced previously – the pressure of eyes. Men who were seated near her or were passing along the carriage were the most persistent, but she also found that women tended to stare at her for longer than seemed necessary, their expressions indecipherable and cool. She had been assured by the Bureau surgeons that her face was based on a computer amalgamation of many thousands of Earth women's faces, and that it was therefore bound to be quite unremarkable to Terran eyes, but she was unable to rid herself of an uncomfortable feeling that somehow there had been a miscalculation.

*You've got to relax*, she told herself. *Acting nervously is only going to make matters worse*. She picked up a discarded newspaper and sheltered behind it, pretending to read as the train progressed slowly and haltingly down the Hudson River valley, but all the while she was absorbing images of the world which drifted by outside. Occasionally she caught glimpses of gardens and was spellbound by their banks of varicoloured blossoms.

She successfully changed trains at Peterson and again – having by-passed New York and Philadelphia – at a new super-junction in Wilmington for the last leg of the journey. The train was old, slow and shabby, and had a broken public address system which made it necessary for guards to patrol the carriages announcing the numerous halts. The sheer frequency of the stops impressed Gretana, but it was the onset of night which gave her her first real indication of the density of the area's population. Nightfall on Mollan meant a generalized plunge into darkness, with some glimmerings of artificial light in the distance, but here the landscape – when viewed from an elevation – was a rich and complex pattern of beaded illuminations whose lines and clusters merged near the horizon into a continuous radiant haze. The unexpected beauty produced an easing of tension which in turn made her aware that she was very tired. She closed her eyes briefly, experimenting with the possibility of sleep, and the sounds in the compartment seemed to grow faint . . .

'That's right, baby – just you snuggle up to old Des and we'll have ourselves some fun.' The voice close to her ear jolted Gretana into wakefulness, but several seconds went by before she realized there was an arm around her shoulders. She tried to start upright, away from the black-clad young man, but he tightened his grip, drawing her into a forced intimacy with his body odour of dank leather and perspiration.

'I don't think she 'ppreciates you none, Des,' said a shaven-headed youth, leaning towards Gretana from the opposite seat. He smiled, revealing teeth which had been enamelled blood-red. 'She don't look too happy.'

'Bull,' Gretana's captor retorted. 'She's gotta get used to me, that's all. What d'you say, honey?' He turned his head and pressed his mouth against her forehead. She felt his tongue flickering on her skin.

Temporarily paralysed with fright, she extended the radius of her awareness to take in the fact that the train was still swaying through the darkness and that the passengers who had been nearby before she slept appeared to have migrated to another section of the carriage. Using all her strength, she pushed herself away from the man's embrace and into an upright position. He tried to pull her back to him but, somewhat to her surprise, she was able to resist him and break free. From arm's length she saw that Des was shaven-headed and crimson-toothed like his companion.

'Hey!' His eyes grew round with wonderment. 'We got ourselves some kinda circus lady here, Sal. A real athletic type.'

'Nice muscles,' Sal said approvingly. He was moving closer to Gretana, a red-grinning apparition, when a chubby man in guard's uniform came through the nearest bulkhead door.

'Rockville next stop,' the man droned, then paused. 'What's going on here?'

'Nothing – take a walk.' Sal stabbed his thumb in the direction of the far end of the carriage.

'I'm going to Rockville,' Gretana said quickly. 'Would you please take my case?'

The guard nodded uncertainly and reached for the case, but Sal stood up and blocked his way. 'Forget it!' He tilted his head and examined the case's dangling name tag. 'We'll look after Greta's bag.

'I don't know these men.' Gretana locked eyes with the guard. 'Please help me. I want to get off the train.'

'This is a personal matter, chief,' Sal said, tapping the

older man's chest with a black-nailed finger. 'You don't want to butt into no personal matter, do you?'

The guard's eyes clouded over as he looked away from Gretana. In that moment the door behind him slid open to reveal two male passengers in the carriage connecting space, looking as though they were preparing to disembark, and the darkness beyond the window was replaced by the slow-gliding lights of a station. Gretana, propelled by anxious strength, lunged upwards, snatched her case from the rack and – with a speed which almost defied natural laws – snaked past the human barriers and reached the carriage's outer door. Within seconds she was down on the station platform and hurrying towards the exit. To her disappointment, the station was a small and unmanned affair with only a shed to house ticket machines and drinks vendors.

'I told you she didn't 'ppreciate you, Des.' The voice came from only a few paces behind her. 'I mean, that was *embarrassing*, man.'

'It all adds to the amusement, Sally boy.' Des did not sound amused. 'You'll see.'

Gretana glanced back and saw that, whereas the two leather-clad figures were very close, the few other passengers who had alighted seemed to have dispersed into the night. She broke into a run, but found it difficult to stride out efficiently with the constriction of the Earth-style skirt and shoes. One of her pursuers gave a derisive chuckle. She reached the concrete apron of the canopied building, ran across it towards the sparse lights of the street beyond and almost sobbed with relief when she saw a man in what she recognized as a police uniform. He was standing with his back against a black-and-white car, one thumb hooked into his belt, the other hand holding a white plastic cup to his lips. Gretana went straight to him.

'Please help me,' she gasped. 'Those men . . .'

Des and Sal, feet slapping noisily, halted when they saw the policeman, but – contrary to what Gretana had hoped and expected – showed no inclination to back away. They exchanged glances, nodded, and moved several paces closer.

'Come on, Greta.' Des spoke in a wheedling voice, as though patching up a quarrel.

'I don't know these men,' Gretana said urgently to the policeman, who had not moved. 'They assaulted me on the train. I had to run to get away from them.'

'Greta, you're taking the joke too far,' Des warned. 'The officer doesn't have time to play games.'

The policeman lowered his cup, scanned Gretana's face with thoughtful grey eyes, then turned to her pursuers. 'You two Crows aren't from around here, are you?'

'No, but . . .'

'In that case, maybe you should get back on the train.'

Des looked affronted. 'I thought this was a free country. I thought a citizen still had freedom of choice about . . .'

'I'm *giving* you a free choice,' the policeman cut in, carefully setting his cup on the roof of the car. 'Do you want to walk on the train, or be poured on?'

'That's nice, from a public servant.' Des glanced from the policeman to Gretana and back again, and a grin spread on his face like the slow opening of a wound. 'I get it – trouble with the old nightstick, huh?'

The policeman unfolded his body away from the car, making himself taller. 'You've got about thirty seconds to hop on that train.'

'We're going,' Des said with mock-sweetness. 'Have a good night.' The two men turned and, flapping their loose black garments like plumage, loped back into the station and broke into an outright run as a bell rang on the train. Gretana waited until they had boarded one of the moving carriages before she dared relax.

65

'Thank you,' she said to the big man at her side. 'I don't know what I would have done if you hadn't been here.'

'I daresay you'd have come up with something,' he replied with an inflexion which she found puzzling. 'Is that your name? Greta?'

'Yes. Greta Rushton.'

'Where do you live, Greta?'

'Silver Spring.' She had to concentrate to recall the assigned address. 'Remington Avenue.'

'You got off the train one stop too soon.'

'I've already told you why,' Gretana said, aware of the beginnings of a new uneasiness. The policeman's youngish face was hard and unreadable.

'So you did.' The policeman looked at his green-glowing watch, then opened the passenger door of his car. 'Get in the car, Greta. There won't be another train for near-enough thirty minutes, and you might as well be comfortable.'

'All right.' Leaving her case beside the car, Gretana got into the vehicle. The interior smelled of rubber and smoke, and a radio mounted on the dash was emitting irregular fizzing sounds. The policeman dropped into the seat beside her and without any hesitation pulled Gretana towards him. His lips came down hard on her own, and at the same time she felt his hand slide under her jacket, the fingers encircling one of her breasts. Shocked, stifled and uncertain of how to react, she held herself perfectly still and tried to dredge up specific knowledge concerning sexual behaviour on Earth.

*The average Terran female,* came the implanted words, *is fertile for approximately three decades, but the tempo of ovulation – set by the planet's huge Moon – is only twenty-eight days, which means that, in contrast to the pattern on Mollan . . .*

'What the hell!' The policeman abruptly pushed Gretana away from him and peered into her face. 'Don't get cute with me, Greta.'

She stared straight ahead, into stellar distances. 'Please let me go.'

'Please let you go!' He studied her from beneath tightening brows. 'You're really playing it straight up, yes?'

She understood the question only by the context. 'Yes.'

'Then why are you wandering around by yourself at night, for Christ's sake? All by yourself and done up like a . . .' The policeman paused, sighed heavily, then leaned across Gretana and pushed open the door. 'Take off!'

'Gladly.' She got out of the car, picked up her case and walked back to the station building. The black-and-white departed immediately with a querulous whine from its electric drive, leaving her totally alone in the darkness of the alien planet. She felt physically sick and afraid, wondering how many more encounters with ugliness there would be before she reached the comparative safety of her apartment. The nearer she came to her journey's end the more hazardous it seemed and, as an ever-present accompaniment to her fears, the Moon was prowling like some obscene animal, far below the eastern horizon.

Incredibly, as far as Gretana was concerned, she was able to adapt to her new life within a matter of weeks.

The apartment had been leased on her behalf by a long-established Bureau worker, based in New Orleans, who had made the arrangements through a local real estate agency. It was part of a small modern block, exclusive enough to allow her to control the frequency of social contacts, but without being in any way ostentatious. For the first few days she spent most of her time in its shaded rooms, adjusting to the basic fact of being on Earth, experimenting with the stored food supply and cooking facilities, and watching a great deal of television.

She also devoted long periods to sitting at a mirror, staring at the stranger's face in the glass – comparing it to those she saw in televised beauty advertisements – and trying to accommodate the idea that, by Earth standards, she might be beautiful. There was no way in which she could be certain, even after prolonged and intensive study, because the two cultures' physical ideals were so divergent. The Bureau's surgeons were not accustomed to dealing with female subjects, and it would have been ironic if, while aiming for the unremarkable median, they had created the exceptional. While such an accident could impair her ability to observe without being observed, its principal drawback would be on the personal level. The repulsiveness of Terran males was enough to cope with in itself without finding that she was a magnet for the appalling crudity of their sexual advances.

In time, however, Gretana developed her own defensive habits and routines. She left the apartment only in daylight hours, she learned to identify safe circumstances and locales, to choose the clothes which drew least attention, to comport herself with a hard, cool disdain which acted as an effective social barrier. The consequent loneliness of her existence, far from adding to the rigours of exile, was something for which she was deeply grateful.

It helped to insulate her and distance her from the daily cavalcade of despair. Pervasive images of statesmen who eyed their opposites in foreign nations with the total blank incomprehension of insects; gold-encrusted churches whose congregations coughed blood; thrill-killers in all their cankered varieties, from the rooftop snipers to the poisoners of school water supplies; corporate despoilers of the environment; Third World freedom fighters who severed the arms of UN-vaccinated children; heroin-billionaires; semi-literate teachers; wars and famines and professional exploiters of refugees; strikers who burned ambulances and turned the sick away from hospitals; testers of nerve gas and tenders of ICBMs . . .

And always there were the children – massively betrayed before they had even been born.

Her instinct for emotional survival forced Gretana, out of sheer necessity, to try stripping the Terrans of their humanity in her thoughts, to try regarding them as organic puppets acting out some incomprehensible black comedy whose final curtain – due, according to Vekrynn, in less than a century – would be a merciful release for all concerned. She was partially successful with regard to the adults, but the betrayal of the children was the source of a raw and rough-edged pain from which there was no escape.

In the early months she fuelled her spirit with hopes that Vekrynn would be physically present at Station 23 to greet her when she returned to make her first cerebric deposition, then she began to pray that he would not. There was a real chance that being with him, receiving a foretaste of her personal nirvana, would make it impossible for her to return to Earth. The actual event, subject of so much anticipation, proved anticlimactic. There was an uneventful trip north to Carsewell, a lonely walk through October mists to the nodal point – its screen of maples now dank and dripping with condensation – and the instantaneous transfer across twenty light years to find that not even Ichmo tye Railt was there in person to receive her deposition. In less than an hour she was back on Earth and numbly making her way south to Silver Spring, hardly able to believe that the interstellar sortie had actually occurred. The bleak reality of Earth, she realized, was threatening to become *her* reality and would have to be fended off with greater vigour, driven back into containment.

Her second and third visits to Station 23 followed the

same unremarkable pattern, conditioning Gretana to believe that the nodal point on Cotter's Edge was so secluded as never to be visited by local inhabitants.

Spring came early in 2004, bringing unexpected relief from a hard winter in which power cuts and commodity shortages had been particularly severe. The mild weather prompted Gretana to make her bi-annual trip to Carsewell a few weeks earlier than usual and to combine the duty with a vacation. She rented an electric car and travelled north at a leisurely pace, making two overnight recharging stops, and it was quite early on a fine April morning when she pulled up on the quiet and now-familiar orbital road west of Carsewell. The sky was bright and busy, and the breezes which disturbed her hair and clothing might have blown from an alternative Earth which had never known pollution. She crossed the spiked-off interstate highway, but instead of going straight up the gradual hill decided to make a detour and approach the crest from the south.

As always, she felt wonderment that such unspoiled tracts of land could exist in a world where tactical nuclear weapons were in use almost daily in squabbles over patches of near-sterile desert. She paused to skry the position of the Moon, and was comforted to find that it was directly below her feet, which meant that the entire bulk of the planet was helping to shield her from its influence. Enjoying the unusual inner peace, she made a meandering approach to the nodal point. On reaching it, she stood in communion for several minutes, savouring the near-mystical pleasure of being at a junction of major skord lines. The ambience was typical – a kind of monastic seclusion combined, paradoxically, with the sense of interaction with the billowing universe. She was drawing upon it, replenishing herself, when the silence was broken by a movement only a few paces behind her.

She spun round in a sudden clamour of nerves. The boy who had got so close before being noticed was about twelve years old. He was supporting himself on two light-alloy crutches, and his eyes were staring at her with disconcerting intensity from a face which had been honed to a narrow triangle by illness. Gretana's initial alarm was lost in a rush of pity.

'Hello,' she said, striving to appear unconcerned. 'Lovely morning, isn't it?'

The boy looked all about him with studied calmness. 'It's all right.'

'You don't seem too sure about that,' she said, smiling.

There was a moment during which his eyes, enigmatic and troubled, held steadily on her own, then he began to turn away. 'I have to go now.'

'You don't have to leave on my account,' Gretana said urgently, starting forward. She checked herself as she saw the change of expression which signalled that he had been hurt and was about to strike back.

'You don't know what I . . .' The rest of the boy's words were lost to her as he fled, bobbing and lurching, into the obscurity of the winding tree-lanes. Sounds of his laboured progress disturbed the air for a few seconds, then Gretana was walled in by silence. She placed the palms of both hands on her temples and waited for the unsettling effect of the encounter to wear off. *This is Earth*, she told herself, trying to erase images of aged eyes in a young face. *Nothing matters here. Nothing makes any difference . . .*

Several minutes went by before she had regained her composure and was able to effect the transfer.

Subsequently, each time she approached the nodal point on Cotter's Edge she did so with extra caution. And, even though the quiet place was always deserted, years went by before she could venture into it without the partial expectation that the same small boy – doomed, yet strangely indomitable – would be awaiting her arrival.


## CHAPTER 6

Phil Barron was almost certain that he was being punished.

There was an unwritten rule that external maintenance work on the end-cap of Aristotle, unless of an urgent nature, was carried out when the space colony was at its monthly maximum distance from the sun. At that time, an engineer venturing out on to the circular platform of the base found that both the Earth and the Moon were below the horizon which was formed by the platform's rim. There remained some distraction due to the habitat's rotation apparently causing the stars to sweep 'horizontally' around the sky at the dizzy rate of two revolutions a minute, but the overall illumination remained constant, making it possible to work efficiently and without vertigo. Barron, as an hydraulics specialist, had been outside under those conditions on several occasions, carrying out routine maintenance on the mirror rams, and had found the experience bearable, if not enjoyable.

But circumstances were very different this time – a fact which was forcibly impressed on him as soon as the outer door of the axial airlock swung open. Earth was nearly 'overhead', describing lazy but noticeable circles in the manner of a balloon tethered by a cord; and not far above the edge of the 200-metre platform the Moon was zooming at neck-twisting speed, briefly silhouetting various structures and attachments. Its gyrations were so unnatural, so difficult for the instincts to accept, that Barron kept seeing it as a huge white floodlight whirling crazily a short distance out from the colony's longitudinal axis. The disparity between the visual and intellectual realities produced an uneasy upward surge in his stomach as he attached a safety line and began moving out towards primary mirror ram No.3.

Barron's suspicion that he was being punished stemmed from the knowledge that the hydraulics leak on No.3's ancillaries had been reported some ten days earlier without any action being taken, and therefore could not have been considered serious. Bo Hardicker had been distinctly cool with him since Barron had organized a protest against a new duty roster, and the section manager was a man who was quite capable of delaying an external end-cap job until the worst possible moment. Shadows moved all around Barron, shrinking and stretching, making it difficult to judge depths and distances, and it occurred to him that he ought to put Hardicker out of his mind and concentrate on the task in hand. One serious mistake at this point would give the section manager all the excuse he needed to transfer him back to Earth.

Although greatly modified since its conception, Aristotle retained one feature of a classical O'Neill space habitat – the three huge longitudinal mirrors which could be splayed out to reflect sunlight into the interior. The opening and closing of the mirrors were the equivalents of sunrise and sunset to Aristotle's inhabitants. According to the original schematic the colony should have consisted of a pair of habitats linked together in contrarotation, an arrangement which was designed to prevent gyroscopic precession, but the need to cut costs had brought drastic revisions. The single tapering habitat that had reached hardware stage was allowed to precess within certain limits, and – so that its inhabitants would not be presented with the spectacle of an apparently wobbling sun – the angles of the big mirrors were continuously adjusted to compensate.

Cost-effective though the system was, it had added to the complexity of the machinery controlling the mirrors, and as a result unscheduled maintenance work was not uncommon. Phil Barron, deciding to complete the current chore as quickly as possible in spite of astronomical distractions, resolutely kept his eyes down as he worked his way out from the zero-G conditions at the airlock. The base of the mirror ram was roughly seventy metres away from the lock, and as he neared it he felt the gently growing insistence with which the rotating end-cap was trying to flick him off into space.

On reaching the machinery cluster surrounding the No. 3 attachment, he anchored himself securely to the alloy grid which served as a perch for repair workers. The light from his suit's helmet added to the confusing inter-play of shadow, and perhaps a minute had gone by before he located the pipe run in which he was interested. He examined its most likely trouble spot, a coupling where it entered an intensifier, and was gratified to see some telltale staining of the metal. It looked as though the job would be straightforward and quick.

He used his radio to request the duty engineer in Systems Control to switch operation of No.3 mirror to the back-up ram, then selected a suitable wrench from the array on his belt. While he worked the Moon kept flitting into and out of his vision, continuously circling, but he refused to acknowledge the messages it was sending to the ancient part of his brain. So determined was he to shut off all extraneous data that the new object which appeared in his sky had completed several revolutions before he raised his head to look directly at it.

The object was a man in a gold-and-silver spacesuit of unfamiliar design. He was poised in space, a few degrees

74

to one side of the Moon, and the fact that he was stationary with respect to the satellite had one implication which disturbed Barron. It almost certainly meant that the newcomer had approached the colony from a separate inertial system – and Barron knew that no arrivals had been scheduled.

He narrowed his eyes and tried to pick out more detail, but seeing was difficult. The colony's rotation was sweeping the figure around the sky, and – as it was some distance beyond the shadow of the end-cap – the metallic suit was blurred by merging haloes of reflected sunlight. While Barron strove to keep the figure in his field of vision it drew nearer, smoothly propelled, and he saw that it was holding an object which could have been a tool or a weapon. He was about to activate his radio when all doubts concerning the nature of the artifact were resolved.

It emitted a nova-bright ray of energy which raked across the end-cap machinery in a hellish three-second burst of destruction, exploding metal into incandescence, shearing through rams, beams, gantries, antennae, pipes, cables and mirror attachments. Clouds of vapour seeded with glowing droplets of metal spiralled outwards into space, obscuring Barron's view of the attacker. He clung desperately to the nearest handrail as he scanned the sky in the plane of the Moon, waiting for a second blaze of radiation, the one that was bound to flare him into oblivion.

The burnished figure appeared above the fast-disappearing rack, but closer now, almost at the rim of the platform. Behind it a huge tumbling rectangle of silver dwindled into the starry background. Barron knew at once that one of Aristotle's main mirrors had been completely severed, but he was totally indifferent to its loss. There was no room for anything in his mind but the shrieking fear of annihilation. He had no expectation of mercy, yet was unable to control a blind reaction as he saw the attacker's weapon being levelled again.

'Don't do it,' he bellowed, straightening up and waving with both arms. 'Don't kill me!'

Incredibly the lustrous mannikin seemed to see or hear him, seemed to hesitate.

'Please don't kill me,' Barron whimpered hopelessly, now positive that showing himself had made his death all the more certain.

There was a protracted moment of delay, a time outside of time, before the enigmatic figure performed a final enigmatic act. It raised its right hand as if in benediction and traced a complex mathematical curve – then it simply ceased to exist.

## CHAPTER 7

Denny Hargate was working the zero-gravity crystal farm at the sunward end of Aristotle. The circular room, located right on the colony's longitudinal axis, was almost completely filled with feed pipes, plastic bubbles of growth chambers and monitoring equipment, but Hargate did not object to the cramped conditions. He could project himself from one point to another with the ease and accuracy of an arboreal monkey, the lack of mass in his atrophied legs proving a positive advantage when it came to beginning or ending a flight. His fingers had the ability to find secure anchorages on seemingly impossible surfaces.

The room had large windows in its inboard wall, and he sometimes paused at one of them to stare at the incredible trefoil perspectives of the colony's interior. From his unusual vantage point there appeared to be three suns, each hanging in a tapering strip of blue-black sky which converged on the distant end-cap. Between the strips, filling in the radial geometrical design, were the colony's three 'valleys' with their compact areas devoted to industrial production, hydroponics, garden villages and grassland. It was a strange and totally unnatural prospect, an enclosed universe in the form of a stylized flower, but in his five months in Aristotle Hargate had learned to regard it with deep affection. This *contrivance*, this flimsy cocoon of metal and glass, had given him mobility, a useful job, the promise of something like a normal life-span – therefore it was a habitat more natural to him than Earth could ever have been. He was at home.

*Denny Hargate*, he would intone while floating at the window, marvelling at the odds he had beaten in order to reach that particular point in space and time. *Citizen of the solar system!*

It was his affinity for the miniature world and its peculiar physics which alerted him, almost before any other colonist, to the fact that something serious had happened. He was alone in the crystal farm, carrying out routine checks on a sensitive batch, when there was a sudden decrease in the amount of light in the room. Unexpected though the change was, it was the barely perceptible tremor accompanying it which sent a frisson of alarm coursing through his nervous system. He twisted in mid-air, looked through the window and saw that the radial pattern of his environment had been radically altered.

One of the reflected suns was no longer there.

The first explanation occurring to him was that No.2 mirror had either been retracted or allowed to splay out beyond its normal maximum, then – with savagely jolting heart – he saw that the two remaining suns had begun a drunken and irregular wobbling. There was no escaping the conclusion that Aristotle had developed a serious instability. The perturbations were too small to generate any noticeable G-forces, but within a short time the mirror alignments had shifted so much that the sun reflections slid off their edges and the interior of the colony was plunged into darkness. In a compartment near to Hargate a man gave a hoarse bellow of alarm. The darkness lasted only a few seconds, then daylight suddenly returned with full intensity.

Clinging to a nylon hand-rope, Hargate saw the frightening alternations of night and day occur twice more before the twin suns raced down the sky and he realized that the No.1 and No.3 mirrors had been retracted to reduce the eccentric forces acting on the colony. As prolonged darkness fell all the interior lights sprang into life, creating brilliant geometries the full length of the colony, but the 'night' which ensued was not normal. The longitudinal strip which should have been closed by No.2 mirror remained transparent, and the Earth and the Moon could be seen batting across it twice in every minute, adding swift-changing variations to the general level of illumination.

*The mirror can't be gone*, Hargate told himself. *It can't be possible to lose a mirror*.

Still gripping the hand-rope, afraid to cast off in case the room shifted violently while he was in flight, he looked all about him and waited for the public address system to dispense reassurance. His outlook had changed. Aristotle, which only minutes ago seemed to possess the stability and permanence of a planet, had somehow been reduced to an entirely different status – that of a spaceship in trouble.

It was incredible and shockingly unfair that something as important as Denny Hargate's continued existence should depend on something as notoriously fallible as human engineering. If something as vital as one of the huge mirrors could simply fall off, who was to say that even bigger disasters could not follow. Who could guarantee that the whole colony was not about to burst open under its internal pressures like a ripe seed pod?

Hargate's heart had begun thudding fiercely and steadily, but with the new thought there came a change in its rhythm, a hint of a more intimate catastrophe. It missed a beat altogether, and Hargate – floating, poised on the brink of the ultimate abyss – had time to consider the possibility that his life had ended. When it came, the next beat was more like a detonation inside his chest than the action of a muscle, and close in its wake there was pain, the kind of pain that draws the mind down into it, obliterating thought.

Hanging there in the solitary dimness of the crystal farm, like a fish in a net, mouth opening and closing silently, limbs making small involuntary movements, Hargate stared down the jewelled tunnel of the space colony and waited.

All he could do was wait . . . .


# CHAPTER 8

Long experience had shown that seven years was the longest period for which it was prudent for a Mollanian agent to remain in one location and with one identity. Beyond that span, no matter how good the agent had been at avoiding close relationships, people began to notice that the man or woman in the apartment down the hall was strangely untouched by the passage of time. They simultaneously became resentful and inquisitive, often without being consciously aware of their own feelings, and that was the signal for the agent to pack up and move on to another town.

'I call it the Dorian Grey syndrome,' Ichmo had told Gretana, showing off his knowledge of Terran literature on one of her early returns to Station 23. 'It's almost as if the Terrans are on the alert for that sort of thing, as if they have a collective unconscious in which there's a suspicion that they've been unfairly treated by Nature. The idea of immortality crops up many times in their mythology and literature, and it's interesting that anybody who is suspected of being immortal is usually presented in an unfavourable light.

'We could be directly responsible, of course – some of our people are bound to have been careless from time to time – but that's all the more reason to be careful now. Always move on at the very first hint that somebody is taking an undue interest in you.'

Gretana had recalled the conversation a number of times – but always with a mild and fairly academic interest – during her stay of seven years in Silver Spring under the name of Greta Rushton. Any special attention from Terrans had been inspired by her physical appearance, and she had soon learned to counter it with a glacial indifference which left the other party humbled or scornful according to his degree of self-esteem, and in either case definitely no longer interested. It had been the same during the seven-year spells she had spent in two other cities in the same region, and now that she was two years into her stay in Annapolis, Maryland it had begun to seem that her technique of repulsing strangers had reached perfection. That was why, quite suddenly, she was worried by the tall man in the slate-grey overcoat.

In an odd way, it had been the garment's lack of distinction which had drawn her attention to it. Two or three times while walking in Carter Park, she had thought: *There's a coat that was made for blending into back-grounds*. Then had come the belated realization that it was the same coat each time, and that in turn had drawn her attention to the wearer – the black-haired man who, by accident or design, seemed to visit many of the places she visited.

He appeared to be about thirty, was no more and no less ugly than any other native of Earth, and had droop-lidded grey eyes which gave him an expression of bored knowingness. It was his eyes which disturbed Gretana most. More than twenty years on Earth had taught her that some of the crudest and most offensive sexual ad-vances could be made through eye contact alone, without a word being spoken, but this man seemed to have different objectives. It was as though he got all the satisfaction he wanted simply by being near her in a crowd, looking at her, *knowing* about her – and, for someone in Gretana's position, that kind of attention was highly unwelcome. It was almost the worst possible kind.

*I'll give it one more chance*, she thought, one sharp and acrylic-bright January morning. *If he's in the park today, watching me, I'll take Ichmo's advice. I'll pack up in the afternoon and move on*.

She breakfasted early and spent an hour conscientiously absorbing TV newscasts, with special emphasis on her part of the United States and how its inhabitants were responding to their physical, political and cultural en-vironment in the year 2025 A.D. The international news was no worse than usual – the smallpox outbreak in the Netherlands was being brought under control; Sarawak had tested a second fusion device in spite of protests from neighbouring countries; preliminary reports were coming in of some kind of major mishap on the Aristotle space colony; and Britain had introduced sugar rationing for a trial period of three months. In the USA the steel, coal and dock strikes were close to being settled, but there had been setbacks in the negotiations on the power workers' and the hospital staffs' pay claims; California police had discovered a partially-completed high-megaton bomb in an underground cavern close to the centre of the Palmdale bulge; in Flint, Michigan, the owner of a sporting goods store had killed his wife by tying her to a chair and hurling a total of 381 darts into her. And in the Annapolis area, because of a westerly wind, temperatures were comparatively high and the radiation count comparatively low.

Gretana took in the news with the practised indifference which preserved her sanity, storing it in a disused room in the mansion of her mind, then left the apartment and walked slowly to the southern entrance of Carter Park. A light snowfall during the night had sunk down through the atmosphere like wine finings, giving the air a sparkle, and so many people were heading for the park that lines had formed at all the weapon detectors. By the time she had passed through she had begun to feel quite warm and she opened her blue duvet jacket to allow some of the crisp air to circulate around her body. Hot food stands were already beginning to do business, the open-air ice rink was in use, and several groups of children – having discovered that the snow was a suitable consistency for throwing – were engaged in good-natured horseplay, the boys crowing with pleasure when they brought off difficult shots. Tall buildings, visible here and there through the trees, formed a mellow pastel background to the entire scene.

As had happened many times in the past, Gretana was both entranced and dismayed. The phenomenal vitality of the Terrans, shown at its best on such an occasion, was a reminder that none of them had any time, that they began to die almost from the moment of birth. When she returned to Mollan in a mere five or six decades, still at the very beginning of her life, most of the darting animated figures around her – including the children – would have been consigned to the grave. How could such a thing be? How could such inequality exist? That small boy over there, the one sitting so quietly and watchfully beside his mother while he tried to comprehend the miracle of snow – what would be left of him when she was attending her first parties on Silver Island in the Bay of Karlth? Would she remember him while she and Vekrynn circled in the spangled twilight? Because, if she did remember, what right would she or any other Mollanian have to dance?

The realization that she was breaking her own rules for non-involvement and survival prompted Gretana to turn away in search of distraction. There was a modern self-heating conservatory in the centre of the park, one of her favourite places, and she walked straight to it. The air inside was heavy with the scent of foliage and blossoms, laden with moisture from a rectangular pool in which red-gold carp nosed and rippled the surface. She paused at a new display of trumpet-shaped purple flowers and after a moment's thought identified them as *Ruellia macrantha*. After the first sensual shock of learning that Earth flowers were varicoloured, she had made a hobby of botany for some years, but found difficulty in relating its scientific terms to the wondrous actuality of the plants themselves. The richly coloured trumpets at which she was looking, for example, were . . .

'I don't think you'll ever get used to them.' The male voice came from behind her and slightly to the right. 'No matter how long you stay here.'

Gretana turned and saw the man in the slate-coloured overcoat. Her first impulse was to hurry away, but years of dealing with predatory Terran men, and some women, had taught her that retreating usually encouraged the other person to advance. It was important to stand her ground. She examined the tall man dispassionately, as though he were another botanical specimen, then returned her gaze to the flowers without speaking.

'I like the flowers, but I'm not too sure about the insects.' he said. 'Have you ever taken a close look at an insect?'

*That's what I'm doing now.* The answer flashed into her mind – to be accompanied by a cold and impersonal stare – but it was dawning on Gretana that the stranger's remarks had an oblique quality about them, an ambiguity which hinted that he might have more than a casual pick-up on his mind. She glanced along the leafy aisles, saw they were almost alone in the conservatory, and decided there could be occasions on which it was only prudent to retreat. The man could be anything from an immigration official to a sex offender, and either way she had no wish to find out.

'Excuse me,' she said, keeping her voice light and unconcerned, and began to walk towards the entrance.

'Of course.' The man waited until she had taken several paces before he spoke again. 'Fair seasons.'

Gretana had taken two further steps before realizing that the final words had been spoken in Mollanian.

She paused – overwhelmed by surprise – and without looking back said, 'Who are you?'

The stranger added a new dimension to her surprise by emitting what sounded like a yelp of laughter. She spun round and saw that he really was laughing – shoulders raised, lean face growing darker as he strove to regulate his breathing. It appeared he was a person for whom laughing was not a superficial action, but a near-painful process which involved his whole body and was difficult to control.

'I'm sorry,' he managed to say, 'but it's *so* much like one of those awful spy melodramas. I knew you'd walk away, so I decided in advance that I'd speak to you in the tongue. You were supposed to stop with your back to me and say "Who are you?" – and that's exactly what you did. It was classic.' He palmed away a tear from the corner of his right eye and gave a ruminative snort of amusement.

Gretana felt some anger and puzzlement, but overriding everything was a growing sense of alarm. 'I've no idea what you're talking about.'

'It's all right,' the tall man said. 'My name is Kelth and I work for the Bureau. Just like you, except that I'm not assigned to any particular area.'

'I'm sorry, but I still don't . . .'

'Look, I know this is something of a shock for you, but I tell you it's all *right*.' He repeated the sentence in Mollanian, then switched back to English. 'We both work for Vekrynn.'

'But . . .'

'I know, I know – there's a strict rule about agents not associating with each other.' The man who had called himself Kelth gave an elaborate shrug. 'I've been here a quarter of a century, and that's a long time for anybody to be on his own – even a Mollanian. And with the whole planet getting ready to blow itself up any year now, I can't see how my talking to you for a few hours is going to make much difference to anything.' He smiled, showing teeth that were almost too regular. 'Except to me, that is – I think maybe I'm a bit homesick.'

'I don't know what to say,' Gretana confessed, still shocked and bewildered. She was deeply worried over the idea of breaking one of the Bureau's strictest regulations, and yet hearing just a few words spoken in her native tongue had made her realize how isolated her existence had become.

'Why don't you ask me how I located you?'

She considered the suggestion. 'How did you?'

'It was simple,' Kelth said, lowering his voice as a couple entered the conservatory. 'All I knew was that there was a female agent in the Annapolis area, but that was all I needed to know. It's easy to spot another Mollanian. If these people had any idea what was going on, if they had any idea what to look for, they could pick us up in no time.'

'I don't understand.' Gretana was unable to shake off a suspicion that she was being tricked in some way.

'Well, we've got these solitary habits, and by Earth standards are practically asexual – two dead give-aways. Also, our general appearances are roughly the same. We're all very tall and well set up in comparison to the average Terran, and there are points of resemblance in our features. The Bureau surgeons don't realize they're doing it because they can't shake our old Lucent Ideal nonsense out of their heads. They give us features which conform to a calculated median, without realizing that on Earth that's a formula for beauty.' Kelth paused and gave Gretana a direct, appreciative look which would have been a danger signal had it come from a Terran. 'I've been here long enough to appreciate Terran aesthetics, and I can tell you Vekrynn's tame sawbones really did a job on you.'

Gretana felt an unexpected flicker of gratification which had the effect of reawakening all her doubts. 'Look, this is wrong. I really don't want to go on with it.'

'There's nothing to go on *with*,' Kelth said. 'We have already committed the ghastly, monstrous, unspeakable crime of saying hello to each other, so we might as well relax for one day and practise the lost art of conversation. I'll tell you what I'll do . . .' Kelth showed signs of being overtaken by one of his unmanageable laughs. '. . . for every hour that you listen to me I'll listen to you for two. How's that?'

Gretana felt a similar urge to laugh and knew it had sprung from a preliminary easing of tension, a foretaste of what it would be like to lay down the burden of constantly being an alien among aliens. The idea was so appealing, her emotional defences so low, that she was predisposed to like and trust the tall man even though he was a stranger to her. Or was he? Looking at Kelth's face as he coped with the task of not laughing, she wondered if they could have met before they left Mollan.

'Do you come from Karlth?' she said, uncomfortably aware that asking the question signified acceptance of his proposal.

'Kelth of Karlth?' He smiled and shook his head. 'That sounds ridiculous. No, I'm from Eyrej province, beautiful home of the dewberry and the snowcake. I'll tell you all about it in boring detail if you like.'

'We'd better go to my apartment.'

'Your apartment!' Kelth allowed his jaw to sag. 'What sort of a person do you think I am?'

Gretana laughed aloud from the sheer pleasure of being party to an exclusive joke, a private communication from one Mollanian to another which meant, for once, that it was the Terrans who were the outsiders. Kelth had been contrasting the frenetic sexual activity of Earth to that of Mollan and giving her an unnecessary assurance that he would honour the behavioural codes of their own culture.

'You know,' she said warmly, 'I'd almost forgotten how to laugh.'

'Sounds as though you suffer from either a bad memory or bad jokes.'

'My memory is excellent,' Gretana replied, wondering why she had experienced yet another flicker of uneasiness as she glanced up at her new companion. She was inherently law-abiding, so the most likely explanation was that her conscience was troubled over the breaking of the Bureau's non-association rule – but the idea that she had seen Kelth somewhere lingered in her mind. She was toying with it, preparing to question him further about his past, when there came a thought which perhaps had been too obvious to occur earlier. Kelth, as a Mollanian, must have undergone surgery to enable him to work on Earth. His present appearance was substantially different to what it had been on Mollan, therefore her memory had to be playing tricks.

Relieved at having untangled a mental knot, she relaxed and began to anticipate the comfort of a day without loneliness.

Kelth had stated his intention to leave at eight in the evening, and Gretana timed the meal for 6.30 so that they could continue talking at a leisurely pace while they ate. The global food shortages had had one benefit as far as she was concerned – a wide variety of vegetable proteins were available in the stores, and she could look after her nutritional needs without resorting to animal products. She planned a menu which in many respects was similar to what they would have had on Mollan, and even – by marinating small grapes in a peach liqueur – managed to approximate Kelth's beloved dewberries. He remained in or near the kitchen while the meal was in preparation and they talked continuously, obsessively, about all things Mollanian – deliberately concentrating on homely trivia – with Kelth breaking into his infectious whole-body laughs each time they touched on a subject that particularly appealed to him.

With the passage of the hours Gretana's conscience had ceased its murmurings, and by the time they sat down to eat she felt happier than at any time since her arrival on

Earth. The starter dishes were good and the surroundings pleasant, she was mildly intoxicated by the conversation, and the darkness beyond the triple glass could have been that of a peaceful Mollanian evening, except for . . . She glanced towards the window on the east side of the room, knowing exactly where to look, and saw that a grain-coloured full moon was rising over the islands of Chesapeake Bay. Repressing a shiver, she went to the window and closed the venetian blind. Kelth's heavy-lidded eyes were intent on her as she returned to the table and sat down.

'That won't change anything,' he said perceptively. 'It's still there.'

'I know – but I'm practising being as blind as a Terran.' Aware that she had sounded callous, she lowered her gaze and stirred whorls of Creemette into her soup.

'These people are every bit as human as we are,' he said gently. 'They've just been unlucky.'

'I know that.' Annoyed at her own verbal clumsiness, she was unwilling to back down. 'I know they can't help being blind.'

'The point is that they would be just as aware of third-order forces as members of any other race if it wasn't for . . .' Kelth paused. 'Sorry – I didn't mean to lecture you.'

'It's all right.'

'Here I am – a first-time guest at your table – and I begin acting as if you were one of Old Father Vekrynn's Preservationist puppets.'

'I told you it's quite all right.' Gretana smiled, determined to hide the fact that she had been disturbed by Kelth's remarks. He appeared to have set out to make it obvious that he had little respect for Warden Vekrynn or the Bureau's central policy, possibly with the intention of sounding out her own views, and her political naïvety was such that she had no idea how to deal with the situation.

Could he have been joking? Or masking loyalty with cynicism?

'Anyway, I expect you'll have noticed by this time that Terrans aren't totally insensitive to third-order forces,' Kelth said, his interest apparently shifting.

'I've seen books on astrology.'

'That's pure mumbo-jumbo, except that they've almost got it right when they talk about the influences of planets when they're in square or trine, but I'm talking about the direct sensing of skord lines. I've travelled quite a bit in Europe and I've seen too many ancient megaliths placed directly on lines for it to have been coincidental. Also, it's amazing how many times you'll find that an old tavern or church has been built squarely on a minor node. They didn't consciously realize what they were doing, of course. They must have looked over an area and decided that one particular place *felt* right for a particular kind of building, without ever knowing what influenced their decisions.

'And you get the opposite effect with modern develop-ments which have been laid out by impersonal planning authorities. You'll get a pub which has been sited way off a line or a node, and the local residents don't want to patronize it, but they can't tell you why. All they know is that it is somehow out of place. There was an eighteenth century English poet called Pope, who was interested in garden layout and architecture, and his advice to planners was "consult the genius of the place". Now, if that doesn't indicate an . . .' Kelth stopped in mid-sentence and blinked apologetically over a poised spoonful of soup.

'I'm afraid you pressed my starter button,' he said. 'When anybody presses my starter button – off I go.'

Gretana shook her head, denying the need for an apology. 'I was interested.'

'Really? I'm glad about that. I've developed a great respect for the people of this planet, you see, and it sickens me the way they're regarded as freaks. Its so *unfair.*'

'They can hardly be classed as normal,' Gretana said, tentatively accepting the role of devil's advocate.

'No, but look at the general galactic situation. We know – in fact, it's basic to our philosophy – that the third-order forces which permeate the universe have a profound effect on living matter, especially just after conception. That's when the raw materials of heredity are sorting themselves into the arrangement for the new individual. It's a crucial time, when even the slightest interference from outside – say, the movement of nearby planets – has a major effect on the biological end-product.

'That's also why the presence of one or more natural satellites is *the* most powerful factor influencing the development of life on any given planet – simply because a moon is the nearest astronomical neighbour. Do you know, Gretana, that every other planet which supports intelligent life is either moonless, or has a very small moon in a remote orbit?

'Even in the latter case, even when the moon is just a distant hunk of rock, studies have shown that the indigenous race is handicapped in its development because of the unstable lunar influences.' Kelth abruptly swallowed the long-awaited spoonful of soup and, as if to make up for lost time, took several more in rapid succession.

'I didn't realize a small moon would make a difference,' Gretana said. 'I thought it was only . . .'

'Even the smallest has its effect.' Kelth cut in emphatically, 'and that's why the Terran culture is unique. Just think of it – a *massive* moon, a quarter of the diameter of the planet, at a distance of only thirty planetary diameters! There's nothing like it anywhere else in the known galaxy.'

Gretana considered her sketchy knowledge of

astronomy and frowned. 'Really? In a hundred billion star systems?'

'There are other planets with giant moons, of course, but none of them has evolved a civilization or even anything approaching intelligent life. This place is a crucible, Gretana. The first humans to skord themselves here must have been desperate for a home – maybe they chose it because nobody would follow – and their descendants probably lost the ability to escape right from the first generation. They've been here ever since, surviving in conditions that . . .

'Well, how can you describe the conditions? When the genetic programme is being assembled the weak, weak, weak molecular forces of DNA and RNA need a neutral environment in which to work – but what's it like here? A volcano? An anthill that somebody has just put his boot through? It's a miracle that the race has been able to survive this long, let alone create a civilization. By all the rules of the game, the Terrans should have degenerated to the level of rabid animals long ago, but somehow they've managed to retain their humanity – and what do *we* do? Do we offer them help?'

Kelth shook his head and an abstracted look in his eyes showed he was no longer addressing Gretana, that he was rehearsing old and painful arguments. 'We feel superior – that's what we do. We stand by with smug expressions on our faces and watch a world full of human beings go under. We help Old Father Vekrynn fill his stupid bloody Notebook.'

Gretana set her spoon down. 'I wish you wouldn't talk about Warden Vekrynn in that way.'

'Why? Is he a friend of yours?'

'I . . .' She decided to avoid personal issues. 'Mollan has always believed in non-intervention with other human worlds. Vekrynn didn't decide the policy.'

'No, but he doesn't oppose it.'

'Why should he?'

'Because it's *wrong*, Gretana.' All traces of humour had deserted Kelth's features, leaving a suggestion of hardness, a hinted capacity for cruelty which she found disconcerting.

'It's wrong to avoid inflicting culture shock?' she said, again feeling icy slitherings far back in her consciousness as she saw the change in Kelth's face. She was almost certain, regardless of logical objections, that his image was lodged somewhere in her memory, but she was unable to make the proper connections. Perhaps it was a matter of the name being . . .

'It's not the inflicting of culture shock that bothers Mollan,' Kelth said forcibly. 'It's the receiving of it.'

'That doesn't make sense,' Gretana countered. 'We are the most advanced.'

'The most static, you mean – the nearest to being dead.' Kelth moved his soup plate away to make room for his elbows as he leaned forward. 'I know you're very young, Gretana, but did it never strike you what a *boring* place Mollan was? We, as a people, have elevated vapidity to the status of a religion. We have a government which is dedicated to ensuring that nothing ever happens and nothing ever changes. We're a scared people, Gretana. We want eternity to be one endless Sunday afternoon – and that's why we don't interact with the other human worlds. It doesn't matter about our non-human contacts, because it's impossible for different species to have any social effect on each other, but we shut out the other humans because we're afraid of their vitality and their potential for change. Don't talk to me about culture shock.'

'I won't.' Gretana cast around for a suitable sarcasm. 'Your ideas are all too new and advanced for me.'

Kelth smiled in mock-kindliness. 'Could it be that *all* ideas are too new and advanced for you? It takes a certain kind of mind to face an eternal Sunday afternoon.'

'Meaning?'

'Meaning that you're a typical product of the Mollanian system of non-education. How many full-scale educational imprints have you taken in your whole life?'

Gretana felt her cheeks grow warm. 'I don't have to . . .'

'How many imprints, Gretana?'

'About twenty,' she said defensively.

'Twenty!' Kelth sighed and closed his eyes for a moment. 'You've been alive for something like eighty years, and out of that time – allowing a generous one second for the making of each imprint – you have devoted a third of a minute to the pursuit of knowledge. Congratulations!'

'I know all I need to know.'

'Not many people can make a claim like that,' Kelth said with overt irony.

'It seems to me that . . .' Gretana, about to protest at being lectured, left the sentence unfinished as an earlier thought returned to her mind. Was it possible that she knew Kelth under a different name?

'It seems to you that my stylus is stuck? Repeating a thing doesn't make it untrue.'

'It isn't the repetition, it's the over-simplification.' Gretana strove to marshal unfamiliar arguments. 'Does anybody ever do anything for a single, clear-cut reason?'

'Probably not. The Bureau's main reason for being so solidly in favour of non-intervention – they don't try to conceal it, don't even see it as something that ought to be concealed – is that they want their sociological data to remain quote valid unquote. The Warden's idea is to stand the uncertainty principle on its head, to observe without having any effect on the subject, and in that way to learn so much about the processes of macro-history that they'll be able to preserve Mollanian society unchanged, exactly the way it is now, for ever. The fact that you can't embalm a body until it's dead doesn't bother them.'

The smile, the sardonic twist to Kelth's lips, acted as a trigger which released ponderous mechanisms in Gretana's memory. An image was retrieved, compared with that of the man sitting opposite to her, and a new name appeared in the forefront of her consciousness – *Lorrest tye Thralen*. Its psychological impact was so great that she almost moaned aloud.

*You must act as though nothing had happened*, she told herself amid the clamour of mental alarms. *Act naturally . . . get close to the door . . .*

'Isn't that a one-sided view?' she said. 'Can outside contact *never* harm a developing culture?'

'What I'm saying is that there are circumstances which not only justify intervention, but which cry out for it. How many worlds did Vekrynn tell you the Bureau was observing? A hundred?'

'I think so.' Gretana spoke casually while she tried to remember which of the locks on the apartment's outer door were actually secured. It would be madness to run for the door and then have to waste valuable seconds fumbling with the locks.

'That figure is slightly historical,' Kelth/Lorrest said. 'Four civilizations out of the original hundred no longer exist. We stood by and allowed four planetary cultures to founder.'

Gretana scarcely heard. All her attention was on the task of raising a spoonful of soup to her lips and, in the most natural manner possible, pretending to find something wrong with it.

'This has gone cold,' she said lightly. 'It wasn't one of my best efforts, anyway.' She got to her feet, picked up

95

the two plates and carried them into the kitchen, her mind still grappling with the enormity of her problem. Crime of any sort was rare on Mollan, and murder was so unthinkable, so contrary to the basic tenets of Mollanian thought, that no case had been reported in Karlth during her six decades in the city. That showed that the memories relating to her visitor were the result of an educational imprint received during the induction given by the Bureau. The initial identification of Lorrest tye Thralen had been slowed by the intervening twenty-three years of experience and overlaid memories, but now that it had been achieved supplementary details were all too readily available:

*Lorrest tye Thralen, member of a radical political group (usually known as 2H), opposed to Mollan's non-intervention policy in general and the work of the Bureau of Wardens in particular. One of several 2H agents who infiltrated the Bureau for subversive reasons . . . others were detected, arrested and put in detention, but Lorrest escaped by murdering a guard. He made his way to Earth, the only place where – with his surgically-altered features – he could avoid recapture, and since then has successfully concealed himself among the planet's population masses. N.B. One Bureau worker who reported seeing him in South America subsequently vanished without trace a short time later and has been presumed dead . . .*

The flurry of decades-old memories concerning Lorrest served to increase Gretana's alarm. She had no idea why he had sought her out, but merely being near him was eroding her self-control at a frightening rate. It was imperative that she get out of the apartment quickly, before losing the slight advantage she had. A Mollanian who could kill was, by definition, an unpredictable psychotic, and the only reaction of which she was capable was to run away. Her instincts craved the sweet sensations of flight.

She rearranged saucepans on the cooker, making sure

the actions were audible, glanced around the kitchen and felt a pang of relief as she saw that her pocketbook and gloves were on a stool near the door which led into the hall. Her credit cards and money were in the pocketbook, which meant that once she was safely out of the apartment she could travel nonstop for a long distance, all the way to the Cotter's Edge nodal point if necessary. The trick was to get outside, quickly and without any fuss.

'That *would* happen,' she exclaimed with a show of homely annoyance. 'I'm completely out of celery salt. *Damn!*'

'It doesn't matter.' Lorrest spoke without turning his head towards the kitchen door. 'I don't mind.'

She laughed. 'It's obvious that you're no cook – I don't go to all the trouble of making greencakes and then serve them without celery salt. Not *ever*.'

'There's no need to . . .'

'No, *please* . . . I'm going to leave you on your own for sixty seconds while I run next door and borrow some from the Harpers. Do you mind?' Gretana was studying Lorrest's back as she spoke. He seemed completely relaxed, at ease with his surroundings, and it occurred to her that he would find her disappearance pretty bizarre if it turned out that she had mistaken his identity. Was that possible? How reliable was a memory imprinted twenty-three years earlier by . . .?

'I guess I can endure the solitude.' Lorrest stretched contentedly and placed his hands on the back of his neck, intertwining the fingers.

'Sixty seconds,' Gretana said. She strode silently to the other end of the kitchen, picked up her pocketbook and gloves, and did a rapid sidestep which took her into the hall. There was a silhouette, an unexpected presence. She gave a low sob as she saw that Lorrest was standing

97

at the apartment's outer door, barring her exit, his eyes filled with watchful reproach.

'You startled me,' she said hopelessly, aware that he had not been deceived, and that the speed with which he had reached the door proved she was physically outclassed. 'I've just remembered that I owe Joanie Harper ten dollars, so I'm bringing my . . .'

She broke off, transfixed, as the tall man's shoulders slowly drew up to the level of his ears. He stooped forward, face rapidly darkening, and it came to her that he was embarking on one of his harrowing bouts of laughter. She backed into the kitchen doorway and stood with one hand raised to her throat, unable to guess what might come next.

'I'm sorry,' Lorrest said, controlling his breathing with some difficulty, 'but you did it again. I *saw* the exact moment you realized who I was, and I guessed you'd make an excuse and go into the kitchen and another excuse to leave the apartment. The only bit I got wrong was the celery salt – I was betting on ordinary salt or sugar or coffee.'

'I want to leave,' Gretana said in a fear-dulled voice. 'Please let me go.'

'I can't do that, Gretana.'

'Why?' Her challenge was born of despair. 'Why not?'

Lorrest seemed surprised. 'I can't let you run out of here thinking I'm a murderer – you could draw a lot of attention to both of us. Besides, there's no need for you to abandon a perfectly good apartment. I'll be leaving soon and you'll have the place all to yourself again.'

Gretana backed further into the kitchen and resisted the desire to sag on to a stool. 'I don't understand.'

'Don't you?' Lorrest followed her into the cupboard-lined alley, his shoulders still twitching with nervous amusement. 'I mean you no harm – I only came to sound you out.'

'Under a false name.'

'We all use false names,' Lorrest said reasonably. 'Making contact was a bit tricky under the circumstances, and that's why I let you see me a few times in the park beforehand. I was hoping the imprint they gave you had faded out altogether.'

'I'll bet you were,' Gretana said, marvelling at her ability to think and speak coherently while alone in a small room with a taker of life. It occurred to her that, with her ignorance of abnormal psychology, she ought to avoid antagonizing or provoking Lorrest in any way. She tried to smile, to soften her retort.

'I'm not a murderer.' Lorrest's face was solemn. 'I'm a citizen of Mollan, just like you, and I'm no more capable of killing another human being than you are.'

'Then why did . . . ?' Gretana stifled the query.

'I should have thought that was obvious.' Lorrest said. 'The Warden knows that observers in the field, people with first-hand experience, are the most vulnerable part of the organization, most likely to be susceptible to the ideas of the 2H movement – so they take crude but quite effective steps to prevent ideological contamination. When there's no conflicting evidence, a lie can be imprinted in the memory just as easily as the truth.'

In spite of the confusion and fear which dominated her thoughts, Gretana was amazed at the audacity of what she had heard. Any Mollanian who knowingly made a cerebral imprint containing false information would be flouting one of the most rigid ethical codes ever devised. His statement that Vekrynn had done so was proof, if any more were needed, that Lorrest was alone and lost in his private reality.

'This is all so . . . ' Gretana paused, aware of the need to conciliate her visitor. 'You're telling me that the murder charges against you are falsifications?'

'Charges plural?'

'There was a Bureau worker who disappeared.'

'Oh, I see. That's all part of the technique. Any time an observer meets with an accident – which is bound to happen now and then – the Bureau says 2H was responsible.' The humorous expression returned to Lorrest's face. 'We ought to be able to sue.'

Gretana shook her head. 'I need time to think about this.'

'Well, if you're not really out of celery salt, perhaps we could . . .' Lorrest gestured towards the dining area.

'Of course.' As she began to serve the main course, Gretana found that her hands were trembling in spite of the fact that she no longer sensed an immediate threat. She did her best to conceal the reaction, encouraging Lorrest to expand on his ideas while she, knowing that a too-quick acceptance would arouse suspicion, pretended to give them impartial consideration. A new short-term goal overshadowed everything else in her life – she had to part company with Lorrest in safety, and as soon as possible afterwards go to the Cotter's Edge nodal point, transfer to Station 23 and report on the day's events. She had no idea what action the Bureau might take, but that was a matter for the future, and merely coping with the present was taking all her resources.

As the minutes went by, however, she found evidence that she was not the Gretana ty Iltha of two decades earlier. Her conditioned dread of being in the presence of a murderer was abating and some measure of self-possession was returning. By the time Lorrest had turned his attentions to the dewberry substitute she felt confident enough to play the role of a near-convert who had earned the right to do some plain talking.

'These are *good*,' Lorrest said. 'You must tell me how you did it.'

'Certainly – on one condition.'

'Name it.'

'That you tell me the real reason you're here.' She met his gaze squarely. 'The story I've heard so far doesn't make sense.'

'What's wrong with it?'

'You took a big risk contacting me the way you did – in fact, you still have no guarantee I won't report everything. And for what? My sympathy or allegiance couldn't make any difference to the 2H movement, otherwise you'd have contacted me long ago.' She kept her tone mild and impersonal, as though solving a party puzzle. 'So there must be something you haven't told me.'

'Not bad,' Lorrest replied, smiling. 'You're not just a pretty face.'

'Calling me pretty by Terran standards hardly constitutes flattery, so there's no point in . . .'

'I give in!' Lorrest set his spoon down and raised both hands. 'You're quite right – I admit you can help me a lot. You see there's a kind of unofficial truce between the Bureau and 2H at present. Vekrynn would like to see us put away, but as long as we're content to skulk around on Earth and do nothing it isn't a big thing with him.'

Lorrest paused to scan Gretana's face in a way that made her feel uncomfortable. 'But that situation is about to change. *Everything* is going to change, Gretana, and when it does Vekrynn is going to take this planet apart to find us. That's why I'm going to need your help.'

'You still haven't . . .' Gretana broke off as urgent new questions invaded her mind. 'What can you possibly do? Break the secrecy?'

'Go around telling people they've got visitors from another world? Warn them they've got to beat their missiles into plough-shares before it's too late? Groups of Terrans have been doing that for a long time and they get nothing but horselaughs. Besides, I'd have to turn the spotlight on myself and the Bureau would pick me up within a day.'

'What, then?'

'I can't tell you,' Lorrest said, his eyes holding hers with white-rimmed intensity. 'You'll know about it when it happens, though. Everybody in the world will know about it when it happens – but I can't tell you anything in advance. That's the way it has to be.'

*Megalomania, paranoia, schizophrenia,* Gretana thought. *How many madnesses are compatible?*

'Everything seems a little one-sided so far,' she said. 'I'm being asked to give my trust and my . . . Exactly what was it you wanted me to do?'

'I doubt if I'll be able to get off the planet without your help – it's as simple as that.' Lorrest gave her a rueful smile. 'We're short of manpower and resources in 2H. We've only been able to find three major nodes on Earth, and the nearest is in Chile, of all places – hardly what you would call a convenient location. The Bureau is aware of all three, anyway, and I know they are permanently watched, so they've got me penned here on Earth, unless . . .'

'I can't do it,' Gretana said quickly, her original fears returning in force. 'It's too much.'

'How can you say it's too much? It's *nothing!*' Lorrest's heavy eyelids slid downwards, censors. 'I'd use the node once only – *once only* – then I'd be gone, and nobody would even know I'd done it.'

'I took an oath.'

'Have you weighed up your priorities? Which is more important to you – honouring a meaningless bit of ritual or helping throw a lifeline to billions of human beings?'

'It's easy to put it like that.' Gretana almost sneered, wondering how far she dared go. 'You're talking about

102

changing the history of an entire planet, and you want me to invest my whole future in some wild plan you won't even discuss.'

'That's the way it had to be,' Lorrest replied. 'Some knowledge is too dangerous.'

'For whom?'

'I see.' Lorrest picked up a table knife and examined it, causing reflections to run like quicksilver on the blade. 'What if I admitted I really am a murderer and threatened to use force on you?'

'I wouldn't be able to believe anything you've told me,' Gretana said steadily. 'And that would be a pity.'

'No psychological manipulations, please.' Lorrest let the knife fall. 'Where do we go from here?'

'I suggest we don't go anywhere for a while – I need a little time to think things through. Does that sound fair?'

'Fair she says!' Lorrest stood up suddenly, almost toppling his chair behind him. 'Have you a television set?'

'There's a portable in my bedroom,' Gretana said, taken aback, feeling her pulse quicken. It appeared that Lorrest's mood had changed again, that the hours of talking had come to an end, and she had no idea what was coming next.

'That's good.' Lorrest walked into the hall, then reappeared in the doorway as he pulled on his grey overcoat. 'I suggest you pay attention to the newscasts during the next day or so – you might see something worth thinking *about*.'

He turned and left, moving with the silent speed that had confounded her earlier, and a second later the outer door of the apartment slammed so violently that the coffee cups she had set out shivered delicately on their saucers. She ran to the door and secured it, then went straight to the bedroom and began to pack an overnight bag.

The familiar task was almost completed when she paused, pressing the back of one hand to her forehead, forcing herself to review the events of the day. There was no doubt that Lorrest's principal reason for contacting her had been that he wanted the location of the Carsewell node, and on the face of it he had bungled the mission, alienating her with his wild talk and irrational behaviour. But was it possible that it had all been calculated?

If he had guessed in advance that she would remain loyal to Vekrynn he might have decided to take advantage of her inexperience, to give her enough of a jolt to send her scurrying to Station 23 by way of the hidden node. It was, now that she thought about it, quite possible that Lorrest was positioned nearby in the darkness outside the apartment, waiting for her to react according to his plan. And if that were the case, she would be better to do nothing out of the ordinary for at least a couple of days and use the time to devise a method of getting to Carsewell without being followed.

A new decision made, Gretana unpacked the overnight bag. With the need for action no longer present, she began to feel a deep weariness – a reaction to the prolonged tensions of the day – and her thoughts turned to the coffee which was percolating in the kitchen. Coffee with just a dash of brandy seemed highly desirable at that moment, no more than she had earned. She put the bag into a closet and, on impulse, picked up the lightweight television set and carried it with her into the kitchen.

## CHAPTER 9

Sedated though he was, the descent through the atmosphere and the landing at the Cape had terrified Hargate.

His sojourn in space had lasted only a matter of months, but that had been enough time for him to become acclimatized to its calmness, to an environment in which all movements were characterized by deliberation, smoothness and silence. In contrast, the final stage of his return to Earth had been a period of confusion, unbearable noise levels and wild buffeting from a dark grey atmosphere that appeared to be entirely composed of clouds, rain and hail. The landing at KSC had been so rough that Hargate had been positive the ship would be hauled away for repair, and yet he had heard it take off again barely two hours later, while he was still waiting to be processed at the emergency reception centre. Earth had become an alien and hostile place, peopled by cold-eyed giants who resented his presence, where the very weight of the air threatened to stop his breathing.

And the threat, he quickly discovered, was no figment of his imagination. He was waiting in line with about twenty other disabled refugees from Aristotle – some of them also in wheelchairs – when he began to sweat profusely and something like a massive cannonball seemed to form inside his chest. It was hard, uncompromising and *real*, leaving no room within his ribcage for the functioning of vital organs. His lungs fluttered against it, but were easily displaced; his heart strove to beat faster, but the warmth and life were being drawn out of it and into the metallic heat sink.

A crushing pain encircled his thorax.

He glanced around the makeshift reception centre – at the concrete floor, steel-trussed walls and unadorned windows with their sections of distant flat horizon – and felt an overriding panic at the notion that this, *this*, could be the last scene he would ever see.

'Pardon me,' he said to the wheat-haired woman who was seated on a bench beside him. 'Can you help me, please?' I think I'm having a . . .'

'Excuse me,' the woman said, smiling abstractedly as she stood up and walked away.

'You don't understand,' Hargate called after her, but stress and the increased weakness of his palate smothered the words in a nasal honking which even to his own ear sounded ludicrous. 'You great bitch,' he whispered and lapsed into silence as an agonizing pins-and-needles sensation swept from his feet up to his thighs, adding to the burden of fear, making it intolerable and at the same time providing him with a completely novel idea.

*Why not die?* he thought. *Everything's screwed up now, good and proper, so why don't you just compose yourself and get ready and ride the big wave that's going to get you to hell out of this mess?*

He took stock of his feelings and found he had not been indulging in private mock-heroics – dying seemed a perfectly good, logical and justifiable response to his set of problems. He subsided in his chair, relaxing, yielding.

*I'm ready now – ready as I'll ever be.*

There was a moment of something like peace, then the planetoid of iron inside his chest began to dwindle and the tide of pain slowly ebbed away from his legs. Hargate lay still, almost disappointed, and experimented with his breathing, taking longer and deeper draughts of air as the internal crisis passed. His surroundings reassembled themselves in his consciousness, resuming their former solidity, and the sounds within the hangar-like building grew louder as though a volume control was being turned up.

He saw that the wheat-haired woman was returning to her seat with a cup of coffee, appraising him from beneath lowered eyelids as she drew near. Reaching for the cup with both hands, he gave her his most dreadful one-sided grin and was rewarded by the way in which she did an abrupt left wheel and walked to another part of the line.

106

*Got you*, he thought vindictively. *That's for not loving thy neighbour.*

Later, when a harassed young medic, a Doctor Costick, asked him if he had experienced any ill effects from the space journey or the return to full gravity, he divulged nothing about the episode. His motives, he realized, were only partly that he had no wish to be hospitalized – the main consideration was that he no longer cared all that much whether he lived or died.

He had a natural preference for staying alive, but not if it meant – as he had done for as long as he could remember – bowing and scraping to the cloaked figure with the scythe, kissing skeletal feet. His stay on Aristotle, his holiday in the sky, had given him some idea of what a normal existence would be like, and he could see little reward in what now lay ahead. *First prize*, he thought, recalling and modifying an old joke, *one more year of Denny Hargate's old life; second prize – two more years of Denny Hargate's old life . . .*

'I'm glad you're okay,' Costick said. 'We haven't much in the way of specialist facilities around here. Do you feel fit enough to travel back to . . . ah . . . Carsewell right away?'

'I can make it, but there isn't much point – I gave up my apartment there when I signed on for Aristotle.' Hargate spoke comfortably, assigning all responsibility for his affairs to the NASA man.

'I see.' The medic unhappily inspected a document. 'How about relatives or friends?'

'What are those things?'

The pattern of furrows on Costick's brow deepened. 'I see you have always attended the Dutchess County neurology clinic in Poughkeepsie. We could probably find you some accommodation near there. How would that suit you?'

'I'm easy.' Talk of a new permanent home on Earth disturbed Hargate, making him realize he had not fully accepted the situation with regard to the space colony. The story which had reached him was that a maintenance engineer called Barron had gone berserk on the end-cap with a powerful cutting tool, and then had given himself up to the authorities. An artificial world was obviously vulnerable to sabotage, but Hargate was reluctant to concede that one man, in a few seconds of technological savagery, could negate what amounted to humanity's last grand dream.

'On the other hand,' he said casually. 'I quite like the climate here in Florida.'

Costick was not deceived. 'I don't think we'll be troubling you any farther, Mr Hargate – as soon as Aristotle became unstable it became uninhabitable.'

'Yeah, but it can't be all that hard to tack on a new mirror and steady the whole thing up again. Maybe in a month or two when they . . .'

'I believe it's a question of cost,' Costick cut in, happy to show that his expertise was not confined to one specialist field. 'Canada, France and Holland have already announced that they're withdrawing from the consortium, and you know what that means – these days we couldn't fly a kite without international funding.'

'I ought to sue this character Barron. Better still, I should kick his balls up into his throat.' Hargate took hold of his right trouser leg and raised one inert foot from the step of his chair, wondering why he was going into one of his set pieces in front of a man who was unlikely to be embarrassed.

'Maybe you'll get your chance – they're holding him right here in KSC in the International Condominium,' Costick said. 'I don't think they know what to do with him.'

'Him and me both.'

Costick glanced at his watch. 'That's not the case, Mr Hargate. I'm going to put you into the hostel for a night or two – at our expense, of course – and that will give you time to have a long talk with our senior placement officer.'

'I'll look forward to that,' Hargate said drily. Within an hour he had been installed in an architecturally unadventurous building which looked as though it had been designed as tourist accommodation back in the days when NASA still believed that Aristotle was only the forerunner of an expanding series of space colonies. It had been reactivated to house the pitiful brigade of which Hargate was a member – the invalids and the chronically ill, whose abrupt return to Earth was sending ripples of annoyance and inconvenience from one side of the country to the other. Hargate did not know whether to be relieved or disappointed over the fact that he had no relatives who would have played sullen games of pass-the-parcel with his reincarnated presence and all the attendant responsibilities. It would have been amusing, for a while anyway, to bowl unannounced on to somebody's patio with a cheery wave. *Hi, gang! I'm back* . . .

He chose to dine in his room, and found the meal amost more trouble than it was worth. The return to full gravity had made drinking particularly difficult. Before finishing his coffee he had soaked the table napkin with fluid regurgitated through his nose, and had been forced to bring extra tissues from the bathroom. In spite of all his caution, a few drops of the coffee found their way into his bronchial tract and, due to a new difficulty he was having with coughing, he spent twenty minutes after his meal in weak heaving and choking which left him exhausted. During that time it grew dark outside the room's single window and he found his thoughts returning to the intriguing, repulsive-attractive idea which had occurred to him in the afternoon. He was not suicidal, he decided on analysis of his feelings – it was simply that he could see some advantages in being dead.

The male attendant who came to remove the tray reproved him for sitting alone in the darkness, and after being startled by the caustic nature of Hargate's response took some measure of revenge by switching on the wall television, unbidden, on his way out. Hargate, swearing bitterly, propelled himself towards the remote control and was on the point of killing the picture when he realized that the tired-looking, stubble-chinned young man on the screen was actually Phil Barron, astronautical engineer extraordinary, perpetrator of history's most expensive single act of vandalism, author of all Hargate's current troubles. Barron, whose black curly hair was prematurely receding, looked angry rather than contrite, and deep indentations which kept appearing at the corners of his mouth suggested he was aggrieved by what the interviewer was saying. Hargate turned up the volume control.

'. . . of people talking about this super-laser I'm supposed to have had,' Barron said. 'What super-laser? I never heard of weapons like that, and even if they did exist somewhere – how would I have gotten hold of one?'

'It has been suggested,' the unseen interviewer put in, 'that it came from an Eastern Bloc country.'

'That, if you will forgive me saying so, is crap.' Barron moved restlessly, highlights on his forehead turning into blue-white shimmers. 'I've been through every loyalty check there is, and . . . and . . . Know what? This business makes me look *stupid*. If I had wanted to sabotage Aristotle I could have done it far better with one stick of dynamite and a timing clock. I wouldn't have risked getting my head burned off – and you can bet your life I wouldn't have made up that character in the funny spacesuit.'

'Oh yes – the incredible vanishing Martian.'

'I didn't say anything about a Martian,' Barron said doggedly. 'All I said was that he vanished.'

'You're positive he was there in the first place?'

Hargate, prompted by a stirring in his subconscious, increased the volume and leaned forward, scarcely breathing, as Barron wearily recounted how a figure in a silver-and-gold spacesuit had appeared in space near the colony's end-cap and had destroyed equipment worth millions of dollars with an unknown type of energy weapon. The story was an incredible one, quite unbelievable, and yet a small boy called Denny Hargate had once learned something very important about the hidden side of reality.

'And that's all there was to it,' the television reporter said. 'This spacesuited figure simply vanished?'

'Well . . .' Barron had begun to speak slowly, as though examining his own testimony for flaws. 'Before it actually disappeared it seemed to give some kind of a . . . I guess you'd have to call it a signal.'

'It waved good-bye to you.'

Barron ignored the facetiousness. 'Perhaps it was more like a *sign*. He did something like this . . .' Barron raised his right hand and hesitantly traced a curve in the air. 'Then he wasn't there any more.'

Hargate, whose heart had begun an irregular pounding, sat back in his chair and thought of the girl, the beautiful and magical girl, he had seen twenty years earlier in a secret place to which he had never been able to return.

The policeman at the main entrance was in his mid-twenties – old enough to have acquired breadth of shoulder and an air of having seen all there was to see; young enough to have retained a peachy smoothness of complexion. His tobacco-coloured uniform was neatly pressed

111

and its multi-hued roundels, reminiscent of historic astronauts' badges, glowed like jewellery. He stared down at Hargate with amused incredulity.

'I'm sorry, sir,' he said. 'There's just no way you could get in to see detainee Barron without a special permit.'

'I'm very glad to hear that – the Centre's finest would be falling down on the job if it allowed just anybody to walk in off the street and have access to dangerous criminals.' Hargate surveyed the bronzed glass foyer of the International Condominium's police headquarters and nodded his approval. 'Now, my reason for wanting to go inside is that I want to obtain one of those special permits you mentioned – so all you have to do is direct me to the appropriate room. Right?'

'Maybe. What's your name?'

'Dennis R. Hargate.'

'And where are you from, Mr Hargate?'

'Until yesterday I was from up there.' Hargate pointed one finger skywards. 'I'm a drop-out from Aristotle.'

'I see,' the policeman said doubtfully. 'What's your business with Barron?'

Hargate, in spite of having resolved to keep his tongue in check, grew impatient. He had been totally unable to sleep during the night, had left the hostel without breakfast and had spent more than an hour searching for and reaching the police building. Now he was beginning to feel tired and ill.

'I just want to visit with him,' he said. 'He's allowed visitors, isn't he?'

'I wouldn't know about that.'

'In that case, why don't we stop wasting each other's time?' Hargate moved his drive control and tried to surge towards the inner doors, but the policeman – with an embarrassed glance towards several passers-by – caught the chair's left armrest and slewed it round, forcing him to stop.

That was the beginning of a public argument which eventually involved Hargate with another policeman, two sergeants and several plain-clothes officers of indeterminate rank, and which got him no further than a cramped office adjoining the entrance hall. As his frustration increased he began to feel flickers of pain in his chest, but he prolonged the scene – capitalizing on the reluctance of the others to crack down hard on a cripple – until an entirely new symptom of his illness made itself apparent. At first his perceived world of giants simply appeared more crowded and confusing than usual, then came the jolting realization that he was experiencing double vision. It was a classic symptom of MPN, one which Doctor Foerster had predicted, but its effect on Hargate was powerfully disconcerting. He was being attacked from within his own *head*. He lapsed into an abrupt silence while he groped in his pockets for the box of Enka-B tablets he had been neglecting to use.

One of the sergeants hunkered down in front of him. 'Say, do you feel all right?'

'Why do you ask?' Hargate queried blandly, guessing that his features now had the additional asymmetry of a squint. 'Don't I look all right?'

It was when the sergeant turned away with a troubled expression, unexpectedly reminding Hargate of his mother when he had thrown verbal acid in her face, that he knew he wanted to go home. The notion of talking to Phil Barron, beguiling in its time, was ill-considered and pointless. What had he been hoping would come of it? An exclusive club for people who saw other people vanish in peculiar circumstances?

Hargate sat with his head down, trying to draw the calmness of *pranayama* from the air, only distantly aware that there were several newcomers in the small office. And when he found that one of them was Doctor Costick, presumably answering a summons from the police, he knew that his plans for the immediate future were complete.

He had done all that could be expected of him. He had tried the bold experiment of living a normal life in a frail travesty of a man's body. He had even ventured into space, something of which only a microscopic fraction of the human race could boast, and through no fault of his own the dice had fallen badly, denying him everything that Aristotle had promised. There was nothing more that he or anybody else could do. It was now time for him to get rid of the pain and discomfort, the hopelessness and sheer indignity of being Denny Hargate.

'Good morning, doctor,' he said, smiling. 'I don't know what was wrong with my memory yesterday – I've just thought of the perfect place for me to stay in Carsewell.'

The fact the he was allowed to leave for the north that day was, Hargate realized, an indication of the vast overload being placed on all the Cape's facilities by the emergency evacuation of the Aristotle colony. Throughout his entire stay the four operational shuttles had been living up to their generic name, the sound of their launchings creating an edgy vulcanic background to the lesser human activities on the ground. The Condominium was heavily populated by journalists of all kinds whose interest had been morbidly stimulated by the fact that the abandonment of Aristotle, the retreat from Lagrange, was probably the last big story concerning space flight. Hargate only escaped predatory reporters by virtue of not matching their preconceptions about how an astronaut ought to look.

His journey to the north took almost two days, a succession of starts and stops in transporter modules which clung for a while to the traction cables of huge nuclear prime movers and released their hold when a change of direction was needed. The gradual deterioration of the weather was appropriate to Hargate's mood, and he was almost gratified by his first sight of snow, grey-white tatters which littered the passing landscapes like discarded newspapers. By the time he reached Carsewell the snow covering was complete and the coldness of the early morning air shocked him with each invasion of his lungs. He could imagine their tissue already beginning to wither, to succumb, path-finding for the rest of his body.

The other passengers who had descended from the same module quickly dispersed, leaving Hargate alone on the platform with the single large case which held all his belongings. Force of habit caused him to ponder for a moment on how to get the case to the baggage lockers unaided, then he remembered there was no need. He was abdicating from such responsibilities. Feeling oddly guilty, he engaged the wheelchair's drive and rolled away towards the station's exit, abandoning the case to its shabby isolation.

Carsewell was in the middle of the slight lull that always followed the morning rush, but he had difficulty in hiring a taxi. Several drivers, deciding that his chair would cause more inconvenience than the fare was worth, ignored his signals, and more than ten minutes elapsed before he was picked up. By that time the cold had penetrated his coat and the rug that covered his legs. The paralysis and debility affecting most of his body precluded shivering, the natural defence against low temperatures, with the result that he quickly began to feel numb.

'Where to?' the taxi driver said as the vehicle pulled away from Warren Station with some sputtering from its ageing electric motor.

It occurred to Hargate that his batteries would be

unable to cope with the rising ground on the direct route to Cotter's Edge, that he would need to approach it from the eastern side. 'Do you know the Reigh place?'

'I only work on addresses, friend. You tell me the address and I'll get you there.'

'Just west of Greenways – I'll direct you,' Hargate said mildly. Under normal circumstances the other man's brusqueness would have inspired a vigorously unpleasant retort, but that too was something for which there was no longer any need. There was no point in fighting battles after the war itself had been lost. He stared quietly and abstractedly at familiar scenery until the taxi had neared the crest of the low hills which bounded the city and was travelling along the perimeter of the Reigh farm.

The driver looked puzzled but refrained from comment when Hargate got out at a cattle gate from which the farm buildings themselves could not even be seen. Hargate felt a playful urge to increase the man's bafflement by handing him all the money he had left as a tip, then decided it could excite suspicion and perhaps lead to interference with his plans. He gave a reasonable tip, watched the yellow vehicle disappear into the bright snowscape, then turned his thoughts to the considerable task of reaching the secret place in a conveyance which had not been designed for cross-country work.

Luckily, the snow covering had been pared thin by the wind and did not create too much drag once he had passed through the gate. He set off on a descending diagonal course towards the leafless maples which were like venous systems etched on horizontal swathes of brilliance formed by the pastures, folds of ground and distant hills. The sky was a sentient blue lens and it seemed impossible that he could reach his destination without being seen, but within five minutes he was safely among the trees and his motor

116

was whining in complaint as the chair balked at their root systems. He used what remained of his strength to turn the wheels, careless of the thorny undergrowths which tore at his knuckles, and – magical suddenness – he was there. The secret place was all around him.

It was almost twenty-one years since Hargate had visited the hidden clearing, and he had never seen it before in winter, but the *feel* of the place was the same, its welcome was the same. There, exactly as he remembered it, was the limestone shelf which formed a natural arm-chair, cushioned now with a white meniscus of snow. There was the spring, rimmed with ice petals, and even the overturned stump was more-or-less intact.

The nasal braying sound of Hargate's breathing began to abate as the stealthy intangibles of the place started to affect him. Its noumenon had not changed either. There was the same solitude without loneliness, the sense of being removed from the world and yet somehow, in a way that defied his understanding, of being at one with all that lay beyond the world.

*I've done the right thing*, he thought, nodding. *It'll be all right in this place . . .*

He grasped one edge of the red plaid travel rug and flicked it away from him, exposing the near-skeletal thinness of his legs, then unbuttoned his overcoat, jacket and shirt. The cold embraced him immediately, slipping intimate arms around his body, a practised lover who fully understood the principle of being cruel to be kind. Hargate endured the sensation without flinching, wondering how long the whole process was going to take. Others might have wanted time to review their lives and make final summations, but in his case there was no need for such embellishments. It was enough to have been Denny Hargate for thirty-two years. He was under no obligation to cap the experience with uninspired metaphors – nonstarter in the Great Race, dealt a losing hand, etc – when all he yearned for was a quick exit.

Hargate closed his eyes and waited.

At first there was considerable pain, from the coldness itself and from the pins-and-needles at his extremities, then the numbness took over and brought an end to all sensation. He was still alive, yet felt free of physical restraint. In the dreamlike state of being, halfway between life and death, the laws of space-time no longer seemed quite so immutable. Perhaps, after all, there was a lingering trace of magic in the universe.

*I wonder if I could do what she did*, he thought, aware that he was sinking fast, and taking nothing but comfort from the knowledge. *I wonder if I could follow her*.

Gripped by a sudden fey elation, an irrational conviction that the best was yet to come, he raised his right hand and retraced – as closely as he could remember it after a lapse of two decades – the design that had been scribed on the air by the loveliest girl he had ever seen.

Nothing happened.

No miracle occurred.

*You always were a fool*, he told himself, deliberately selecting the past tense, jeering at his own disappointment. *Right to the end* . . .


# CHAPTER 10

'He did something like this . . .' The tired-looking young man hesitantly moved his right hand through a complex downward curve. 'Then he wasn't there any more.'

Gretana, who had been watching the television relay from the Cape with some interest, felt a near-physical impact as the content of the young man's words and

118

actions stormed through her mind. She froze in the act of unbuttoning her blouse, went to the set and pressed the retro-record switch. Her second and third viewings of the crucial part of the interview proved superfluous – she had known first time round, with jarring certainty, that Phil Barron had been imitating a Mollanian transfer symbol. His claim that the spacesuited figure had then vanished, rendering his story incredible to almost any other listener, was all the proof she needed. The inescapable conclusion was that the Aristotle space colony had been sabotaged by a Mollanian.

She sat down on the pliant edge of her bed, staring with unfocused eyes, forgetting the summary of the news about the abandonment of Aristotle and the fierce international recriminations it was causing. Lorrest had told her to pay attention to the news, to be on the alert for evidence of 2H's activities – and there was no doubt that sabotaging the colony was interference with Terran affairs on a grand scale. It was almost certain that the renegades had located a minor transient node – a fortuitous, drifting intersection of local skord lines – which had enabled one of their number to carry out a guerrilla attack on Aristotle. Even Barron's assertion that the saboteur had stopped short of killing him was indirect evidence that he had encountered a Mollanian, but that only served to deepen the central mystery.

*Why had they done it?*

In what way could the destruction of Earth's first and only beachhead in space serve the aims of Lorrest and his organization? Given that he was acting from some kind of misguided altruism, she would have expected him to assist the Terrans to spread into space and away from the chaotic third-order forces of the Earth-Moon system. It seemed to her that Lorrest had slammed a door on the Terrans, trapping them on the ill-starred planet as effectively as he was.

119

She remained motionless, blouse partly undone, more convinced with each passing second that she was caught up in something far beyond her understanding, and that there were vast ramifications she had not even glimpsed. *Everybody in the world will know about it when it happens*, Lorrest had told her. *Vekrynn is going to take this planet apart to find us*. Was this what he had meant? Was this enough to prompt the Warden to institute a determined manhunt – or was it only a beginning?

The abrupt realization that she was completely out of her depth brought Gretana an unexpected sense of relief. Changing her mind about undressing, she stood up and went to the bedroom closet to fetch her overnight bag, comforted by the fact that her duties were now so clearly defined.

It was time to report to Warden Vekrynn.

The batteries of the rented car were growing weak by the time she reached Carsewell in the grainy light of dawn.

Lingering fears about being followed by Lorrest had led her to take a circuitous route and to expend extra energy by completing most of the journey at night. The result was that by the time she reached the southern approach to Carsewell her lack of speed was beginning to make the car conspicuous. Anxious though she was to reach the nodal point, she knew better than to break one of the most basic rules of her trade. She called in at a suburban service station to exchange batteries, only to be told by a grinning, Zapata-moustached attendant that a local power failure had depleted the stock of ready-units. All he could offer was a recharge which was going to take at least an hour.

Gretana, suddenly aware of how tired she was after the protracted drive, decided to accept the recharge. She went into the deserted coffee shop, determined to relax until the car was ready. The attendant, perhaps under the impression that her decision not to press on had something to do with his personal charm, followed her to the counter and straddled the stool next to her. Gretana spoke to him quietly and earnestly for some thirty seconds, at the end of which he stood up and walked away with a thoughtful expression.

Again it occurred to Gretana that she was not the person she had been twenty-three years earlier. A sudden yearning to go home, to be done with Earth and all its futility, turned her thoughts towards Vekrynn. While sipping black coffee she wondered if what she had to report would be sufficiently important to guarantee a meeting with him. The prospect of seeing the Warden again in person was both exciting and unnerving, a foretaste and at the same time a reaffirmation of all that the future promised. Lately, in spite of all her efforts, her vision of that endless golden Sunday afternoon . . . no, that had been Lorrest's derogatory phrase . . . of that succession of calmly joyful decades had been growing strangely two-dimensional, and she needed Vekrynn to restore its solidity.

As soon as the car was ready she drove through Carsewell to the west side of the city and parked on a little-used dirt track near the perimeter of the Greenways housing development. Ten minutes of brisk walking in the diamond-faceted morning air brought her to where nothing but the old highway separated her from the sloping pasture which led up to Cotter's Edge. She crossed over, negotiated the snow-filled drainage ditch and began the ascent towards the nodal point. The flawlessness of the white curvatures ahead of her, proof that she was the first to take the path since the snow had fallen, raised the question of how many Mollanian observers used the same route to Station 23. She guessed the number would have to be quite small to prevent the area of the node attracting too much local interest and perhaps acquiring an odd reputation.

On reaching the cover of the trees she kicked some compacted snow off her boots, and – already sensing the other-worldliness, the *connectedness* of the place – made towards the hidden clearing. Rehearsing the address of Station 23 in her mind, she skirted a clump of undergrowth, went to step down into the invisible aura of the node itself and jarred to a halt, a shocked whimper escaping her lips.

Encountering another person in the clearing was a rare and surprising event – it had happened only once in more than two decades – but its strangeness was compounded by the intruder's appearance.

Sitting in an electrically-propelled wheelchair was a frail, hollow-shouldered man, possibly in his early thirties, whose lop-sided face had been eroded by illness and pain. Here was a man, Gretana knew immediately, whose lifespan would be only a tiny fraction of her own, short even by Terran standards, but who knew more about suffering than she could ever comprehend. A reddish plaid rug lay on the ground beside his chair and his concave chest was exposed to the hostile chill of the winter air. The man's face was mottled with blue, and small fast-fading feathers of condensation testified to the weakness and rapidity of his breathing.

*He's dying*, she thought, chastened, prey to all the lacerating emotions she thought she had learned to suppress. *He came here to die!*

Overwhelmed by a combination of uncertainty and pity, she held herself as still as one of the surrounding trees while her mind wrestled with a terrible suspicion. There was something about the man's tortured face, something about the set of his chin and the incongruous smoothness of his brow . . .

*Is this the same little boy? The one who fled on his crutches?* Gretana felt a coldness which had nothing to do with the environment. *Is this what twenty years of illness . . .?*

The answer to her questions was both unexpected and dramatic. Under her petrified gaze, the man in the wheelchair raised his right hand and brought it downwards through the air in what was undoubtedly an attempt to reproduce a Mollanian transfer symbol.

She understood at once that the crippled boy and man were the same person, and that at some time in the past he had seen her or some other Mollanian agent depart for Station 23. The event would have seemed like magic to the Terran, especially as a child, and the impression it must have made could be gauged from the fact that he had chosen to spend the last minutes of his life here. Inspired by a last guttering of hope, he had tried to set foot on the same invisible road. Predictably, his gesture had brought no result. The whole principle of sympathetic congruency was dependent on a number of factors – an understanding of the basic philosophy, a disciplined effort of will, an awareness of the mathematical relationship between primary location and the target node.

None of these had been available to the man in the wheelchair, however, and with the failure of his untutored attempt to skord he appeared to have given up his hold on life. He had lowered his head, folded his hands in his lap, and the movements of his chest were fast becoming imperceptible. His very submissiveness – like that of a small animal curling up to die – magnified Gretana's pain. She pressed the heels of both hands to her temples. Something had to be done, but nothing could be done. To try summoning medical aid would only . . .

'Over here, Ed,' a man shouted from somewhere nearby. 'She's in here.'

Gretana spun round, dry-mouthed, and through the trees glimpsed a tall, heavy-set man in the crimson cap of a hunter. He was carrying a shotgun and beckoning to a companion. She reached the centre of the clearing without being conscious of any physical effort or lapse of time. For a second she feared that the distractions of the situation would scramble her thoughts, but her mind reacted positively, assembling the elements of the transfer equation with special rapidity.

She lifted her right hand, poised herself for departure, and in that precise instant the man in the wheelchair raised his head, opened his eyes. She saw his look of disbelief merge in wonderment, then he was reaching towards her with both hands in a kind of supplication. There was a splintering of twigs, a rattling of undergrowth near the edge of the clearing.

Unable to check herself, driven by a complex emotional reaction, Gretana took one of the outstretched hands, and at the same time used her right hand to sculpt a unique quintic mnemo-curve in the cold air.

The transfer took place.

# CHAPTER 11

It was night on 82 Eridani I, and Field Station 23 looked exactly as it had done when Gretana first saw it. The buildings on the edge of the circular plaza were throwing up a wash of light which overpainted all but the brightest stars, and there was the same sense of inner emptiness which told her that no planets swam in that region of space. There was, however, one vast difference in the circumstances of her arrival.

Beside her, at the centre of the radial mosaic, the

crippled Terran was struggling into an upright attitude in his wheelchair.

Propping himself up on his arms, he looked at her and at the backdrop of angular luminosities. For a moment his asymmetrical features registered a blend of surprise and jubilation, and then – an abrupt reminder of why she had yielded to instinct – he slumped back unconscious, head lolling on to his chest. His hands slid from the chair's armrests to swing limply beside the wheels.

'No, *no*,' Gretana breathed. She caught the handgrips at the back of the chair, turned it and began pushing it towards the station's reception chamber. Lines of tesserae pulsed amber and white beneath her feet as she overcame the chair's inertia and began to pick up speed. There was a movement of silhouettes ahead, accompanied by shouts and the sound of running feet, then Ichmo tye Railt was beside her and using his superior strength to drag the chair to a halt.

'What do you think you're *doing*?' Ichmo's ill-proportioned face was taut with anger and shock. 'You've got to go back.'

Gretana shook her head. 'I can't do that.'

'You haven't any choice in the matter,' he shouted, overwhelming her with the sheer volume of sound as he pushed both her and the wheelchair back towards the centre of the plaza. 'You're going right now.'

'There were Terrans near the node. They might have seen me leave.'

'You'll just have to wait till they leave.'

'That could take an hour,' Gretana insisted. 'This man will be dead by then – and you'll be responsible.'

'*I'll* be . . .!' Ichmo released his hold and stepped back from Gretana, looking bemused. 'That's the most unfair thing I've ever heard. You're pulling me down with you.'

'You've got to decide your priorities,' she said coldly,

two decades on Earth having accustomed her to verbal in-fighting. 'Is your career more important than the life of another human being?'

'This is the first time anybody has done this.' Ichmo looked at the inert figure in the wheelchair and averted his gaze, but not before Gretana had seen the flicker of revulsion in his eyes. 'Why are you here? Your next deposition isn't due for some time.'

'I have to make a special report.'

'If it's about the space colony business, we already have a . . .'

'I don't care what you have,' Gretana snapped. 'This man needs attention right now, and I'm going to see that he gets it.' She pushed the wheelchair past Ichmo, knowing as she did so that she was acting out of character, compensating for the uncertainties and alarms that were growing within her. It was quite possible that in the entire history of the Bureau no observer had ever broken the rules so flagrantly and spectacularly as she had just done, and she had no idea what the consequences would be. In particular, she could not anticipate Vekrynn's reactions. All she could do for the moment was try to avert the final tragedy for the man in the wheelchair.

'Is this somebody you got friendly with?' Ichmo said, pacing beside her.

'I don't even know his name.'

Ichmo looked distraught. 'Do you know what's wrong with him?'

'I'm not sure. He's been ill most of his life, but right now he's suffering from exposure.'

'What do you expect us to do for him?'

'He needs heat most of all. And medical aid.'

'But we haven't any doctors here.' Ichmo moved ahead to open the door to the reception chamber. 'And even if we had, they wouldn't know anything about Terran medicine.'

Gretana made no attempt to conceal her impatience. 'Are you telling me that after five thousand years of stuffing data banks with information about Earth we haven't the means to diagnose and treat a single illness?'

'That isn't our function,' Ichmo grumbled.

'Well, I suggest that we start being flexible about our function.' Gretana said in a deceptively mild voice, 'otherwise you'll have a corpse to dispose of.'

Only later, while sitting alone beside the Terran's bed, did she appreciate how heedlessly wilful she had been in threatening Ichmo with having to see a cadaver, a bleak experience which rarely befell any Mollanian. Another surprising aspect of her behaviour was that, for the first time in her life, she had interacted with other Mollanians without even once remembering her lack of beauty and letting herself be influenced by it. *Am I changing?* she wondered. *Is this what Vekrynn was talking about when he said the Lucent Ideal was a parochial concept?*

The room in which she was sitting was quiet except for occasional snuffles from the unconscious Terran, but for an hour it had been a centre of activity. Doctors had been summoned across light years from other Bureau establishments, specially prepared medication had been administered, officials of unknown rank had conferred with each other and had departed without speaking to Gretana. She had been isolated, made to feel as alien as the Terran himself, and knew without being told that she was to be dealt with by Vekrynn in person.

It was ironic, she decided, that her wish to meet Vekrynn again was being granted under such strange circumstances. He was bound to be angry, and the thought of it filled her with foreboding. She could only hope that the importance of what she had to report about Lorrest tye Thralen would be weighed against the seriousness of her crime.

In the confusion following her arrival at Station 23, Ichmo had neglected to enquire further into the reasons for her return, and now she was regarding the information as something like a trump card to be played at the most advantageous moment. And underlying her concern for her own future was the question of what was to be done with the pitifully frail Terran. Dennis Hargate, former inhabitant of Aristotle – as his papers identified him – appeared to be sleeping off a deep exhaustion, and if he remained unconscious until after Vekrynn could be consulted it might be allowable to teleport him back to Earth. He had seen little and possibly would remember or understand less, and it was almost certain that any story he told on Earth would be regarded as a product of delirium. That being the case, there was room to hope that the whole incident could be tidied up and forgotten, and that . . .

'Where am I?' Hargate said abruptly, disturbing the utter silence of the room with a thin nasal voice. He had not moved in any way, but his eyes were open and staring at the featureless ceiling.

Gretana, her nerves tingling, glanced around the room and saw there was little to distinguish it from any apartment on Earth. There was nothing about her Terran clothing to arouse suspicion, and if Hargate could be induced to go back to sleep – perhaps to be kept sedated – it could still be possible to return him to his own world.

'There's nothing to worry about,' she soothed. 'You're in hospital.'

'You wouldn't lie to me, would you?'

'Of course not.'

'If I'm in hospital, why have I been laid out in my street clothes?'

The observance of the little Terran complicated Gretana's tentative plans. 'You're going to be all right.'

'I can tell I'm going to be all right – that wasn't the question,' Hargate said. 'I want to know where I am.'

The note of impatience in his voice was another surprise – she would have expected bewilderment or panic. 'Not far from Carsewell,' she floundered.

Hargate raised his hands a short distance and allowed them to fall 'How many light years?'

'I don't understand,' Gretana said, suddenly aware that the fragile occupant of the bed, physically handicapped though he was, had an uncompromising flinty intelligence and that her chances of manipulating him were approximately nil.

'The place I saw isn't on Earth – you aren't keeping it secret – and there aren't any other suitable worlds in the solar system.' Hargate's voice was weak and he continued to stare at the ceiling. 'That means I'm in a different star system – so I'm asking you if it's close to Sol . . . or in a far part of the galaxy . . . or in a different galaxy altogether. It's important for me to know where I am. Do you understand?'

'Twenty light years,' Gretana said, coming to terms with the new facts of the situation.

'So it's 82 Eridani, assuming you go for G-type suns. Thank you. It makes me feel less helpless when I know exactly where I am, though in this case . . .' Hargate's voice faded out for a moment, and when it returned he sounded almost like a child. 'It was as good as a religion to me, you know . . . as good as magic . . . knowing there was a different game going on somewhere . . . with different rules . . .'

The halting words gave Gretana an intuitive and empathetic glimpse into a life other than her own, a life claustrophobically bounded by dark palisades of sickness and pain and all the wretched parameters of Earth, yet one which was lit from within by courage and imagination.

And she, Gretana ty Iltha, had once regarded herself as the unluckiest creature in the universe because of a slight disproportion of her features. Shamed, prompted by a blend of curiosity and respect, she stood up and approached the bed. Hargate stared up at her for several seconds, and she saw his eyes widen in recognition.

'I thought I dreamed that part,' he said. 'I saw you about twenty years ago, and you're still twenty . . . It's a bigger game than I thought, isn't it?'

'I'm not allowed to say anything.'

'Oh? And were you allowed to kidnap me?'

Gretana had almost begun an indignant retort when she realized that Hargate was attempting to manipulate *her*. 'The only reason I don't seem to have aged is that my people have a much longer life-span than the people of Earth,' she said, refusing to be ruffled. 'Two decades is a very short time to us.'

'Really? And roughly how long do you manage to peg on for?'

'On average . . .' Gretana paused, oddly embarrassed. 'Five thousand years.'

'*Five thou . . .!*' Hargate raised himself up in the bed, then fell back on the pillow, smiling his one-sided smile.

'It's a result of biological engineering,' Gretana said quickly. 'The norm for a human planet is very much less.'

'You mean a mere couple of hundred years or so.'

'About seven hundred.'

'*Christ!*' Hargate lapsed into silence, and when he spoke again his voice was bitter, reflective. 'What did we do wrong? Was it something we said?'

Gretana, uncomfortably aware of having disclosed too much, considered trying to explain that the presence of its giant, bloated Moon made Earth a seething cauldron of third-order forces which wreaked havoc on the genetic inheritance of every creature conceived within its influence; that the disruption of the sub-molecular building blocks at the most delicate phase of their existence was recipe for sickness and unreason; that conditions on Earth were so unfavourable for civilization that it had even been theorized that an offshoot of humanity had been planted there by an ancient and malevolent experimenter. The explanation would be meaningless unless set in the entire Mollanian context, and if she provided that she would be compounding her crime against the Bureau. On the other hand, a man like Hargate was capable of deducing or guessing a great deal about the Bureau's activities from what he already knew . . .

Resolving to confine herself to historical and philosophical generalities, Gretana began to expand Hargate's mental horizons. Through much of the discourse he lay quite still, his eyes glittering and yet abstracted, like someone who was receiving a prolonged fix with a much-craved narcotic. Only when she reached the central issue was there an adverse reaction.

'You're laying an awful lot of blame on the poor old Moon, he said. 'I can't . . . I mean, it's hard to accept that these third-order forces you talk about, forces you can't even feel, could cause so much harm.'

'*You* can't feel them – most non-Terrans would be very much aware of them.'

'But, according to what you say, you've been on Earth for years and they haven't had any ill effect.'

'That's because I'm an adult human,' Gretana explained again. 'The vulnerable stage in an individual's history is in the days following conception. I'm talking about humans now – there are many other races, differently structured, whose adult members couldn't think of entering the Earth-Moon system for even a day. Others will risk very brief visits in specially shielded ships.'

'At least it's an answer to the Fermi paradox – where is

everbody?' Hargate frowned at the ceiling. 'If two smallish bodies like the Earth and Moon set up all these bad
vibes, how about binary stars?'

The point was one which Gretana recalled very clearly
from an imprint. 'As far as we know, no planet of a
multiple star has ever evolved any kind of life.'

'I suppose it all fits. It isn't even a pun to call us
lunatics – the word directly associates the Moon with
madness. It's all so . . .' Hargate became silent again, his
eyes sombre as he considered the history of his own world
from a new vantage point.

'Perhaps you should get some sleep.'

'*Sleep!*' A corner of Hargate's mouth twitched. 'You
know, some of our philosophers and most of our religious
leaders always claimed that we had a special place in the
scheme of things – but I don't think the galactic freak
show was what they had in mind.'

'It isn't like that,' Gretana said, repressing a pang of
irrational guilt. She began to outline the doctrinal reasons
for Mollanian non-interference with other human worlds,
then went on to the work of the Bureau of Wardens.
Having started to speak, she found that apparently separate subjects were deeply interconnected. When dealing
with recent events it proved difficult to avoid certain
areas, and – with some prompting from Hargate – she
confessed her belief that it was a Mollanian renegade who
had sabotaged the Aristotle space colony. Somewhat to
her surprise, Hargate's interest in the fate of the space
habitat was short-lived. He kept returning to the basics of
Mollanian science and philosophy, particularly to the
principles of non-cursive travel.

'Does that mean that Mollanians don't use spacecraft at
all?' he said.

She shook her head. 'We use them, but mainly for bulk
transport of raw materials and local travel where there

aren't any convenient nodes. They aren't suitable for interstellar travel because of the light barrier. When it's necessary to put a ship into another system, the components are usually skorded there separately and assembled.'

'I see.' In spite of the growing signs of tiredness, Hargate remained fascinated. 'Do you think that somebody from Earth – me, for instance – could learn to skord?'

The idea was totally new to Gretana. 'It might be possible – your ancestors must have had the ability.'

'What's it like? How do you feel when you just *step* from star to star, world to world, and see everything change?'

'I don't know. I've only travelled to Earth.'

'Huh?' Hargate stared at her with incredulous blue eyes. 'You mean you could have walked the galaxy and you simply never bothered? My God, woman!'

Gretana was disturbed by an uncanny sense of having taken part in the same conversation at an earlier time, then it came to her that Hargate's tone was exactly the same as the one Lorrest had used during their single meal together. All at once, it seemed, every man she met – hunted murderer or house-bound Terran – was assuming the right to treat her with open scorn. A surge of indignation sent her back to her chair. She had taken only two paces when she heard a flurry of movement and a low gasp. She turned and saw that Hargate, apparently having attempted to detain her, was lying askew on the bed. He was clutching his side and his eyes, opaque with pain, were locked with hers.

'Don't go,' he whispered, trying to smile. 'I'll let you beat me at Indian wrestling.'

It dawned on her that Hargate, unaware that she too was under confinement, had assumed he was going to be left alone and the prospect had scared him. She went to the bed and, concealing her dismay at how light and feeble he was, helped him rearrange his limbs in a comfortable position. As a member of a disease-free race, she found it chastening to touch his wasted frame. The little Terran, unprepared and with zero physical resources, had been through experiences which could have reduced others to incoherence – and yet he had dared to criticize her way of life. Gretana gave a grudging smile as she realized that Hargate was quite unrepentant – he had pleaded and joked, but had not actually apologized.

'What's funny?' he said tiredly, watching her with half-closed eyes.

'Perhaps you are,' she replied, aware that for the first time in their strange relationship she had begun to see him as a human being. 'I've been answering all your questions – when do I get to hear something about you?'

'Apart from my triple career as a male model, tennis champion amd computer designer, there isn't much to tell.' Hargate allowed himself to be coaxed into an account of his life which grew more and more episodic as the effects of weakness and medication drew him closer to unconsciousness. In between times, Gretana told him something of her own past and hopes for the future, not really sure whether he was awake or asleep, and as she too grew tired it occurred to her that she had been waiting a long time for Vekrynn to arrive.

*Perhaps what I've done won't seem all that terrible to him*, she thought, drifting into a sleepy euphoria. *Perhaps, he'll understand . . .*

# CHAPTER 12

The domed blue ceiling of Vekrynn's office was like an empty sky, and the sparse furnishings – devoid of individuality – were a reminder that the room's nominal occupant viewed the material world with an Olympian perspective. There was a lack of warmth which had nothing to do with the air temperature, rather a sense of coldness seeping backwards from the end of time.

Intimidating though the ambience was, Gretana was unable to look anywhere but at Vekrynn tye Orltha himself. Years on Earth had insensibly accustomed her to the proportions of Terran males, with the result that the Warden seemed more than ever like a titanic statue moulded in all the noble metals. The gilt helmet of closely waved hair, the platinum of the embroidered tunic, the brown eyes needled with gold – all had the effect of irradiating the surrounding space. As she approached him she felt a sudden faith that his resources were more than enough to render her problems insignificant.

'Fair seasons, Warden,' she said, with more confidence than she would have thought possible an hour earlier.

'You,' Vekrynn replied, ignoring the greeting, 'are even more stupid than you are ugly – and, believe me, that means *stupid*.'

'Sir, I . . .' The insult roiled through Gretana's mind, demoralizing her with its crudity, and all at once it was as though she had never been to Earth. She was the Gretana ty Iltha who had lived a sequestered life in a Karlth suburb long ago – pathetic, unlovely and vulnerable.

'I'd like to know what you thought you were doing. What made you bring that object here?'

'There was no time to . . .' Gretana, who had been unconsciously drawing herself up into her old mirror-watching attitude, was jarred by the word which Vekrynn had applied to Denny Hargate. She dredged up the self-control to make her shoulder muscles relax, to stave off the prickling that had begun to blur her vision.

'He isn't an object,' she said quietly, numbed by her temerity in challenging the Warden. 'He's a human being, and he was dying.'

Vekrynn came towards her, looming. 'Is that supposed to be something new on Earth?'

'It's new for each person it happens to,' she said, willing herself not to back down in response to the overwhelming psychic pressure being exerted by the Warden.

'This is incredible,' Vekrynn half-whispered, drawing near. 'I never thought that you, of all the observers I've recruited, would have the . . .' His eyes hunted over her face, speculative and oddly cautious, then he turned and walked back to his desk. He sat down in the high-backed chair and when he looked towards Gretana again she was surprised to see that he was smiling.

'You made me lose my temper, Gretana ty Iltha, and that is quite an achievement,' he said. 'Now, let's see if you can distinguish yourself even further by correctly divining *why* I got angry.'

Gretana was disconcerted. 'I broke the law. I disobeyed a prime directive, but there was no . . .' Her voice faded as she saw that Vekrynn, still smiling, had begun to shake his head.

'Laws. Directives. Regulations. They're very important to us, but at the same time they are only abstractions, which mean they are quite *un*important compared to some other things – for example, a human life. I know you acted on impulse, but what's going to happen to this poor creature Hargate now? He can't be sent back to Earth,

136

knowing what he does, and there is no place for him in our society.' Vekrynn waited for his words to take effect.

'From what I've been told, Hargate is a very sick person, in all probability one whose intellect and experience are severely limited, even by Terran standards. I can arrange to have him institutionalized, of course, but the severity of the culture shock that would involve is inconceivable. In your attempt to be kind you have condemned him to end his days in isolation from everbody and everything he knows and cares about, in total confusion and bewilderment.'

'I didn't think of it like that,' Gretana said, aware that she was being truthful on two separate levels. In skording with Hargate to Station 23 she had acted with absolutely no thought for the future – nor could she, now that she knew him, imagine the acid-tongued and quick-tempered Terran being intimidated by alien surroundings. He would possibly be afraid, but – another fragment remembered from conversation with Lorrest – it was the Mollanians entrusted with his welfare who were likely to experience culture shock. Thoughts of Lorrest reminded Gretana she had not yet told Vekrynn the reason for her unscheduled return. It should have been the first thing to be discussed, but the Warden had been too busy telling her she was stupid and ugly . . .

'Let's go on with the guessing game,' Vekrynn said. 'Give me two more reasons for being angry with you.'

Gretana, still unable to gauge the Warden's mood, shook her head. 'I'm sorry.'

'One of them is the harm you've done your own career – I'm supposed to return to you to Mollan for arraignment – the other is the fact that you have involved me. You see, I have no intention of surrendering a member of my team, and that means I must commit certain infringements and do a lot of talking and go to a lot of trouble that I wouldn't otherwise have had.' Vekrynn took time to produce a wintry smile. 'I'm a busy man, young Gretana, and I would have been happy to forgo all this.'

'I'm quite prepared to return to Mollan and accept the . . .'

'Nonsense! You're going back to Earth, where you can be of some service to the Bureau, and the Terran is going with me.'

'Where to?' Gretana said, having difficulty in keeping up with the pace of the exchange.

'I have a private estate – a retreat, you might call it – on Cialth. It's a very pleasant world and I have permanent staff there, so the Terran will be well looked after. He will be my private guest for as long as it takes for him to . . . for the time remaining to him.'

The resentment caused by Vekrynn's opening remark began to fade from Gretana's mind as she strove to modify her attitudes towards him. She had hoped for clemency and understanding, but it had never occurred to her that a man in the Warden's position would personally shoulder the responsibility for her ill-considered actions.

'Don't stand there dreaming,' Vekrynn snapped. 'Go back to the Terran, put him into his conveyance and bring him out to the node. I'll be waiting for you there.'

'But I . . .'

'Do it *now!*' Vekrynn's eyes projected ancient and overwhelming authority.

Gretana nodded and almost at once found herself hurrying through the long ante-chamber where three-dimensional star maps floated in the dimness. The corridors and offices of the station were unnaturally deserted, and she wondered if people were keeping out of Vekrynn's way or if he had ordered a general clearance for reasons of his own. She entered the room which had been set aside for Hargate's improvised treatment. He was still asleep, lying exactly as she had left him, looking too ill and broken to be alive. The incongruity of his Earth-style clothing was an indictment to Gretana. She worked both hands under the slight figure and, once again daunted by his lack of body mass, placed him in the wheelchair which had been parked in a corner. Hargate grunted noisily during the process, and by the time she had arranged his legs in positions of apparent comfort he was wide awake and alert.

'If you've finished taking liberties with my person,' he said, 'would you mind telling me what's happening?'

Gretana copied his tone, sparing herself explanations. 'You're going on a wonderful vacation to a planet called Cialth. You're going to be very happy there.'

'How about you?'

'I'm going back to Earth.'

'I don't think I like the sound of this.'

'I don't think either of us has any choice in the matter,' Gretana said firmly, grasping the handles on the back of the chair and propelling it into the corridor.

'What's all this crap about me going on a vacation?' Hargate demanded, twisting to look up at her. 'What's going on here anyway?'

'The Warden is taking you to one of his private residences.'

'Why should he do that? I don't want to go with him.'

Closing her ears to his protests, Gretana wheeled Hargate at speed along the corridor, through the square outermost chamber and out into the permanent floodlighting of the central plaza. Hargate lapsed into stillness as he saw the herculean figure of the Warden of Earth waiting at the focus of the nodal mosaic. It was as though Vekrynn's psychic energies had reached across the intervening space and swamped all activity in the little Terran's nervous system, imposing complete paralysis. Gretana, in spite of comparative familiarity, felt that she was breasting concentric rings of numinous power as she went towards Vekrynn, and she could only guess at the effect on Hargate. It occurred to her that it would be almost impossible to find two men who were more dissimilar in every circumstance of their existences, and hers was the responsibility for bringing them together.

'This is the man I brought from Earth,' she said, using English for Hargate's benefit. 'Sir, this is Dennis Hargate.'

Vekrynn glanced down at Hargate, turned away immediately and spoke in Mollanian. 'It has occurred to me that we may be under observation here. I want to create the impression that I am personally escorting you to one of the Bureau's administrative centres, but the subterfuge won't work if we are seen using different mnemo-curves for different destinations. It embarrasses me to behave like a conspirator, but you have managed to limit my options.

'The three of us will transfer together to a disused site, one I can reach without using a physical mnemonic. When we get there I'll give you the address of your assigned node on Earth. You will go directly to Earth and resume your duties, and I will transfer the Terran to Cialth with me. Is that clearly understood?'

'It's quite clear,' Gretana said, still using English, 'but shouldn't we explain what we're doing so that . . .?'

'I am breaking certain laws on your behalf,' Vekrynn interrupted. 'In return I expect your discretion. I also expect you to understand, if it doesn't place too great a strain on your intellect, that explaining my actions to an inhabitant of Earth hardly constitutes discretion. You will therefore speak nothing but Mollanian until we part company – an event I hope will take place in the very near future.'

'I'm sorry,' Gretana said, her thoughts thrown into

disarray by Vekrynn's reversion to open insult. *No subtlety at all – in case I miss the point*, she told herself. *That kind of insult is an insult*. The implication was that Vekrynn's famed diplomacy was a myth, or that the current situation was placing him under a far greater strain than she had imagined. She turned to Hargate and saw that he was staring up at the Warden with a curious intensity, his eyes reflecting the surrounding lights as miniature diadems.

'Are you ready to go?' Vekrynn took Gretana's left hand in his right.

'Of course.' Gretana caught one of Hargate's hands and tried to raise it into the tripartite clasp which was usual when three people were skording together, but before the union could occur Vekrynn drew back with sudden force.

'You hold the Terran,' he said, and something in his expression told her that he had already begun to formulate the address of their destination in his mind. She had time for one upward glance to where the brightest stars penetrated the canopy of radiance, for one pang of wonderment over the realization that they were about to vault across the sky, then there was the familiar sense of *loosening*.

Gretana gasped aloud as yellow-and-orange brilliance washed over her in a silently explosive dazzle. They were at the centre of a nodal mosaic which differed from any that she had seen before in that it was composed of reddish tesserae and was overgrown with honey-coloured moss. At the perimeter were ruins of buildings which might once have been part of a Bureau station, and beyond there was a fantastic forest of transparent amber trees whose branches appeared almost to burn with refracted and mirrored sunlight. The sun itself was gold fire in an awning of gold, and its heat probed immediately at every opening in Gretana's tweed suit.

'Move away from the Terran,' Vekrynn said, releasing

her hand. She did as instructed, trying to ignore Hargate's spasmodic twitch of alarm as he divined what was happening.

'This world is more than two hundred light years from Earth, but it is linked by a major skord line to your Carsewell node, so you will have no difficulty in returning there in one step.' Vekrynn's uniform and hair shimmered as he recited the relevant Mollanian transfer equation. He concluded by ordering her to leave immediately.

Gretana hesitated. 'May I have a minute to say goodbye to . . .?'

Vekrynn seemed to grow taller. 'Go . . . *now!*'

'You can't leave me.' Hargate's twanging voice was urgent, and he was leaning forward in his chair as though trying to launch himself towards her. 'For Christ's sake, you can't leave me here with . . .'

His words were lost to Gretana as, with the new equation still fresh in her mind, she raised her right hand and curved it down through the bright air.

The transfer, the guaranteed miracle of Mollanian mind-science, took place.

It was late afternoon in the state of New York, and the approach of dusk had been accelerated by the snowfall which was general throughout the area. The snow was in the form of small and quite solid particles which descended vertically with no tendency to float. Gretana could actually hear it sifting downwards like salt through the trees which screened the nodal point on Cotter's Edge. She remained perfectly still, numbed by the knowledge that she had stood on three widely separated worlds in little more than a single minute, and tried to adjust to this latest version of reality.

The little clearing was permeated with a chill grey sadness which was accentuated by the stray gleams of light

142

visible on the tree-fragmented horizon to the east. On the ground beside her, now stippled with white, was the plaid travel rug which Denny Hargate had discarded when she had seen him . . . How long ago?

Gretana looked at the calendar display on her watch and her bemusement increased as she confirmed that the incredible sequence of events had begun on the morning of the same day. So much had happened since then that she could scarcely remember her reasons for returning to Station 23 in the first place . . .

*Lorrest!*

The abrupt recollection of the renegade's name was accompanied by the almost painful realization that she had actually been in Vekrynn's presence without telling him why she was there. One explanation was that she had allowed herself to be swamped by fears, worries and distractions; another – doubtless to be preferred by Vekrynn – was that she had been stupid. His opinion of her intelligence was low, but what would he say on hearing that she had travelled twenty light years to deliver an important report, incidentally committing the monumental blunder of taking a native Terran with her, and in the end had returned to Earth without passing on the vital information?

In spite of the winter temperature, a tingling warmth ascended Gretana's face as she visualized the Warden's all-too-likely reaction. Elongated seconds, each one bringing nightfall a finite step nearer, dragged by while she stood – alone and undecided – in the twilight, listening to the furtive whispers of the falling snow.

# CHAPTER 13

The bet was not all that sizeable – six bottles of a good malt were involved – but it had been placed with great solemnity, and Hector Mellish was genuinely excited over the outcome. His fingers had a distict tendency to tremble as he worked to align his twenty-centimetre refracting telescope in accordance with the given coordinates, and he suspected the unsteadiness had nothing to do with the cold inside his small observatory. He paused to check the time and to take a sip of neat whisky from a shot glass.

'Better go easy on that stuff,' Parker Smith advised, stirring slightly in the companionable darkness. 'Don't forget I'll be taking most of your supply home with me.'

'We'll see, we'll see,' Mellish said, smiling at his friend's presumption. Their lives in Asheville, North Carolina, seemed to have been spared the degradations that were so common throughout the world, and sometimes Mellish felt that he was not sufficiently appreciative. The two men had shared an interest in amateur astronomy for more than ten years, with Mellish doing most of the practical observation and Smith largely concerning himself with stellar physics. Smith was a computer expert, but he prided himself on his classical mathematical skills, and that had been the origin of the bet.

They had been sitting indoors one cloudy night, drinking and smoking and chewing the fat. Mellish had expressed admiration for the work carried out more than two centuries earlier by the German mathematician Karl Gauss, whose techniques for orbit computation had enabled astronomers to relocate the newly-discovered minor planet of Ceres after it had been lost for weeks behind the sun. Smith, belly and mind suffused by alcoholic warmth, had claimed the ability to perform a similar computation without modern aids, and had promptly been challenged. The resultant argument had ended with Mellish undertaking to provide a two-month record of Ceres' movements, from which Smith was to predict the planetoid's position for a month later.

Zero hour for resolving the wager was ten o'clock at night – a time which was less than five minutes away. It would, of course, have been easy to make a forward adjustment in Smith's figures and check his accuracy at any convenient time, but such a course had no appeal to Mellish's sense of the dramatic. It had to be a make-or-break affair at the predestined moment, with ceremonial triumph for the winner and ignominy for the loser. To that end, Mellish had even gone as far as sketching and memorizing the positions of the few background stars that would be in his field of view, and he knew he would be able to identify the wandering asteroid within seconds of looking through the eyepiece – provided it was there to be seen.

'Sure you don't want to cancel the bet?' he said, playing the game to the hilt. 'Whisky is a hell of a price these days.'

'Not when you get it the way I'm going to get it,' Smith replied comfortably.

'Your funeral. Want to check these settings?'

'No – I guess I can trust you that far.'

'Damn right.' Mellish stared at the glowing figures displayed by his watch, and on the instant of their changing to the new hour he switched on the electric drive of his telescope, counteracting the Earth's rotation and freezing one tiny section of the heavens in the instrument's field of view. 'Who's going to have first look?'

'It's a mere formality – you go ahead.'

'Too kind.' Mellish stooped, put his eye to the telescope and adjusted the focus screw. The circular blurs of radiance he had seen shrank to points which wavered slightly because of atmospheric turbulence, and there – almost perfectly centred in the image – was Ceres.

Mellish accepted at once that he had lost the bet, but he decided to prolong the suspense Smith was pretending not to feel. He continued peering into the eyepiece, making satisfied grunting sounds while he examined the speck of light that was Ceres. He was deeply impressed by the ability Smith had demonstrated, to pinpoint – using nothing but a pencil and jotting pad – the location of an errant ball of rock in the vast tract of space between the orbits of Mars and Jupiter. Ceres was some 700 kilometres in diameter, registering as only a glowing mote despite the great power of the telescope, and to a non-mathematician like Mellish its presence at the predicted spot was almost magical.

'What's the hold-up?' Smith said at last. 'Have you gone to sleep?'

'I hate to tell you this, but . . .' Mellish paused, tantalizing his friend, and was taking a final look at the asteroid when something very odd occurred.

The remote point of light ceased to exist.

Mellish gazed at the place where it had been, fully expecting it to reappear, and his mind grappled with the problem of what had happened. His first thought was that Ceres had been occulted by a dark body – possibly one of the cargo-carrying airships which were experiencing a minor resurgence – but as the seconds slowly went by the evidence against that theory mounted higher. To block off the light for such a long period the occulting object would have to subtend a considerable angle, and nothing in Mellish's experience had the necessary dimensions. It was as though Ceres itself had simply disappeared.

'Something pretty weird has just happened,' Mellish said. 'Ceres has vanished.'

'My God, I've heard of welshers,' Smith replied scornfully, 'but this is the . . .'

'You don't get it!' Mellish straightened up and grasped the other man's arm. 'It was *there* – right where you said – but now it's gone. I was looking straight at it when it went.'

'Behind a cloud?'

'No. Take a look outside, Parker – the sky's clear.'

'This is one of your jokes, right?'

'I'm not joking,' Mellish snapped, suddenly aware of how difficult it was going to be to convince Smith. He returned to the telescope, checked that the asteroid was still not visible, then set about the daunting task of persuading his friend that he had witnessed something momentous taking place in the heavens. The argument went on for many minutes, with Parker Smith slowly reaching the conclusion that his computations had been wrong and that Ceres would be found in another part of the sky. It was only then that Mellish got the idea of bringing in an outside authority.

'There's an easy way to settle this,' he said, trying to sound calm. 'I'm going to call the Hartmann Observatory.'

Smith snorted with amusement. 'Good idea! Please can I have my asteroid back.'

'You'll see.' Mellish led the way out of the hand-built dome that covered his telescope, stamped up the back garden path and went into the house. He turned on lights, ushered Smith into his library with exaggerated courtesy and picked up the telephone. The local observatory's number was well known to him and he was able to key it in without consulting a directory. He was greeted by the steady bleeping of the engaged tone. Irritated by the delay, he was on the point of setting the instrument down when he noticed that, according to the phone's information display, eight other callers were waiting to get through to the same number – an indication that the observatory was exceptionally busy for that time of night.

Without speaking, Mellish pointed at the glowing digit and was amply rewarded when – for the first time in the course of their disagreement – Smith met his gaze with eyes which had begun to show doubt.

# CHAPTER 14

He knew he was making a big presumption, because Vekrynn had looked directly at him only once, and only for a fraction of a second. Even when Hargate encountered people from his own culture it was not always possible for him to judge them accurately, and in this case he was dealing with a totally alien being – an awe-inspiring giant with a range of experience beyond Terran comprehension. But Vekrynn was human, nevertheless, and he had reacted as a human, and Hargate had been watching his face with all the morbid sensitivity which on occasion made him almost telepathic . . .

*This man*, he thought, *is my enemy. This super-being, who was strolling from star to star at the time of Cheops, wants me dead*.

The intuitive discovery was no stranger than any of the revelations that had come to him during the day, but it differed from the others in that it demanded more than wonderment. If at all possible, he had to avoid being left alone with Vekrynn – and Gretana was already raising her hand in the gesture he had come to know so well. Hargate leaned forward and called out his plea for her to stay, but his voice failed as her hand curved downwards. She disappeared on the instant, and all at once the sun-scoured plaza he shared with Vekrynn had the feel of an arena.

Hargate moved the control lever under his right hand into the drive position and sent his chair whirring across the mosaic pavement in the direction of one of the gaps in the circle of derelict buildings. Vekrynn turned imme-diately, eyes triangulating on Hargate, and came striding after him. The fact that he considered it unnecessary to run added to Hargate's feelings of sick apprehension.

The chair rocked wildly as it struck clumps of yellow moss, a reminder that it was completely unsuited for rough ground. Hargate narrowed his eyes against the encroaching light as he passed through the gap. The light blazing from the amber forest was so intense that it seemed to constitute a physical barrier to his progress, but some distance to his left he saw the beginnings of a path through the trees. He made a sharp turn by momentarily stopping his left-hand wheel, then accelerated towards the track, cursing the machine's sluggishness as he went. Its batteries, already drained by the difficult approach to Cotter's Edge, were too weak for speeding.

He had almost reached the path when Vekrynn, still moving without haste, stepped out of a ruined doorway in front of him and stood with his arms spread wide in a nimbus of reflected light. Hargate braked violently and, realizing the futility of trying to flee, brought his chair to a halt a few paces away from the Mollanian. There was a moment of throbbing silence.

'There is no need for you to be alarmed,' Vekrynn said, speaking very slowly and distinctly. 'I have made provision for you.' Hargate produced a sneer, 'I'll bet you have.'

Vekrynn paused, his eyes fixed on a point above Hargate's head. 'I want you to come with me.'

'And I,' Hargate replied, 'want you to piss off.'

The silence descended again while Vekrynn considered the remark. 'It is natural for you to be frightened and confused,' he said, still speaking with exaggerated care, 'but I can assure you that . . .'

'I'm not frightened, and I'm not confused, and I'm not a moron – so you can take the marbles out of your mouth.' Having begun a verbal offensive, Hargate decided to follow through. 'And I demand to be taken back to Earth.'

'Earth? Very well – if that's what you want.'

'That's what I want.'

'As you wish,' Vekrynn said. 'All you have to do is return with me to the centre of the plaza. I can't explain it to you, but it is important that you position yourself exactly at the . . .'

'Hold on,' Hargate said quickly. 'Gretana said you wouldn't let me go home. She said you were taking me to some place called Cialth.'

Vekrynn's face was almost hidden in webs of light rays. 'You can be properly looked after on Cialth – as some compensation for the way we have infringed your rights as an individual. However, if you prefer to go back to Earth I have no objections.'

'But . . .' Hargate's suspicion that he was being manipulated grew stronger. 'What if I blab everything I know?'

Vekrynn chuckled. 'Who would believe you? Besides, you would be arriving at a very isolated spot at the beginning of a winter night. It is likely that within a very short time you would be . . .' The Mollanian transferred his gaze to another point in the distance. 'In all probability you would . . .'

'Die is the word you're looking for,' Hargate said, feeling a secondary stirring of intuition. According to the

fantastic scenario Gretana had unfolded earlier, the lumi-
nant giant standing before him had been alive for something like fifty centuries – approaching the limit for a
Mollanian. Even for the Warden of Earth there eventually
had to be an ending. How would such a being regard the
imminence of death? It was difficult enough for Terrans,
the unwitting mayflies of the interstellar community, to
come to terms with personal extinction – so how would a
man like Vekrynn feel as he neared the end of his
lifespan? Sated? Philosophically resigned? Perhaps that
would be true for some Mollanians, but Hargate had a
sudden conviction that Vekrynn felt otherwise . . .

'I'm neglecting important duties,' Vekrynn said, his
voice growing louder. 'You must go back to the centre of
the plaza immediately.'

Hargate looked up at him, squinting into the light.
'What if I decide to stay right here?'

'Again, the choice is entirely yours. This is an uninhabited world, with no food or water, but if it suits you to
remain here . . .' Vekrynn turned to walk away.

'Wait!' Hargate reviewed the few options that were
open to him, and reluctantly reached for his drive control.
His belief that the Warden wished him dead had not
altered, but on the other hand Gretana had told him the
Mollanian reverence for life was so great that homicide
was virtually unknown among her people. He would,
regardless of how apprehensive he felt, have to trust
Vekrynn would stop short of murder when it came to
tidying up his affairs.

'I've thought things over,' Hargate said. 'Earth has
nothing for me – so I'll go to Cialth.'

'A wise decision,' Vekrynn indicated the doorway from
which he had emerged. 'This is too narrow for you. We'll
go back through the gap in the wall.'

'Right.' Hargate looked ruefully at the forest of

translucent amber trees, wishing there had been a chance to examine them properly, then it came to him that he had become remarkably blasé in a very short time. He had decided to abandon his home planet for ever, was now about to flit instantaneously to yet another remote and unknown world, and could feel almost no emotional reaction. So much had happened during the day that his mind was overloaded, his capacity for surprise diminished. What he needed now was time to rest and reflect, to process the information, and yet one personal truth was already emerging from the blur that was his consciousness. He wanted to be with Gretana again. Looking at the flawless, changeless beauty was like an excursion into the past, a return to the bright land of illusion, magic and hope.

'After I get to Cialth,' he said, turning the chair, 'will I be able to see Gretana?'

'It should be possible – though not often.'

The noncommittal answer reassured Hargate he was not being lured or tricked by Vekrynn into travelling with him to, say, a detention centre or worse, but it was too vague to be satisfactory. 'How often?'

'As often as she wishes.'

'Do you practise being evasive?' Hargate began to drive forward. 'Or is it a natural gift?'

Vekrynn, still averting his gaze, fell into step beside the slow-moving chair. 'I have nothing to say to you.'

'Why? What are you afraid of?'

'Afraid!' Vekrynn glanced down at Hargate, his face registering scorn as they moved on to the reddish tesserae of the circular plaza. 'I can't think of a less apposite word.'

*This is incredible*, Hargate thought. *This man is supposed to be a diplomat who has had thousands of years to practise verbal fencing – and yet I can rattle him every time.*

The only explanation suggesting itself was that his presence was placing the Mollanian under near-intolerable stress. It was possible that a member of a disease-free race, one in which physical perfection was the norm, could suffer when confronted by crippling illness – but was there more to it with Vekrynn? Was the fear of death that Hargate had sensed in him earlier so great? Could it be that Hargate, whose life expectancy could conveniently be measured in months, was a reminder to Vekrynn that he too was mortal and that the message was one the big man could not bear to contemplate? Trying to comprehend Vekrynn's viewpoint, Hargate looked up at the resplendent figure pacing beside his chair, felt an unexpected pang of sympathy and snorted with amusement. The idea that he, of all people, should feel sorry for a man who possibly had many centuries ahead of him was more than a little ludicrous.

'Why do you laugh?' Vekrynn said.

'All us crazy people do it,' Hargate replied mildly, noting that Vekrynn had sounded both curious and piqued, like a child who felt he was being excluded from a joke. It occurred to him that he really had been presumptuous in trying to psychoanalyse a member of an alien race. All the emotions and character traits he had assigned to Vekrynn were the result of conjecture – with no allowance for the fact that the man had been justifiably angry, and in all probability also shaken and embarrassed. The real evidence was that Vekrynn could simply have vanished and left Hargate to perish in this gaudy crucible of a world, instead of which he was taking considerable pains to keep his ward alive.

They reached the centre of the radial mosaic. Hargate, now familiar with basic skording procedure, stopped his chair and extended his right hand to Vekrynn. The Mollanian advanced his own hand slowly and with obvious

153

reluctance until the contact was made, then he closed his eyes. In spite of Hargate's mental and physical tiredness he felt a surge of excitement at the prospect of once more making that miraculous leap across space, of achieving what no reasonable member of his race could ever have expected to achieve. He scanned his surroundings, taking in every detail of the exotic scene, trying to anticipate the instant at which everything would change. The ruined buildings shimmered in the hot air, and the forest beyond was a bedazzling amber fire which challenged the senses, and in the midst of the brilliance something seemed to move. Hargate blinked rapidly and tried to focus his eyes on what might have been a dust devil or a fragment of mirage . . .

The transfer took place.

It was mellow evening on a world where the air had an incredible glassy clarity.

From the hummock on which he was sitting Hargate could see streams, wooded areas, plains, lakes, and mountains which did not act as a barrier to sight, but which receded in range after range in such a way that trying to follow them with the eye induced a giddy sensation of flight. Hargate was conscious of never having seen so much at one time, of the new world crowding itself into his head, expanding his mind. He rolled his chair forward a few paces, unable to do anything but gape, then – with an abrupt narrowing of perception – realized that the ground beneath his wheels was a springy lime-green turf.

For an instant he was unable to decide why the sight of it had produced stirrings of unease, then it dawned on him that he had been expecting to find one of the radial mosaics used by the Mollanians to mark the 'stations' in their transportation network. He had also been expecting to find at least some of the amenities of civilization, and their total absence suggested that either Gretana or Vekrynn had lied to him.

Hargate turned in his seat, barely in time to see Vekrynn complete a Mollanian mnemo-curve and cease to exist.

'Come back, you . . .!' He rolled towards the spot where Vekrynn had been standing, momentarily unable to accept what had happened, then brought the chair to a halt and looked around him, seeing the vast, calm world in a different light. Its predominant feature now was its sheer reverberating emptiness.

'Looks like I was right about you the first time, Vekrynn,' he said aloud, and immediately resolved not to speak again. The stillness of the environment had engulfed his words, absorbing their vibrational energies, symbolically confirming his belief that he was the only human being on the entire face of the planet.

In retrospect it was obvious that Vekrynn *had* wanted him out of the way, permanently silenced. The Mollanian had been too squeamish to carry out a straightforward homicide, but with the fantastic powers at his disposal such physical crudities were quite unnecessary. By abandoning Hargate on an uninhabited world – presumably one which was never visited by other members of his race – he had eliminated him as effectively as a soldier could have done with a machine gun. This way would take a little longer, that was all – exactly how much longer depending on whether death came by starvation, exposure or . . .

*How big would an animal have to be before I could spot its traces?*

*How big would an animal have to be to do me in?*

*And, while we're at it, is there any guarantee that I could even recognize an extraterrestrial animal even if it was staring me straight in the balls?*

Hargate glanced towards a group of palm-like trees a

short distance away to his left and considered taking shelter among them, then came the disquieting realization that other creatures might have had the same idea. There was even the further possibility, one he was in no position to discount, that the trees themselves could be dangerous. All he knew for certain about the nameless world on which he found himself was that his present location offered no urgent or obvious threat – therefore there was no point in moving away.

There was no point in doing anything at all, not even in feeling anger or hatred towards a man who had retreated light years beyond his reach; not even in trying to emulate the Mollanian transfer symbols, which were only a reflection of precise and subtle mental processes. Earlier he had wished for peace in which to reflect on the events of the long day, and now – like the granting of a final request – he had been absolved of every one of life's petty obligations.

He turned his chair to face the sinking sun and locked his wheels. The silence pressed down all around him, from horizon to distant horizon, as he turned up his collar, squirmed into a more comfortable position and waited for the appearance of alien constellations.

He had all the time in the world in which to think.


# CHAPTER 15

Lorrest tye Thralen, in spite of his many years on Earth, had never quite shaken off his Mollanian fear of heights. He could recall with amusement his earliest decades in Eyrej province, when he too would never have considered running without first donning an exercise mask to protect his face in the event of a fall. In his opinion that was one of the more ludicrous of his people's foibles, evidence of their obsessive preoccupation with physical beauty as expressed in the Twenty Rubrics of the Lucent Ideal.

He had often told himself that the acrophobia which was universal on Mollan, making buildings of more than one storey extremely rare, was merely an extension of the same attitude, that the principal reason for it was the dread of what the impact with the ground could do to face and form. That being the case, he – who had scrupulously discarded all that was petty and parochial in his upbringing – should have been able to perch on a high ledge with the same equanimity he showed in, say, driving a car. But it had not worked out that way.

A short distance beyond the window of his fifth-floor hotel room were the rusting beams of an adjoining steel-framed building which had never been completed. At times he would stand for long periods by the window, concentrating all his attention on the reality of the beams, bringing their flanges and cleats and welds into intensely sharp focus against the blurry background of the street, but no matter how he tried he was never able to identify himself with the construction workers who had routinely put the steelwork in place. And as for the men who ventured far higher, the erection crews on skyscrapers, their minds and lives were beyond his comprehension.

A common Mollanian rationalization was that, with only a few decades of life at stake, the Terrans could be much more casual about the risk of death, but Lorrest was inclined to reverse that reasoning. The shorter the term of life the more precious each day had to be, and the physical courage often displayed by Terrans – as compared to the cautious nature of the average Mollanian – was another indication that they had begun to differ generically from the interstellar human stock. Against all the odds, the savage riptide of lunar forces which played havoc with

157

their initial genetic structuring had created something positive in addition to all the predictable malaises. That vital essence was worth preserving, as far as Lorrest was concerned, no matter how great the cost or effort . . .

He was standing by the window, watching dust motes march and countermarch in a ray of lemon-coloured sunlight, when his telephone sounded at precisely the arranged hour. He allowed it to bleep eight times, part of the 2H identification code, then picked up the instrument and slipped a scrambler disc into place across the mouth-piece.

'Fair seasons, Haran,' he said, speaking in English. 'It looks as though Phase Two has gone off all right.'

'Phases One and Two were the easy parts,' Haran tye Felthan replied stolidly. 'Warden Vekrynn couldn't care less about what we did to the space colony, and until recently he hasn't had any reason to concern himself with Ceres – but it's all different now, Lorrest. He's bound to have heard about the disappearance by this time, and he's bound to have connected it with us, and with any kind of computer survey of the possibilities he's bound to . . .'

'You're bounding faster than a kangaroo,' Lorrest cut in. 'Has there been much public reaction in France?'

'Practically none. Up to the present six different organizations have claimed responsibility for flattening the Eiffel Tower, and the average citizen here finds that more interesting than astronomers losing a ball of rock.'

'They'll learn,' Lorrest said cheerfully. 'It's been quiet here too. A few stargazers-are-scratching-their-heads stories in the magazine programmes . . . nothing more . . . but they'll learn. *Everybody's* going to learn.'

'Lorrest!' There was a brief pause, and when Haran spoke again he sounded edgy and depressed. 'I didn't get the scheduled check call from Orotonth this afternoon.'

'It could be a foul-up in the telephones.'

'Could be, but if the Bureau has picked him up he'll have told them everything he knows.'

'Which isn't very much.'

'Except that he knows you're in Baltimore,' Haran said. 'Think about it, Lorrest. If Vekrynn has any inkling of what is happening he'll think nothing of spending a million, a billion, to pull you in before it's too late. You've got to be careful.'

Lorrest snorted his indignation. 'When was I ever not careful?'

'Do you mean within the last week? How about your going off on your own and trying to recruit that woman in Annapolis? We're not a religious organization looking for converts, man. We're up to our necks in a very danger-ous . . .'

'Point taken,' Lorrest said quickly, unwilling to discuss his tactical blunder of a few days earlier. 'But you wouldn't be talking like that if I'd got the location of the north-east node out of her.'

'And I wouldn't be talking to you *at all* if she'd turned you in.'

'Let's not hold a post-mortem,' Lorrest said, using a favourite formula for dismissing any consideration of his impulsiveness. The reminder that one of his personal foibles could have endangered the most important plan ever conceived by 2H left him feeling guilty and nervous, and when he had finished the telephone conversation he prowled around the apartment several times, scowling at the floor and trying to define his position with regard to the outside universe.

One of his most serious problems, as he saw it, was that he tended to regard everything as a kind of game. Haran was justified in sounding so serious, so *dire*, but at the same time – and knowing perfectly well that his colleague was right – Lorrest was unable to repress a flickering of contempt and amusement. He could remember how in his second decade he had heard for the first time about the doctrine of Preservationism and the role of the Bureau of Wardens. The idea of studying the rise and decline of civilization on a hundred human worlds for the sole purpose of ensuring the Mollanian culture could continue indefinitely had struck him as being both egocentric and craven. On learning that the observation was done in secret, and that there was never any intervention – even when a civilization was spiralling down into final extinction – because 'the data would have been invalidated', he had unhesitatingly declared the policy to be criminal, callous and inhuman.

He had become an activist and had published articles stating that Mollan, as the probable fountainhead of mankind, had a moral obligation to unite, guide and where necessary aid the younger human cultures – but always there had been the faint sense of solving an abstract problem or taking part in a college debate. The requirement was to work out what was right or wrong and to cast a vote, to support one's chosen team and wave its colours. Even when he had joined 2H and had been told to infiltrate the Bureau of Wardens, even when he had undergone the drastic cranial and facial surgery and had been sent to Earth, even when he had been arrested and had escaped to become a fugitive in an alien society – he had retained a sneaking suspicion that his life had not really begun. To use a Terran colloquialism, he had always been waiting for the main feature to start. Now people were assuring him that the main feature was well under way, and he could not quite believe them . . .

*This is bad*, he thought in unexpected panic. *There's a world and all its people at stake and all I do is drift!*

The room suddenly seemed small and oppressive, and the sunlit world outside correspondingly more inviting, a better place in which to think. There were three days to wait until the 2H plan reached it irrevocable climax, and at any point up to a few hours before zero all the years of planning and work could be negated by his making a single mistake. It was essential that he should pull himself together and get his thinking straight, and a plunge into the bright winter chill seemed as good a way as any to begin. He took his slate-grey overcoat from a closet, put it on and went out into the corridor.

There was a sign at the elevator saying it was operating that day, but he decided against paying the surcharge and went down the nearby stair. As an after-effect of Haran's call and his bout of introspection, he was abnormally alert when he reached the bottom flight. At another time the four tall men shouldering their way into the lobby through the glass doors might not have drawn his attention, but on this occasion he picked them out at once and recognition jarred him to a halt.

*Mollanians!*

The word clamoured inside his head as he backed up the stairs to the first corner. One of the men had gone to the reception desk, one was heading for the hotel's rear entrance, another was approaching the elevator bank and the fourth was walking directly towards the stairs. Their behaviour was odd by normal standards, Lorrest realized, but understandable if the object was to seal off the building. He turned and sprinted towards the upper floors, easily taking the steps four at a time, his heart thudding with a fierce excitement. At the third floor he swung into the short transverse corridor and ran to its end, where an emergency door opened on to the fire escape. His instinct was to throw the door open and launch himself down the outside stair without checking his speed, but a warning voice sounded above the thunder of blood.

He slid to a halt, very gently opened the door and looked down the fire escape.

A big man was waiting in the alley below.

Lorrest closed the door, his mind grappling with the fact that the man had been standing with one hand thrust inside the unzipped front of his quilted jacket. *Weapons? Would Vekrynn's men use weapons against him?*

The answer came immediately, impelling him backwards towards the hotel's main stair in an urgent loping run. He carried defences against certain kinds of radiation weapons, but there was no guarantee his pursuers would not employ drug darts. He reached the stairs without encountering anybody and was going up them in great leaps, two to each short flight, when it occurred to him that he was running blind. Any hiding place he might chance on would be discovered sooner or later, and there was no escape route in the upper part of the hotel, unless . . . unless he dared to take what was, for a Mollanian, an unthinkable risk . . .

At the fifth floor he deflected himself into the corridor and got to the door of his own room just as the elevator's arrival light came on. He stabbed his key into the lock, sidestepped into the room, began to bolt the door behind him then realized that doing so would be a clear indication of where he was. The desk clerk spent much of her time in the back office and would not have been able to tell his pursuers for sure whether he was in or out, and it was up to him to make them believe they had been unlucky.

He ran to the window, threw it open and climbed out on to the ledge. Cold breezes tugged at his clothing as he closed the window, and when he turned the shifting of parallax made the steel skeleton of the adjacent structure appear to sway like the masts of a ship.

Lorrest stared at the nearest floor beam, mesmerized. It was perhaps three good paces away from him, a distance

162

he knew he could leap with ease, but a measurement in paces implied the reassuring support of the ground. Here there would be nothing but cold clear air beneath him, and if he were to make a bad jump – perhaps hampered by his overcoat – he would go down and down, and there would be lots of time to anticipate what was going to happen to him when he hit the pavement, or perhaps a perimeter fence and then the pavement, or perhaps a ledge and a perimeter fence and then the pavement . . .

*This must be the main feature*, he thought in bemused wonderment as he saw angular patterns flow beneath, evidence that he had made the leap and was flying through space. His feet came down on rusted metal. He caught hold of a stanchion for momentary support and, now totally committed, ran along the narrow aerial pathway of a floor beam to where the massive stump of an incompleted central column offered some concealment. Belatedly aware that he could have attracted the attention of other residents of the hotel, he worked his way round to the far side of the column, hunkered down and nestled into the boxlike space between its flanges.

A sudden eye-of-the-storm calm descended over him as he realized he had done all that was possible for the time being. If he had been seen by the Mollanians he would know about it soon enough, and if any Terrans had noticed him there would be some kind of outcry – but for the present all he could do was crouch in his strange geometrical eyrie and survey the deserted wasteland of the building site below. And force himself not to think about falling.

As the protracted minutes went by he gradually came to accept that he had eluded the Bureau's agents. They would certainly have gone into and searched his room, but Mollanian conditioning would have prevented them from considering the vertiginous metal pathway to freedom.

Unfortunately, one problem led to another. If the Mollanians believed he would soon return to his hotel they were bound to keep watch on all the entrances, and if he wanted to clamber down to the ground inconspicuously he would have to wait for the cover of nightfall.

The thought of making the climb in darkness caused Lorrest to press himself closer to the chilling metal of the column and he diverted his thoughts to the problem of getting safely through the next three days. Haran had been right when he said that Vekrynn would spend unlimited amounts of money to pick up a key member of 2H before it was too late. There were not enough Bureau agents on Earth to form a really effective search team, but there was little doubt that the Warden would have enlisted every conceivable Terran agency, legal and illegal, to track him down. A trumped-up criminal charge would be enough to bring in the police, and the lure of really big money would take care of the rest.

Trying to ignore the cold which was spreading through his body, Lorrest analysed his chances of remaining undetected in the city for the greater part of a week and decided they were dangerously low. His best course would be to get off the planet altogether, but as that was impossible he would have to consider isolating himself in a rural area, even though the weather was against him. At another time of the year it would have been easy enough to fill his pockets with canned food and spend the time hiding out in the forest land on the eastern side of the Allegheny range, but there was a limit to what even a Mollanian constitution could stand. It looked as though he would have to find and move into a disused house, and that had its own set of risks.

*All this should have been arranged in advance*, he thought. *We're a bunch of amateurs, behaving like amateurs. I suppose our excuse has to be that there aren't*

*any experts in this line – nobody has ever done to a world
what we're going to do to this one.*

To his surprise, Lorrest managed to doze for short
periods during the two hours he had to wait for nightfall.
When he finally decided to return to the ground the steel
framework on which he was suspended had become a
cube of mysterious darkness, its components patchily
illuminated by greenish glimmers from the street. Telling
himself that the lack of visibility would help dispel vertigo,
he straightened up tentatively. His legs were numb and a
tingling stab of pain hinted that the return of blood
circulation would be far from pleasant. He gripped the
flanges of the column, began a shuffling turn in preparation for climbing down it, then made the appalling discovery that he was getting no nerve signals from his feet. It
was quite impossible for him to decide if he was standing
squarely on a floor beam or teetering on its extreme edge.

He shifted his weight slightly, trying to assess the
situation, and suddenly – there was no perceptible lapse
of time – flaking corners of metal were ripping upwards in
his hands like saw blades.

Before he had time to understand that he was falling,
before he had time to scream, the beam on which he had
been standing smashed into his outflung left arm just
above the elbow. Brutal though the impact was, it
checked his descent sufficiently to let him throw his legs
and right arm around the column. He clung to it with a
desperate ardour, pressing his loins and torso and face
against the abrasive steel, while he fought to damp down
the panic that was exploding through his system.

Reality . . . nightmare . . . reality. As the giddy swings
in his perception faded away he moved his left arm and
knew at once that he was badly hurt. The pain that
invaded his body by way of the shoulder left no doubt that
a bone had been fractured. With it came the uncomprom-

ising message that if he was to complete the long climb to the ground he would have to do it immediately and quickly before the anaesthesia of shock wore off and the *real* pain began.

Moaning quietly, he slightly relaxed his grip on the flanges of the column and allowed himself to slide to the floor below, checking his descent often enough to prevent a lethal build-up of speed. Windows in the hotel glowed with placid light, a group of youths ran noisily through the fenced-off alley at the rear of the building site, and the siren of a nuclear engine sounded dolefully in the distance, but Lorrest remained locked in a private purgatory.

By the time he neared the ground his right hand was slipping on a copious lubrication of blood. He dropped to the rough concrete of the column's foundation, almost fell, and stood swaying in the darkness while he tried to formulate new plans for a future that had suddenly become very much more dangerous.


# CHAPTER 16


A panel of food manufacturers and health officers were defending the new practice of introducing insect protein – discreetly tagged as 'approved natural ingredients' – into products intended for human consumption.

Gretana had been trying to follow the arguments, particularly those of an assertive man who kept popping live mealworms into his mouth, but her television set was losing its ability to cope with serious power fluctuations, and the picture size and sound levels were changing almost continuously. She had forgotten to buy new batteries, which meant it was hardly worth the trouble of switching over to internal power. Her living room, illuminated by the mandatory low-wattage fluorescent tubes, seemed cheerless and uninviting, but she knew there was little chance of sleep if she went to bed.

The late evening and night seemed to stretch out before her like a Mollanian lifespan. Warden Vekrynn had told her that in his service she would have no need of a life recorder with which to preserve happenings of interest. Her experience on Earth had ratified his promise, but nothing could have prepared her for the mind-numbing rush of events in the past forty-eight hours.

She had a cold inner certainty that her lapses in conduct, especially the failure to make a full report to Vekrynn, were casting long shadows into the future, and yet she continued to leave things unresolved. What made it worse was the feeling that virtually everybody she knew would have acted with much greater decisiveness. Even the embittered little Terran, Denny Hargate, in spite of all his dreadful handicaps, would have plotted his own course through the tides of circumstance and it would have taken a great deal to deflect him, whereas she . . . *You're a typical product of Mollanian non-education*, a remembered voice told her. But that had not been Hargate. It had been . . .

The pounding on the outer door of her apartment was totally unexpected.

She jumped up and listened for several seconds before realizing there was nothing peremptory in the sound. It was slow and deliberate, as though the person responsible assumed right of entry, and somehow that had the effect of increasing her alarm. With one hand holding her blouse closed at the throat, she considered the range of possibilities and with ready prescience selected the most likely.

*Lorrest tye Thralen.*

She went to the door, irrationally choosing to move in complete silence, tilted her head and said, 'Who's there?'

'William McGonagall, poet and tragedian,' came the

167

immediate answer, followed by a pause in which she heard laboured breathing. 'Don't make me laugh, Gretana – I'm hurt.'

She opened the door and saw the tall figure clutching his left arm. 'What do you want?'

He shook his head. 'Can't do any more funny answers – I've got a broken arm.'

'You can't stay here.'

'I believe it's a greenstick fracture . . . typical Mollanian resilience . . . but I'm not used to this kind of pain, Gretana, and they're hunting me.'

Gretana's fear increased. 'You can't stay here.'

'Tell you what,' Lorrest said, moving forward and forcing her to retreat. 'Why don't you do what women in your position are supposed to do? You could bring me in and tend to my wounds and pretend to be sympathetic, but all unknown to me you've sent a secret signal to Vekrynn.'

'That's impossible, and you know it.'

'Yeah – I'm not stupid.' Lorrest walked into the kitchen and turned to face her and she saw that his face was haggard. He unbuttoned his overcoat, withdrawing his left arm from the sleeve with great care, and draped the garment over a stool.

'Don't you think you're presuming a lot?' Gretana said.

'Not really.' Lorrest's smile became a grimace as he slipped off his jacket and began to unbutton his shirt. 'If you were the hotshot Preservationist you think you are you'd have tipped the Warden off about me and I wouldn't have made it to the top of your stairs.'

'I see.' Gretana's sense of responsibility increased. Previously she had only suffered forebodings, but here was confirmation that in a single dereliction of duty she had influenced a train of events about which she had no understanding. She watched in silence as Lorrest partly took off his shirt to reveal a left arm which was so massively bruised that between elbow and shoulder it had the appearance of being carved from a blackish marble veined with green. The ghastly discoloration extended down Lorrest's left side, indicating that the muscles there had been torn by the impact which had wreaked such spectacular damage on his arm.

'You're really hurt,' she exclaimed. 'What happened?'

'A bunch of the Warden's men showed up at my hotel and I went out on some steelwork next door to get away from them. Then I did something you're not supposed to do on steelwork – I fell off.'

Gretana weighed up the story, one Mollanian to another. 'You climbed around a high building?'

'They were carrying weapons. I had to get away.'

She sighed her exasperation. 'Are you still claiming the Warden would harm you?'

'Harm me?' Lorrest looked thoughtful. 'For the time being Vekrynn will do everything in his power to make sure I'm not harmed – that's because I know something he needs to know – but if he gets his information he'll do me harm, and that's for sure. The sort of harm you inflict on an ant when you stand on it.'

'That's ridiculous,' Gretana snapped. 'What are you going to do about that arm?'

'Could you fix up a splint?'

'If I do that will you promise to leave?'

'Leave?' Lorrest appeared to weigh up the idea. 'For you, sweetheart, I'll get off the planet altogether. All you have to do is tell me where . . .'

'Forget it!' Gretana's former fears were displaced by anger. 'Why is it that people like you can never listen to reason?'

To her surprise, Lorrest smiled in what could have been genuine pleasure. 'I do believe you're turning into a political animal,' he said mildly. 'The first big hurdle is the realization that nobody on the other side is capable of seeing the obvious. Once you're over that, though, you come to the second and even bigger hurdle – what are you going to *do* about these people who can't see the obvious? You can arrange to demonstrate to them that you're right and they're wrong, but that can take an awfully long time, and at the end of it . . . guess what? . . . they still can't see what you've so carefully laid out in front of them. That brings you to the well-tried solution – stop them seeing anything at all.'

'You think you know everything,' Gretana said. Acutely aware that the retort had been both predictable and inadequate – exactly the sort of thing to trigger one of Lorrest's painful laughs – she went to a drawer and took out a bamboo place mat. 'Would this work?'

'Could do, if we bind it around my arm and fix up some kind of a sling. I knew you'd help.'

'I'm not helping with anything – all I want is for you to get the hell out of here.'

'Don't pretend to be tough.'

'Do you know I've been to Station 23? That I went back to report on you?'

Lorrest glanced around the apartment with narrowed eyes. 'What did they say?'

'Nothing. I didn't get to make the report.'

'Oh? Why not?'

Gretana hesitated, wondering why she was further entangling herself. 'I took a Terran back with me and it caused a bit of a furore.'

'You took a . . .' Lorrest's shoulders gave a preliminary heave and he sat down on the nearest stool, his face already darkening. 'That's wonderful. I'll bet Vekrynn wasn't pleased.'

'He was furious.' Gretana smiled in spite of herself,

170

comforted by Lorrest's reaction. While padding the bamboo mat with cotton and binding it around his upper arm, she described how she had seen Denny Hargate at the nodal point and how on sheer impulse she had teleported him with her to Station 23. She noticed however that Lorrest's expressions of amusement became muted as she outlined the subsequent events, and by the time she finished speaking his face had acquired a look of brooding solemnity.

'You sound as though you liked this man Hargate,' he said.

'He's about the most sarcastic and short-tempered being I've ever met, but I suppose I did start to admire him in a way. You know, before I left Mollan that would have sounded grotesque.'

Lorrest gave her a wry smile. 'Well, the thing you've got to keep uppermost in your mind is that when you first saw him he was obviously *trying* to end his life.'

'Yes, I could see he was . . .' She broke off, suddenly suspicious. 'What are you trying to say?'

'I'm saying you almost did Hargate a favour. He wanted to die anyway, so when Vekrynn . . . ah . . . disposed of him he was only doing what Hargate wanted.'

'Stop it!' Gretana threw her scissors on to the kitchen table and they slid along its surface with a metallic chittering. 'I won't listen to that kind of talk.'

'Sorry. I just don't want you to feel guilty.'

'You're still doing it. You . . . *you* are still calling Warden Vekrynn a criminal.' She tried to give a scornful laugh, but it emerged as something closer to a sob, further increasing her anger and frustration. 'Why didn't I tell the Bureau you were here?'

'There's only one reason,' Lorrest said equably. 'In your heart you didn't really want to. If you'd been genuinely determined to turn me in nothing could have stopped you. Think about it.'

'I am thinking about it.' Gretana made the effort to clamp down on her emotions, realizing that coldness and self-control were the best weapons against provocation. 'I want you to go away from here and never come near me again.'

'So be it,' Lorrest said, apparently unruffled. He worked his splinted arm back into his shirt sleeve with some difficulty and began fumbling with the buttons. Gretana, disdaining to help, walked into the adjoining room and switched off the television set. Abruptly, and against her better judgement, she yielded to a desire to establish once and for all that the unwanted visitor was impervious to logic.

'Just tell me one thing,' she said, returning to the kitchen door. 'Warden Vekrynn has everything that Mollanian society can offer – wealth, power, honour, privilege – so why should he descend to being the sort of person you think he is? What would he *gain*? Can you give me one shred of motive?'

'Not really,' Lorrest replied, picking up his jacket. 'He's a raving megalomaniac, of course – but merely saying that somebody is crazy isn't analysing his motives.'

Gretana raised her eyebrows. '*You* are saying that *he* is insane?'

'Isn't it obvious? Look at his big project, his famous Notebook. Do you know that he has taken imprints of the summarized depositions of every observer the Bureau has ever stationed on Earth?'

'What's wrong with that?'

'It can't be done, child – that's what's wrong with it.' Lorrest paused and softened the pedagogic manner with which he liked to impart information. 'There's an upper limit to the number of our imprints the brain can usefully

172

accommodate. For most people it hovers around the thousand mark, and some highly gifted individuals can cope with three or four thousand – but Vekrynn had zapped himself with at least a hundred thousand. A tenth of a *million*, Gretana. I don't think it does him any harm, any more than overfilling a bucket does it harm but it gives you a clue about how he regards his own intellect. A definite god complex, I'd say.'

Gretana struggled with unfamiliar concepts. 'Even if what you say is true, it still doesn't make him a murderer.'

'Doesn't it? Perhaps what we would regard as culpable homicide he would see as justifiable insecticide. I'm telling you, Gretana, your friend Hargate was too much of an inconvenience to be let stay around.'

'You're a liar.'

'Did you actually go with him to Cialth and see him installed in some kind of rest home for sick Terrans?'

'No. I told you Vekrynn was trying to protect me – we went to a disused Bureau station first of all, then we split up.'

Lorrest stopped in the act of donning his jacket. 'A disused station? Was it bright and hot? All bright and hot, and yellow and orange, with a kind of forest made of barley sugar all around it?'

Gretana nodded. 'That's sounds right.'

'It must have been Branie IV. There was an observational headquarters there for one of the human civilizations we let go down the tubes about six centuries ago. If Vekrynn abandoned your friend there the heat will have killed him off within a day, but I don't think he'd have done that. The skord connections are good from Branie IV, and quite a few travellers still go through there. It would be bloody awkward for Vekrynn if somebody found a desiccated Mr Hargate, spinster of this parish, sitting there in his pushchair. He'll have dumped him somewhere else, but unfortunately – especially for Hargate – we've no way of knowing where.'

'Wrong!' Gretana was triumphant, eager to drive Lorrest into a trap of his own devising. 'I went back to try to put things right with Vekrynn.'

'So you really were going to fix me.'

'Naturally.' She met Lorrest's gaze directly, enjoying the moment. 'But there was nobody there when I arrived, and I thought I was too late. I went to have a look at your barley sugar forest while I decided what to do next, then I thought I heard voices and I turned back. I was just in time to see Vekrynn and Denny Hargate leave.'

'For Cialth?'

'Where else?'

'I don't know.' Lorrest looked thoughtful. 'What was the mnemo-curve like?'

Gretana hesitated and, employing her Mollanian talent for a special kind of mathematics, traced an exact copy of the gesture Vekrynn had made on the instant of departing with Hargate.

'It wasn't Cialth,' Lorrest said emphatically.

'How do you know?' Gretana demanded. 'You haven't memorized every reciprocal address in the sector.'

'No, but I know the general form they take. Look.' Abandoning the attempt to put on his jacket, Lorrest set the garment down and gave her an impromptu lecture on descriptive topography as used in the Mollanian transfer system. 'So you see,' he concluded, 'wherever Vekrynn took your friend it wasn't to Cialth. Show me the curve again.'

Reluctantly, feeling that once again she was being out-manoeuvred, Gretana began slowly recreating the symbol with her right hand. She had used only about a dozen skord addresses in her life and had regarded each one as being an arbitrary set of mathematical elements. Lorrest's approach, treating *all* addresses as part of a unified system and being able to predict relationships between them, was so far superior to hers that it smacked of being unfair. *Who decides these things?* she wondered, completing the curve. *Who teaches one person to enjoy using and developing his mind, whilst allowing another to . . .?*

'It isn't even in the human sector!' Lorrest hugged his immobilized left arm to his side and began pacing the length of the narrow kitchen. 'For some reason Vekrynn has dumped your friend, your tame Terran, about . . . let's see . . . about two hundred light years inside the Attatorian sector. There must be a Type One world there that nobody else from Mollan has ever seen – but how did old man Vekrynn latch on to it in the first place? And *why?* Why would he . . .?'

'I'm glad you've got around to asking yourself that,' Gretana cut in. 'You keep building up these fantastic accusations against the Warden, with no real evidence, and you expect me to believe them. Well, I still *don't* believe them and you're still on your way out of here. Come on!' She picked up Lorrest's jacket and held it ready for him. Lorrest obediently slipped his arms into it and allowed her to draw it over his shoulders, an action which made him seem oddly childlike in spite of his size and physique.

'That's a very good point about evidence, and I'm glad you made it,' he said, turning to face her. 'I don't quite know why it is, but I'm becoming obsessed with the notion of making you see reason. Maybe it's the sheer magnitude of the challenge. Anyway, I've worked out how to give you all the proof you need.'

'How?'

'Through Denny Hargate, of course, I'll go after him and fetch him back to Earth. In all probability he's already dead, but if he's still alive he can testify for himself. Either way you'll have your evidence.'

175

She closed her eyes for a moment, exasperated. 'Now you're being ridiculous.'

'Don't dismiss it like that,' he said quickly. 'All you have to do is tell me where to find the Bureau's east coast node, and I promise you I'll bring him back. Why are you shaking your head?'

'E for effort,' she replied, borrowing a Terran expression, 'but I'm not talking. I've already let Vekrynn down once and I'm not doing it again.'

'I thought we had established that your true loyalties are with Helping Hand.'

'Is that what you call yourselves? Helping Hand?'

'Yes. It doesn't sound sinister enough for the Bureau's propaganda, so they refer to us as 2H. But that's what we're doing here on Earth, Gretana – we're giving these people the helping hand they need.'

'By sabotaging the space colony?'

'There was a good reason for that,' Lorrest said. 'It was part of the plan.'

'Oh, yes. The plan you're not allowed to divulge, but when it comes to a head everybody in the world will know about it.' Gretana smiled faintly, remembering her resolve to be coolly unconcerned. 'You don't seem to have any idea how crazy that sounds – and you're *still* demanding everything and giving nothing in return.'

'Only for your own good.' Lorrest walked to the other end of the kitchen and stood for a moment facing the window, and when he turned his face was troubled and irresolute. 'Can I trust you, Gretana?'

*I can show Vekrynn I'm not a fool*, she thought, hiding a powerful surge of excitement. *The thing is not to appear too eager* . . .

'I thought I was the specialist in corny dialogue,' she said. 'Does anybody ever admit to being untrustworthy?'

176

'You're learning,' Lorrest replied, and when he spoke again his voice was subdued. 'We're going to . . .'

'Yes?'

He made an unconvincing attempt to grin. 'We're going to destroy the Moon.'

Gretana had never acquired a taste for neat brandy, but the shock it administered to her tongue was oddly comforting, a sensual link with the humdrum world. She took repeated sips from her glass, all the while keeping her gaze on Lorrest. He had tucked his left arm inside his jacket just above the first button, improvising a sling, and now was seated at the dining table. He had taken only one drink from his glass and was flicking its rim with a fingernail, producing ringing sounds which turned the surface liquid into an oscilloscope of transient bright circles. His expression was one of tiredness and elation.

'We're very lucky on Mollan, never having contracted religion,' he said, 'but as a result we're linguistically deprived. I mean, the word you're looking for now is blasphemous – you *feel* that what we're about to do is blasphemy – but, being a godless Mollanian, you don't have access to the appropriate expression.'

'I can think of others just as appropriate,' Gretana countered. 'How about wild, insane, hare-brained . . .?'

'You're not doing too well – those mean more-or-less the same thing, and they don't really express your gut-feeling that it's terribly wrong for mere human beings to start meddling with the Grand Scheme.'

'How about impracticable? Or improbable?'

'The plan is practicable, even with 2H's limited resources.' Lorrest's tone was becoming surer. 'There's a minor planet in this system, name of Ceres, with a diameter of about seven hundred kilometres. I presume you've heard about its disappearance?'

'Yes, but . . . What has that to do with the Moon?'

'We put a bank of mass displacement units on Ceres and drove it out of orbit. It's on its way to the Moon right now, accelerating all the way, and in two days from now there's going to be one hell of a collision.'

Objections swarmed in Gretana's mind, reinforcing her instinctive rejection of what she had heard. 'I don't understand. It said in the news that Ceres had ceased to be visible, but if has only been moved . . .'

'We screened it. Optically, magnetically, gravitationally – every way you could think of – to stop the Bureau using deflectors on it when they deduce what's going on.'

'They'll find it,' she asserted, her confidence springing from faith in Warden Vekrynn's omnipotence rather than any appreciation of the technical problems involved.

'No doubt,' Lorrest said. 'The Bureau will compute its rough position, then they'll find some way to deactivate our screens and make the asteroid visible – but it will be close to the Moon by that time, and we've taken steps to make sure their deflectors won't be effective. Fireworks night will go ahead as planned.'

'I can't imagine the Moon just breaking up.'

'It won't happen immediately.' Lorrest spoke as though explaining some minor mechanical process. 'It won't be a head-on collision, you see. What we've got to do is strike the Moon a glancing blow at a precisely calculated angle and start it spinning fast. Very fast. The rotation will set up gravitational stresses in the Moon and tear it to pieces, and the pieces will go on spinning and breaking up into smaller pieces and scattering themselves. According to our calculations, the end result will be a whole swarm of little moonlets strung out along the Moon's orbit. All the second-order and third-order forces will be pretty well neutralized, especially gravity, which is why we had to force an evacuation of the Aristotle colony. The Lagrange

178

points will have ceased to exist, and for a while there's going to be enough chaos on Earth without a runaway space colony to worry about.'

'What sort of chaos?'

'Well, for example, there'll be no more lunar tides. All tidal energy schemes will have to be abandoned, coastlines are going to change, major sea ports are going to silt up.'

Gretana gave an uncertain laugh. 'Helping Hand!'

'Exactly. And having demonstrated in an impressive manner that we exist and mean business, we're going to come out in the open. We're going to put ships into Earth's orbit, make direct contact with heads of state, help to stabilize the world situation until the new generations of Terrans appear – the ones who haven't had their genetic blueprints distorted.' Lorrest raised his brandy glass as though proposing a toast. 'You're lucky, Gretana – you're going to witness the birth of a new world.'

'And how many of the people who actually inhabit this world are going to be *un*lucky?'

Lorrest frowned. 'Meaning?'

'The period of chaos . . . culture shock . . . reduced energy supplies . . . food and commodity shipments disrupted . . . How many Terrans are going to die as a result?'

'You can't look at it like that,' Lorrest said impatiently. 'If we do nothing the whole bloody lot are going to die sooner or later. Sooner, if you ask me.'

'What if I don't ask you?' She kept her voice level. 'What if I don't regard you as any kind of authority?'

Lorrest slammed his glass down on the table, spilling some of its contents. 'I get it – you're not going to give me the nodal point.'

'I never said I would.'

'You *are* learning, aren't you?' Lorrest stood up, his

179

face hardening as she had seen it do before, losing all trace if its characteristic amiability. 'What next? A quick jaunt to Station 23 to report me to Vekrynn?'

'No, I'm prepared to keep this to myself – as long as you never come near me again,' Gretana said, and to give the lie more credence added, 'Besides, I have no intention of leading you straight to the node.'

'We reached this stage once before,' Lorrest replied, slipping his right hand into the pocket of his jacket, 'but the situation is more urgent this time. I need that location, and you're going to give it to me – whether you want to or not.'

Gretana rose to face him, keyed-up and apprehensive, but not fully believing the threat of force. She was still formulating a reply when from the direction of the hall there came a violent pinging sound – half-explosive, half-electronic in nature – and a small metallic object slid into view on the parquet floor between the dining area and the kitchen. Heart stopped, mind numbed by the certainty that she was close to a grenade which was on the point of detonating, she threw herself backwards, collided with the table and was turning to run when her identification of the object was completed. It was the main lock from the apartment's outer door. In the same instant a squat-bodied man with protuberant pale eyes and a down-curving gash of a mouth came running into the room. He was holding a weapon which appeared to be a laser pistol.

'Nobody move,' he ordered in a hoarse voice. 'Don't nobody move.'

Gretana forced her speech organs to manufacture distant sounds. 'What do you want?'

'Shut it.' The intruder examined her briefly and dismissively, eyes as unsympathetic as those of a deep-water fish, and turned his attention to Lorrest. 'The hands, big man – hoist 'em.'

'Gladly.' Seemingly unperturbed, Lorrest raised his right hand almost to the ceiling and spoke in conversational tones. 'Would you mind saying what you want?'

The stubby man gestured with the pistol. 'Get the other hand up.'

Lorrest smiled apologetically. 'I'd like to oblige, but I've got a broken arm. I don't usually walk around doing this Napoleon imitation.'

'You better hold real still,' the man said. 'You so much as fart, I burn your arm off.'

Keeping the pistol trained on Lorrest, he felt in his overcoat pocket with the other hand and produced a small object which resembled a photographic light meter. He pointed it at Lorrest and made scanning movements. Gretana watched him with a sense of alarm which increased with every second. Violent crime was rife throughout the country, but it would have been too much of a coincidence if she and Lorrest had fallen foul of a casual raider at this particular time – and the intruder appeared to be unusually well equipped. The implication was that he was acting for the Bureau of Wardens, as a kind of bounty hunter, but what other inferences could be drawn?

'So you're carryin' no hardware, just like they said.' The man put the scanning device away. 'You got a coat?'

Lorrest nodded towards the kitchen. 'In there.'

'I'll pick it up on the way out. Walk in front of me.'

Lorrest took one step towards the kitchen, but halted directly underneath the fluorescent light fitting, his face unnaturally shadowed. 'This woman doesn't know anything about me. She has never seen me before.'

'She never seen me before, neither.' The small man looked at Gretana, and for the first time there was a flicker of animation in his eyes, a door opening at the end of a long dark passageway in his mind. She saw the pistol in his hand swing towards her. Its movement seemed to grow slower with every degree of rotation, but the effect was subjective – a thin sad voice warned her that her life was ending, that she was on the edge of oblivion, and her mind had reacted by seizing on the single moment that remained, attenuating it, reluctantly yielding it up by the microsecond.

In that cryogenic state of perception she saw with an awful clarity everything that happened as Lorrest reached higher with his upraised hand, snatched the fluorescent tube from its clips, and – turning it into a two-metre glass spear – drove it with all his strength into the stubby man's face. It hit him on the bridge of the nose, shattered into little daggers which gouged through his eyes, then shattered again under the continuing impetus of the thrust to wreak further hideous damage. He fell backwards, howling, his pistol turning towards Lorrest. With the light tube in his hand reduced to a bloody spike, Lorrest went down after him. Gretana turned and ran to the bedroom as the howling abruptly ceased.

*Death is real!* The words shrilled silently inside her head. *I've seen a butcher at work, and I've smelled the blood . . .*

'Gretana!' Lorrest was standing in the doorway, and even in the reduced light from the other room it was obvious that his right hand was wet and red. 'Playtime is over – you are *now* going to tell me where that node is.'

'I can't, she said. 'I can't.'

'Think again.' He came towards her, reaching out with the hand which was wet and red, his face an inhuman mask. 'Think again, Gretana.'

'Near Carsewell, New York,' she heard herself whimper as she tried to avoid the hand. 'On a ridge called Cotter's Edge, just west of the Greenways enclave.'

'Thank you.' Lorrest retreated and left the room, and a

few seconds later she heard a rush of water from the bathroom. She buried her face in a pillow, trying to suppress a gory kaleidoscope of after-images, and waited for any sound which would indicate that Lorrest had left the apartment. There was a brief silence and then, with the unexpected suddenness of a reptile attack, something warm and pliable fell across her legs. She sprang upright with a sob of panic to find that Lorrest had returned to the bedroom and had thrown one of her overcoats on to the bed.

'On your feet,' he said tersely. 'Let's go.'

She raised her hand, symbolically warding him off. 'Go? With you?'

'What did you expect? If one man traced me here others could do it and, believe me, there's no way you could get out of telling them where I'd gone. Besides, you don't want to go on sharing your apartment with a corpse, especially if the police come nosing around.'

'You're the killer. *You!*'

'In our special circumstances, that hardly matters. On top of all this, I need you as insurance.'

'I don't understand,' Gretana said, pushing the coat away with a trembling hand.

'Don't you?' Lorrest's smile was barely recognizable as such. 'I don't trust you any more, Gretana – you've been too long on Earth. The only way I can be sure that node location is correct is to take you with me. If it is, you can skord yourself off to Station 23 – which would be the safest place for you anyway – and blab everything you know to the Warden. Perhaps he'll give you a vacation.'

Gretana dredged far into her reserves and found the strength for defiance. 'Perhaps he'll give you one.'

'He'd have to find me first – and there's an awful lot of galaxy out there.' Lorrest tilted his head and stared for a moment in the direction of the unseen Moon. 'And in two days' time nothing the Warden does is going to make any difference.'

# CHAPTER 17

The animal had been watching Hargate all day.

Its body was the best part of a metre in length and had an asymmetrical green-and-grey pattern which camou-flaged it so effectively that Hargate was still unable to decide whether it was shaped like a beaver or a wolf. He was equally uncertain about the creature's intentions. When he was wakening from a doze he would notice a clump of grass a few paces away and while he was trying to recall if it had been there earlier the clump would blink a green-gold eye, letting him know he was under close surveillance.

Shouted swear words and sudden movements of his arms were always enough to drive the creature off – it scuttled away *backwards*, eyes filled with mute reproach – leaving him to speculate about whether it had been motivated by friendship, curiosity or hunger. The third possibility seemed the most likely to Hargate, and he was deeply uneasy about his prospects during the coming hours of darkness.

After being abandoned by Vekrynn on the previous evening he had resigned himself to, and had almost been reconciled to, the idea of dying of exposure while the bright ciphers of alien star groupings wheeled overhead. It would have been a more dignified and exotic death than he had ever anticipated, even in his brief sojourn in the Aristotle colony, but the night had remained warm, and at dawn his physical condition had been comparatively good. He guessed that the Mollanian drugs and other therapies were helping sustain him because, during the second day, apart from occasional bouts of double vision and pins-and-needles in his legs, his chief source of discomfort was hunger – and the attentions of the alien quadruped.

By mid-afternoon it seemed to him that the creature – he had dubbed it a bealf – was becoming bolder and more persistent with its approaches, that it would soon have to be deterred by something more concrete than bellowed obscenities. Trying not to lose sight of his adversary while it inched its way through the grass, he took inventory of his resources.

The weakness of his arms precluded the use of club or missile, but there was the possibility that draining some electrolyte from his chair's batteries would provide the semblance of a useful weapon. A major drawback to the scheme, however, was that he had no suitable lightweight container from which to hurl the acid. He scanned his surroundings and steadied his gaze on the clump of palm-like trees some two hundred metres away. Could their resemblance to terrestrial palms extend as far as the production of large, thin-shelled nuts? He had no idea what the odds might be, but the chance of finding a source of armament and food in one place was something he could not ignore.

*At least I don't want to die any more*, he thought, sardonically amused. *Vekrynn had made me realize that being dead isn't everything in life.*

Hargate switched on his power circuit and tentatively advanced the drive lever a short distance. The chair stirred itself reluctantly, but by using all his strength on the wheels he got it to lurch forward out of the grooves it had created in the turf. He glanced triumphantly in the direction of the bealf and saw it slowly backing away, eyes intent.

*Didn't think I could move, did you? Well, friend bealf,*

*with any luck that's nothing to the next surprise you're going to get.* Grinning malevolently at his thoughts, Hargate urged his chair towards the trees, aided by a slight incline.

'Don't leave,' a man's voice said from close behind him. 'We've got things to talk about.'

Gasping for air, Hargate slewed himself around and saw that a very tall, black-haired man had materialized at the spot from which Vekrynn had disappeared. He had his left arm tucked into the front of his slate-grey overcoat and in his right hand was carrying an ordinary plastic shopping bag, garishly decorated, which stood out as totally incongruous in the alien setting. The newcomer looked like a Terran – he did not have the extreme breadth of skull that Hargate had observed in Vekrynn and other Mollanians – but the fact that he could skord was significant, and possibly threatening. Could it be that Vekrynn had sent someone to complete his work for him?

'Maybe I'm too busy to talk,' Hargate said, trying to make his voice hard. 'Who are you?'

'I'm Lorrest tye Thralen.'

'That tells me bugger all.'

The stranger's smile was unexpectedly boyish and amiable. 'I'm a friend of Gretana and an enemy of Warden Vekrynn – is that any better?'

'Some.' Hargate saw the tall man's image become two, realized he was squinting again and fought to bring his eye muscles under control. He had persuaded himself that he was prepared to die in a short time, with an entire alien world for a marker, but now that it no longer seemed necessary he could admit to himself just how much he wanted to stay alive.

'Well, I must say I'm glad to . . .' Hargate stopped speaking and swallowed as he heard a tremor come into his voice. 'Are you just going to stand there and grin?'

186

'Sorry, sorry, sorry!' Lorrest came towards him with exaggerated deference. 'I thought you might be dead by this time, but I took a chance and brought some beer and sandwiches. May I presume that you eat such humble food?'

Slightly disconcerted, Hargate watched in silence as Lorrest took off his overcoat, spread it on the grass and emptied the contents of his plastic bag on to it. As well as the cans of beer and wrapped sandwiches there was a packet of chocolate chip cookies.

'That looks good,' Hargate said. 'I don't know how I got so hungry inside a day.'

Lorrest glanced at the sun. 'You've been here more than a day, chum. An Earth day, I mean – this planet must turn a lot slower.'

'I never thought of that.' Hargate looked around him, freshly reminded that he was far from home, and his gaze fastened on the crouching form of the bealf, which had advanced to within twenty paces. 'Say, are you carrying any weapons?'

'No.' Lorrest swivelled his head, taking in the panorama of mountain ranges. 'Why?'

'I'm nearly certain that thing wants to eat me.' Hargate pointed at the bealf. 'I'd like to put a hole through it.'

Lorrest snorted with amusement. 'Gretana said you were a rough-cornered type, and I'm beginning to see what she meant.' He tore off part of a sandwich, squeezed it into a ball and lobbed it towards the attentive animal. The bealf seized the morsel in its jaws, then backed away until it was lost to view in the grass.

'It's nice having so much food you can afford to throw it away,' Hargate grumbled. 'Don't forget I was dumped here to starve.'

'Okay – let's talk about that.' Lorrest handed Hargate a

can of beer and a sandwich. 'Better still, let's talk about everything.'

The hour that followed was one of the most singular of Hargate's life. On a personal level, he found he could relax and communicate freely with the Mollanian, in spite of the vast dissimilarities in their backgrounds. Their conversational styles meshed so perfectly that Hargate soon felt a rapport, even though he guessed that Lorrest was using some rehearsed diplomacies, and the feeling was good. Right from the start he was able to drink beer without embarrassment, although its fizziness increased the regurgitation through his nose, quickly soaking his handkerchief. During each bout of Hargate's coughing Lorrest, neither staring nor pretending to be completely unaware, waited patiently until the talk could continue. And the story he unfolded was a seething white wave in Hargate's mind, obliterating old concepts, strewing others in startling new patterns.

'I can't quite take this in,' he said at one stage. 'The Moon is another *world* – I can't imagine it being destroyed.'

'It's as good as done,' Lorrest assured him. 'Less than two Earth days left to it.'

Hargate considered the incredible statement. 'And is there nothing Vekrynn and the Bureau can do to save it?'

'Not a thing, though they won't realize it until it's too late.'

'I don't get you.'

'We have allowed for the fact that they'll locate Ceres and hit it with enough thruster rays to deflect it,' Lorrest said. 'What Vekrynn doesn't know is that we were lucky enough to find a major node on the surface of the Moon, in the Ocean of Storms. We have aimed Ceres exactly at the node, and we have put a special kind of machine there – a cone field generator – and it will activate itself

188

about five minutes before the impact is due. When that happens Ceres will be snapped back on to its scheduled path, and . . . bingo!'

Hargate tried to visualize the colossal energies involved in flicking a minor planet around like a marble. 'This machine, this cone field generator, is it something like a powerful magnet?'

'Yes, except that it works by locally modifying a few geometries. I don't know if I could explain it to you.'

'That's all right – I've crammed enough new stuff into my brain already. But if that sort of machine is so good, why doesn't Vekrynn use one to pull Ceres really off course?'

Lorrest gestured with a beer can. 'No anchorage. Any ship the machine was mounted in would simply be drawn towards Ceres – not the other way round.'

'I see.' Hargate's thoughts returned to the basic issue, the one he found hardest to incorporate into his world picture. 'But will pulverizing the Moon really make any difference? Gretana told me something about how these second-and-third-order forces of yours affect living matter, but . . . Our bodies are two-thirds water, so I can visualize a slight tidal effect, perhaps, but what else?'

Lorrest's manner became didactic. 'Don't dismiss water so quickly, my friend. Mollanian science is a long way ahead of Earth's – and we're still arguing about the structure of water. The hydrogen-to-oxygen bond is so weak that a glass of water, no matter how simple and stable it may look, is like a single giant molecule constantly reforming and rebuilding itself. Even in *warm* water there are short-lived regions of ice crystals that form and melt millions of times every second. Water is uniquely flexible and fragile, which makes it the perfect trigger substance for biological processes, and – believe me – both the structure of water and the chemical reactions taking place in it *are* affected by cosmic influences.'

'I suppose forces that you, as an adult, can actually feel must be able to affect us,' Hargate conceded. 'What's it like, being able to sense skord lines and the movements of planets and such?'

'I hate using clichés, but how do you explain sight to the . . .?' Lorrest paused to stare at Hargate. 'But that's not exactly the case, is it? As a boy you found the Bureau's Carsewell nodal point by yourself, and you knew the place was special. How did that feel?'

Hargate considered the impossibility of describing in full the emotional experience of a childhood visit to Cotter's Edge. 'I didn't feel any planets tugging at me.'

'It isn't like that. It's . . . Look, the world we're on now has no moons and there are no other planets in the system. Do you feel any difference?'

Hargate tried to turn his senses inwards, to locate a special reservoir of tranquillity. 'Perhaps,' he said, unwilling to acknowledge his failure. 'Do you think I could learn to skord?'

'That's something I'd dearly love to know.' Lorrest's face, in one of its rapid changes of expression, showed a hint of anger. 'We on Mollan are the only one of the known human cultures who use sympathetic congruency for interstellar travel. The ability is almost certain to be present or latent in all the others, but a cornerstone of our Government's policy is that we don't make contact, don't spread the knowledge. It would result in outsiders arriving on Mollan, you see, bringing new ideas and attitudes, disturbing the peace of the long Sunday afternoon. A man like Vekrynn would rather die than face up to change and growth and uncertainty.'

'I don't think he'd rather die.' Hargate went on to talk about his intuitive belief that Warden Vekrynn had a pathological fear of death.

'I know he wants to be immortal, but that leaves a lot

still to be explained.' Lorrest made a sweeping gesture which took in the surrounding vistas of plains and mountains, lakes and seas. 'For instance, what are we doing *here*, two hundred light years inside a non-human sector? Nobody else on Mollan even knows about this world, and I wouldn't have found out if Gretana hadn't back-tracked on herself and seen Vekrynn's mnemo-curve. Why does he come here?'

'Perhaps he just keeps the place in reserve, for losing trouble-makers.'

'Perhaps, but I doubt it.' Lorrest stood up, signalling an end to the strange picnic, and looked around with sky-mirrored eyes. 'Have a look at that stream over there.'

Hargate concentrated his gaze on a ribbon of silvered water about a hundred metres from the hummock upon which they had eaten. 'What about it?'

'Do those stones in it look like stepping stones to you?'

Hargate swore as he realized that in all his hours of surveying the same scene he had overlooked the clear evidence of human interference with the environment. 'Stepping stones to what?'

'There's only one way to find out. Come on.' Without hesitation, Lorrest grasped the back of Hargate's chair with his right hand and began to push. Hargate fully expected Lorrest to leave him at the side of the stream and cross it alone, but on reaching the bank the tall Mollanian moved to his side, threw his right arm across the chair and lifted it clear of the ground. Four long steps took the two men and the machine to the other side of the stream in as many seconds.

Impressed by the display of strength, Hargate said, 'Next time you might have the manners to ask my permission.'

'Next time I might throw you in. Lorrest got behind the chair again and urged it in the direction of a wooded area which lay about a kilometre ahead.

'What are you hoping to find anyway?'

'I've no idea,' Lorrest replied. 'All we can deduce is that when old man Vekrynn came here he had one thing in mind. Secrecy. Concealment. And those trees make the best hiding place in this area.'

'You're wasting your time,' Hargate sneered. He repeated the statement more than once as the wheelchair bounced and rocked on the uneven ground, and in between times he swore volubly and slapped at tiny winged creatures which rose up from the disturbed grass.

'I'm glad to see somebody else doesn't like bugs,' Lorrest said, inconsequentially. 'We don't have them on Mollan, you know. Most of the pollination is done by birds. Our flowers are all white, like our birds, and they imitate birdsongs to attract business. It's quite an experience for a Mollanian when he sees the kind of flowers you have on Earth.'

'Shove the botany lecture – I'm not interested.' Hargate made an ineffectual attempt to halt the chair by applying the brakes. 'If you want to blunder around in those trees and risk getting your ass chewed off by monsters that's all right with me, but I demand to be left out in the open where at least I can see what's . . .'

His voice failed as shiftings of parallax caused by the chair's rapid progress suddenly opened an avenue deep into the trees to where something large and apparently with a surface of polished gold reflected the sunlight. The object's curvatures shone with a buttery lustre. Before Hargate could announce what he had seen Lorrest, now breathing hard from his exertions, gave a satisfied grunt.

'Vekrynn always had a weakness for shiny things,' he said. 'It wouldn't even occur to him to camouflage an aircraft.'

'What makes you so sure it's an aircraft?'

'This is bad submarine country, *mon ami*. We'll take a closer look.'

On being propelled into the vicinity of the machine, Hargate was able to confirm that it had been designed for flying, although the centrally positioned wings seemed too small for the fuselage and no control surfaces were in evidence. It appeared to have the capacity of a rail carriage and, now that he could examine it closely, Hargate realized that the aircraft was old. The golden skin, which had appeared immaculate from a distance, was dulled in some places and was peeling away from an underlying grey metal in others. On the side of the fuselage was a painted inscription in blocky characters which Hargate took to be Mollanian.

He pointed the lettering out to Lorrest. 'What does it say?'

'It roughly translates as Peninsular Educational Tours,' Lorrest said, shaking his head in bafflement. 'This grows curiouser and curiouser. One disadvantage of being able to skord from point to point on a planet, the way we do on Mollan, is that kids can grow up with no idea what the territory is like in between. Some educational authorities try to put that right by flying them around in aircraft like this one.'

'What's it doing here?'

'That's something else I'd like to know. This is the safest aircraft ever devised – three entirely independent means of staying aloft – so it's a logical type for a man like Vekrynn to use, but did he steal it? And how did he get it here? I daresay an assembly robot could have put it together for him quickly enough, but he'd have had to skord it out here bit by bit, and that would have taken a lot of his time. I just don't get it.' Still shaking his head, Lorrest walked right round the aircraft once, then went to a large door forward of the wing. It resisted his attempts to open it. Apparently undeterred, he took out a brown wallet, riffled through its contents with great care and finally removed from it what appeared to be a rectangle of ordinary writing paper. He held the paper in the palm of his hand and pressed it against the aircraft's skin, close to the door handle, for about ten seconds. Pausing to give Hargate a parodied conspirator's wink, he tried the door again and this time it swung open immediately, revealing a roomy interior.

'That's a smart piece of paper,' Hargate commented.

Lorrest nodded, putting the white scrap back into his wallet. 'It's a machine, of course, but I subscribe to the idea that no electronic device is perfect until it's smaller and lighter than the original design sketch. And, luckily, I know this type of aircraft well. Let's get you on board.'

'In there?' Hargate was taken aback. 'Are you going to fly it?'

Lorrest's shoulders heaved once before he frowned and clasped his left arm. 'No more feed lines like that, *please*. Naturally I'm going to fly it.'

'But where to?'

'The plan is to fly it to where Vekrynn flies it, and find out exactly what he has tucked away on this planet. It seems an interesting way to pass a few hours.'

'How will you know where he goes?'

'You have just picked out the major weak point in the scheme,' Lorrest said, wheeling Hargate towards the open door. 'A lot depends on whether Vekrynn has ever been stupid enough to let the plane take him to his destination under automatic control. If he has, it'll be fairly easy to duplicate the flight plan; if he hasn't, if he has always done the flying himself, the job will be a lot trickier. To be honest, it would probably be too much for the equipment I have with me – so keep your fingers crossed.'

Lorrest, again displaying a surprising degree of

strength, lifted Hargate and the wheelchair under his right arm and with a single turning movement got them into the aircraft. The interior was a single large compartment, with a pilot's seat and controls in the nose. Ranged around the sides were chairs, desks and storage cupboards which, despite their distant origin, had an obvious kinship to Terran classroom furniture. As further evidence that children tended to be the same everywhere, many of the desks and adjoining window frames had been drawn on and scribbled on with coloured inks.

Hargate, noticing a small object on one of the desks, rolled himself closer to it and found the stub of a perfectly ordinary pencil, the ends of which showed unmistakable signs of having been chewed. Intrigued, he picked the pencil up, but dropped it immediately when its outer casing crumbled into yellowish dust, suggesting that it could have been lying there for centuries. It came to him that no amount of similarities between Terran and Mollanian children could outweigh the fact that the latter measured their life expectancies in millennia. The disparity was something he had been too busy to brood upon, but now the sheer unfairness of it darkened his mind and mood. He turned and wheeled himself to the front of the aircraft, where Lorrest had knelt down and was beginning to remove panels from the control console.

'Is it true what Gretana told me?' he said. 'Do people on all the other human worlds live for seven hundred or eight hundred years?'

'That's the norm.' Lorrest continued working as he spoke. 'Seven or eight centuries.'

'The first part of our Christian Bible quotes figures like that. It says that Methuselah clocked up nearly a thousand years – do you think that's the way it might actually have been?'

'I doubt it,' Lorrest said abstractedly. 'That implies that

something happened quite suddenly some thousands of years ago to degrade Terran biomechanisms, and it doesn't seem likely to me. I'm more inclined to believe it has always been that way. I'd blame it on the . . .'

'The Moon! Unstable lunar influences!' Hargate squirmed in his chair. 'When you get on to something you really stick with it, don't you?'

'It's the only way, my friend.' Lorrest smiled as he again opened his wallet and selected a rectangular scrap of paper from a slim bundle. 'I'll bet you anything you like that Vekrynn doesn't even know that tools like this exist.'

'Is there anything about us that you *can't* blame on the Moon?'

'His mind is as stagnant as Mollanian technology itself, and that's saying something.'

'How about the shape of our heads? Or the smell of our socks?'

'The design of a Mollanian artifact can remain unchanged for thousands of years. If it weren't for organizations like 2H there'd be virtually no creative thinking.'

'Scrotum fillers to you,' Hargate snapped, wheeling his chair away. He positioned himself at the rear of the cabin, scowling, refusing to acknowledge the wave Lorrest gave him a minute later when the aircraft's door swung itself shut. He expected to hear engines starting up, but within a few seconds there was a change in the quality of light streaming in through the windows and he realized the aircraft was rising vertically, in total silence. At a height of about a hundred metres the movement was translated into horizontal flight and the landscape began to flow beneath with increasing rapidity.

Hargate studied the complex of geographical features. The incredible clarity of the air seemed to suspend the rules of perspective, creating a new kind of space in which distant peaks perched confusingly on the slopes of nearer mountains, and in which remote blue seas hung in flat suspension above middle-ground lakes. He tried to visualize what they would find at the end of the flight – a secret pleasure dome, perhaps, or a simple hermitage – but the wealth of microscopic detail quickly became numbing to the mind, making it expedient for him to turn his attention to the aircraft's interior.

'How old do you reckon this flivver is?' he said to Lorrest, reopening communications.

'Five or six centuries at the most,' Lorrest replied. 'After that you start getting too many structural failures and it's easier to switch to a new machine.'

'I see.' Intrigued by the possibility that the aircraft had been ferrying Mollanian children around their world at the time of Columbus, Hargate prowled about the cabin, opening drawers and lockers, occasionally discovering traces of occupation. In one place he found a small engraved bracelet, in another a magnifying glass – apparently commonplace objects which, because of their origins, he saw as archaeological treasures, worth stowing away in his pockets.

He had almost completed his meagre plundering when he noticed, tucked into a recess below a window, a complicated metal object which looked like an engineering instrument in some respects and in others like one of the mathematical sculptures he had once constructed for a living. It had a central spine from which sprouted numerous slim telescopic rods, all finely graduated, terminating in a glittering strip of silver. Hargate stared at it with a greedy quickening of his heart, intuitively identifying it as having something to do with Mollanian instantaneous travel. He snatched it from the recess and went forward to where Lorrest was sitting in the nose of the aircraft.

'It's a child's trainer,' Lorrest explained, taking the

object and casually remoulding the bright strip to a new shape. 'They use it to set up basic mnemo-curves.'

'How about me?' Hargate reached for the trainer with covetous fingers. 'Do you think I could learn to skord?'

Lorrest gave him a searching glance. 'You keep coming back to that, don't you?'

'You don't understand – this is what I had in place of religion. As a kid, I only saw Gretana once at Cotter's Edge, but that was all I needed. I never told anybody about seeing her, but all my life I *knew* there were people to whom the ordinary rules didn't apply, and that was very important to me. As far as I was concerned, you see, we had a bad set of rules. It comforted me to know there was a bigger and better game going on somewhere. I suppose I was nursing a secret hope that some day I'd be invited to play. Does that sound crazy to you?'

'I think I understand,' Lorrest said. 'But why is it so important for you to skord?'

'It's part of my personal mathematics. I like the idea of reducing time to the status of an ordinary dimension, and that's because I'm short of time.' Hargate hesitated, wondering if he could ever get his point of view across to the Mollanian. 'I've only got a year or so left – perhaps a lot less – and I want to make the maximum use of it. Mathematically speaking, I want to extend myself in three dimensions to compensate for deficiencies in the fourth.'

Lorrest gazed at him for a few seconds, his eyes becoming lensed with tears. 'Why is there no justice, Denny?'

'What do you mean?'

'When I think of the way most of my people squander all those centuries they've grabbed for themselves . . . those pale ghosts of human beings . . . while you've got enough courage for . . . for . . .'

198

'Courage my ass,' Hargate put in. 'How about it? Can you teach me to skord?'

'I honestly don't know. Right from infancy Mollanians are aware of living in a matrix of third-order forces, and that seems to give us an in-built mathematical faculty that a Terran might never be able to acquire.'

Hargate refused to be discouraged. 'Come on! I know all about homeomorphism and algebraic topology and theory of functions, and I've read Riemann and Hu and Wilder and people like that. You can't be all that much smarter than I am. What do you say?'

'Your Terran maths might be a handicap. You'd have to unlearn some of it.'

'So I'll unlearn – what do you say?'

Lorrest smiled helplessly. 'Well, we're going to be airborne on autopilot for a few hours before we reach Vekrynn's *pied-à-terre*, or whatever we're looking for . . . Maybe I could force some elementary maths into your skull.'

'And I'll pay you back,' Hargate promised. 'I'll try to force some elementary manners into yours.'

The structure was a featureless slab of concrete, like a single huge building block that had been dropped in a forest clearing. Mosses and vines had attached themselves to much of the surface without softening the uncompromising lines. Only in one place, where a fallen tree formed a sloping catwalk from ground to roof, had the environment made any headway in obliterating the unnatural intrusion.

'No attempt at concealment here,' Lorrest commented. 'Either Vekrynn was confident nobody would get this far, or he realized that if they did they weren't going to be put off.'

Hargate ran his gaze over the wall towards which he was being propelled and picked out the faint outline of a door which also seemed to be made of concrete. 'It doesn't look much like a country residence.'

'No, it has to be a store, a glorified strongbox. The only question is – what's inside?'

'I'll bet it takes more than one of your intelligent playing cards to open it.'

'Unbeliever!' Lorrest brought the wheelchair to a halt and went towards the door, already opening his wallet. 'The locks are undoubtedly the best that Vekrynn could buy, borrow or steal, which means they were probably manufactured on Mollan around the time the Normans were invading England. Our establishment engineers are handicapped, of course. One thing about our longevity that nobody seemed to anticipate was the stultifying effect on designers – it's very difficult to find materials that last as long as we do.'

Hargate sniffed noisily to express a bitter amusement. The tranquillity of the surrounding forest and the mellow coppery radiance from the setting sun reminded him of the long summer evenings of boyhood, those evenings on which time seemed to relent and cease its persecution, but he was not deceived. The caravan was still winding its way towards the dawn of nothing. In the solitude of the previous day he had persuaded himself that, as far as the mathematics of eternity was concerned, there was no difference between a lifespan of four decades and one of four millennia – all fractions with infinity as the bottom line had to equal zero – but one had to be in a certain mood to accept that kind of reasoning . . .

'Hurry up, for Chrissakes,' he said with a kind of nasal snarl. 'It's bloody boring sitting here.'

'Patience, patience,' Lorrest said, unperturbed, continuing to explore the surface of the door with one of his apparently ubiquitous white rectangles. 'It's just a matter of finding the right place for my calling card.'

A moment later he gave a low exclamation and stepped back as – with the loud report of a long-established seal being broken – the door retreated a short distance into the building. It stopped, then slid sideways to reveal a short corridor ending in another door which had a circular window. A pale amethyst light streamed through the glass. *Has the light been on all the time*, Hargate found himself wondering, his mind seizing on the irrelevancy, *or is there a fridge door switch?*

Holding the card aloft and slightly ahead of him, Lorrest walked slowly to the inner door. He pushed it open a little, satisfying himself that it was unlocked, and came back smiling. 'It's all right. I didn't think Vekrynn would have gone in for automatic weapons, but associating with people like you has made me suspicious.'

'Yeah, you look suspicious.' His melancholia displaced by curiosity, Hargate urged his chair forward and through the outer doorway. Lorrest held the inner door open, allowing him to roll into a long chamber which occupied the entire volume of the building. The cold, delicately-tinted light had no obvious sources, coming equally from walls, floor and ceiling, making it difficult to judge dimensions and distances. Hargate, who had half-expected an Ali Baba's cave of rare treasures, was slightly taken aback to find that the chamber was bare except for a single deeply-cushioned armchair which faced a row of seven metal boxes. The boxes were desk-sized, had numerous flush-mounted panels in varying shades of blue and were massively bolted to the floor, a detail which gave the whole assembly a curious old-fashioned appearance. Hargate was reminded of twentieth century electrical power installations.

'What is it?' he said, not hiding his disappointment. 'Some kind of relay station?'

'Hardly.' Lorrest went forward and stood for a moment

by the chair, his face registering an excitement that was almost manic in its intensity. 'If I'm not mistaken . . . Denny, I can't *believe* this.'

'Believe what?' Hargate said irritably. 'How about letting me in on . . .?'

Lorrest silenced him with an upraised hand and lowered himself into the deep chair. He touched no controls that Hargate could see, but a few seconds later a screen-like area of white luminescence sprang into existence in the air above the centre box. After a barely perceptible delay the screen blossomed with what Hargate had learned to recognize as Mollanian script.

'What we have here,' Lorrest said, speaking slowly, 'is a copy of old man Vekrynn's famous Notebook.'

'Is that all?'

Lorrest gave him a wry smile. 'I don't think you understand. Vekrynn is determined that his great opus, *Analytical Notes on the Evolution of One Human Civilization*, will live forever, become part of the Mollanian heritage and all that stuff. He's so afraid of the idea that it might be lost that he maintains, at his own expense, five up-dated copies of it on five different planets, and naturally he has made certain their whereabouts are known to everybody who could possibly be concerned.'

Hargate studied Lorrest's face, trying to solve the puzzle it represented. 'Is this a sixth copy that nobody knew about?'

'You've guessed it.'

'I still don't see why you're wetting yourself,' Hargate said. 'From what you say, it would be in character for him to have a reserve copy.'

'*Here?* On a world far outside the human sector? On a world no other human knows about?' Lorrest shook his head as the writing on the screen began to change. 'No, there has to be another reason. My guess is there's

202

something special about this one, and I'd like to know what it is.'

Hargate chuckled. 'You're becoming obsessed, man. Vekrynn isn't worth the time or trouble.'

It's no trouble, and I've got a little time to kill.' Lorrest settled back in the chair and the characters blazoned on the insubstantial screen hovering above the middle cabinet began to change.

'Have fun,' Hargate said drily. Anxious to conserve what little power remained in his batteries, he rolled his chair away manually and began a circuit of the oblong chamber, hoping to find something of interest he had missed at first glance. The journey was disappointing – not even a scuff mark differentiated one blank wall from another. Losing interest in the interior of the building, he propelled himself back to the entrance, opened the door and went along the short corridor to the threshold of the alien world. The sun had not quite disappeared below the horizon, but there was little diffusion in the pure air and night was already advancing down the sky in merging bands of blue-green.

He shivered luxuriously, in spite of the ambient warmth, as he made yet another attempt to accommodate the knowledge that he, Denny Hargate, who as a child had not been able to drag himself more than a few city blocks without becoming exhausted, had travelled farther from Earth than any other member of his race. It was more than he could ever have expected. His private religion, his faith in that first miracle at Cotter's Edge, had paid off in the form of something like a trip to heaven. If he had any cause for complaint it was that providence had not granted him the travelling companion he would have chosen – Gretana was the high priestess of Cotter's Edge, and she should have been the one to accompany him. He could almost have reconciled himself to the prospect of dying in a couple of years or less on condition that he would be able to look at that incredible face every day, to replenish and fecundate himself and thus counteract the slow withering of his soul.

It was, however, most unlikely that he would ever see Gretana again. She was many light years distant and he had no way of even guessing the direction in the darkening vault of the sky, where the unfamiliar star groupings were again beginning to emerge. Could it be that loneliness was an unavoidable by-product of total mobility? From what he had learned of the Mollanians, theirs was a *cool* society in which individuals – freed from all the restraints of forced physical proximity – had forfeited the ability to form close personal relationships. Gretana saw her parents as remote and uninterested figures, which fitted his thesis, but another possible explanation lay in the Mollanians' fantastic longevity. Lorrest had mentioned the difficulty of producing inert materials which could match a Mollanian lifespan; how then could a fragile thing like human passion hope to endure when the parties concerned went on for centuries, *millennia*, with no sign of change? *Perhaps poignancy is all*, Hargate mused. *Perhaps . . .*

The deep quavering sob which came from immediately behind him almost stopped Hargate's heart.

He flailed himself around in his chair and saw Lorrest staring down at him. The Mollanian's face was a near-luminous mask, flowing and distorting in an interplay of emotions Hargate was unable to identify. He shrank back into his chair, suddenly afraid as Lorrest dropped to his knees, covered his face with his hands and began to sway, all the time emitting the inarticulate whimpers which can be wrested from humans by insupportable grief.

'You'll never forgive us,' he said, after a time, each word a separate expression of pain. 'You'll never forgive what we have done to you.'

Feeling oddly self-conscious, prompted by instinct, Hargate leaned forward and gently placed his hands on Lorrest's bowed head. And the tableau remained unchanged for many minutes, silhouetted in amethyst radiance, while the representative of one world made his confession and the representative of the other tried to give personal absolution.


# CHAPTER 18

'Fair seasons, Gretana! I must apologize for keeping you waiting,' Warden Vekrynn said with a handsome smile. 'The past few days have been somewhat . . . unusual.'

'I quite understand, sir.' Looking at Vekrynn across the broad expanse of his desk, Gretana again realized the futility of trying to anticipate his reactions to anything. She had been certain, especially in view of the recent demands on his time, that the Warden would have been even more brusque than on the last occasion they had met. Instead, he appeared relaxed and cheerful. There was even a trace of excitement in his manner, which had the effect of making him seem humanly approachable to an unprecedented degree.

'I'm sorry, too, about the way I treated you. I was trying to deal with some very important, very urgent matters at the time, and the last thing I needed was an inquisitive Terran dumped in my lap.' Vekrynn renewed his smile. 'Nobody ever did that to me before.'

'I panicked,' Gretana said, the Warden's unexpected courtesy increasing her dread of what was to follow.

'So did I, a little, but that doesn't excuse my mistreatment of a co-worker. I hope you understand that we have been going through a crisis. I've been forced to move ships and large quantities of equipment into the vicinity of Earth – all because of a missing asteroid.'

Gretana took a deep breath. 'Lorrest tye Thralen was in touch with me days ago, trying to win me over to 2H. I tried to tell you, but somehow I didn't.'

To her astonishment, Vekrynn looked unconcerned. 'I don't know what I'm going to do with you, young Gretana,' he said mildly.

'But he came back, and . . . and I had to tell him how to find the Carsewell node. I'm responsible for his escape from Earth.'

'I know – Ichmo has already given me the gist of your report. I'll say this much for you – when you do something wrong you do it in the most spectacular manner possible.'

'I . . .' Gretana's sense of unreality grew stronger. 'I was afraid to tell you. I was sure you'd be . . .'

'Furious?' Vekrynn leaned forward and rested his elbows on the desk, creating an inverted pearly image of himself on the polished surface. 'Don't get the wrong impression. What you did was a very serious infringement of regulations, and this time you'll hardly be able to avoid some kind of punishment, but the important thing right now is that the madmen in 2H have made a fatal mistake over this Ceres affair. Their attempt to destroy Earth's satellite has failed, and the very fact that they made it is going to bring real trouble down on their heads. The Bureau will now get all the Government backing it needs to deal with them. It doesn't matter where Lorrest tye Thralen has slunk off to – I'll be able to find him.'

'Perhaps I can help,' Gretana said, still bemused by the Warden's casual acceptance of her misdeeds. 'He said he was going to find Denny Hargate, and I have an odd idea that he really meant it.'

'I don't think he would go to Cialth.'

'According to Lorrest, Hargate isn't on Cialth.' Gretana paused, filled with an unaccountable sense of imminence, of probabilities shifting and resettling like great juddering wheels of chance. 'I went back to Branie IV when I was trying to complete my report, and . . . I saw you leave with Hargate.'

'You saw what?' Vekrynn jumped to his feet, his face now mirroring shock and anger.

'I saw you leave with the Terran.' Gretana lowered her head, unable to withstand the ferocious pressure of Vekrynn's gaze. 'According to Lorrest, the mnemo-curve you used would have taken you into the Attatorian sector, but . . .'

The massive thudding sound that immediately followed her words caused Gretana to flinch. She jerked her head upright, half-convinced she had provoked Vekrynn into violence, and saw that he had fallen forward on to his desk from the standing position, supporting the upper half of his body on his hands. His head projected towards her from the gantry of his arms and shoulders, and for a long moment his face was quite unrecognizable. The mouth had been stretched into a grin, but it was the vacuous, mirthless grin of a half-wit, and the gold-needled brown eyes were staring through and beyond her into a universe she never wanted to visit. She gazed back at him in dread, unable to move, until at last his old identity emerged through the stranger's features like a developing photographic image.

'You will stay in this room till I return,' Vekrynn said, striding to the door. 'You will not communicate with anyone.' He opened the door, made an adjustment to the lock, then went into the outer corridor, slamming the door behind him. Gretana knew, without having to be told, that she was a prisoner.

*What have I done?* she thought, drifting her eyes around

the blue-domed office she had first seen a long time earlier, in the days of her innocence. *What have I done?*

*And to whom?*


# CHAPTER 19

Hargate realized there were two courses he could follow – he could brood on what he had learned about Warden Vekrynn and quietly burn up with hatred; or he could avoid the self-punishment by concentrating his thoughts on the recent wonders that had entered his life. And, in spite of a history of indulgent bouts of negative thinking, he chose the latter option. He wheeled himself across the aircraft to where Lorrest was sitting at a side window, broodily watching the changing landscapes below. Hargate took the Mollanian travel trainer from its storage place between his right hip and the back of the chair.

'Look, I know you don't think there's much chance of my ever being able to skord,' he said, 'but what if we forget the big stuff for the time being? Wouldn't it be easier for me to try jumping between two minor nodes? Two that aren't very far apart?'

Lorrest, whose face was still drawn and had a bruised look around the eyes, gave a half-smile. 'You're not going to give up on this thing, are you?'

'So I'm a stubborn little bastard. How about it?'

'Denny, I'm surprised that you even want to speak to me.'

Hargate sighed with exasperation. 'Who's got the one-track mind now? I've told you a dozen times – you can't shoulder the blame for something Vekrynn did long before you were born. For God's sake snap out of it and do something useful.'

Lorrest grimaced and pushed his hair up off his forehead. 'I'll call out made-up addresses, and you practise visualizing them and setting them up. Okay?'

'Fire away, teach,' Hargate said. In the hours that followed he gave all his attention to the task of adapting his mind to Mollanian concepts of formalist maths. He found the work absorbing, and only rarely did his concentration waver enough to let him take note of the shrill and gleefully malicious voice which seemed to heterodyne with the sounds of flight. And Seth lived after he begat Enos eight hundred and seven years . . . and all the days of Cainan were nine hundred and ten years . . . and Mahalaleel lived after he begat Jared eight hundred and thirty years . . .

It was Lorrest who tired first and asked Hargate if he wanted to break off.

'Not yet, but I think I've done enough on these fake addresses,' Hargate replied. 'Suppose I was at home, at the Cotter's Edge node, and I wanted to skord up to your node on the Moon. Exactly where is it?'

'I don't think I should . . .'

'What difference does it make? Who could I tell?'

Lorrest stared at him closely for a moment, then shrugged. 'Do you know the geography of the Moon all that well?'

'Like the back of my hand.'

'All right. Try to visualize a spot about one-fifty kilometres north-east – inverted compass, by the way – of the Mayer crater.' Lorrest went on to specify a precise set of grid coordinates, and waited with a look of humorous scepticism while Hargate struggled, using his newly ingested Mollanian maths, to throw a conceptual bridge between Earth and Moon. Scowling ferociously, Hargate picked up the travel trainer and slowly – with some help from the computer in his watch –  shaped its working surface into a complex curve. He was gratified to see Lorrest's expression change.

'You did it!' the Mollanian exclaimed. 'You actually got it right!'

'Do you have to sound so surprised?' Concealing his pleasure, Hargate collapsed the trainer and started the same calculation afresh, determined to improve his speed. He worked on it single-mindedly for more than thirty minutes, oblivious to his surroundings, and was taken by surprise when Lorrest suddenly gave a theatrical groan of misery.

'Denny, how long are you going to keep it up?' Lorrest said, gently pounding his own forehead. 'Give me a break, will you?'

'What's the matter? I'm being quiet.'

'You're being quiet, but you're creating a kind of third-order whirlpool all round yourself, and its driving me crazy. If you ever manage to direct that energy properly you may actually be able to skord by yourself some day.'

The words came as a revelation to Hargate. 'You mean you can feel what I'm doing?'

'*Feel* it! This is one of the reasons we encourage Mollanian children to discard trainers as soon as they can. Anybody who's using one tends to act like a giant radio station that's drowning out its neighbours. Kids sometimes use the effect to play tricks on adults – shunting them off to places they didn't want to visit.'

'This is great,' Hargate said. 'I really feel as if I'm getting somewhere.' Ignoring Lorrest's complaints, he returned to his mental exercises with the trainer and continued until when, near the end of the flight, Lorrest raised the question of his immediate future.

'In one hour and three minutes,' Lorrest said, looking at his watch, 'your Moon's going to get zapped into smithers, and I'd like to be on Earth to see it happen. The view will be just as good from Carsewell or from Valparaiso – which would you prefer? Valparaiso should be warmer, but you'll have the problem of being an illegal immigrant.'

'Won't you be there to get me out?'

'Hardly! The Bureau keeps a continuous watch on the few nodes discovered by 2H. I'll be arrested as soon as I arrive.'

Hargate frowned. 'In that case it isn't worth going.'

'At that stage I'll *want* to be taken back to Mollan.' Lorrest's eyes became unfocused as he was drawn into his inner world. 'With the Moon destroyed, I'll be too famous – notorious, I should say – for Vekrynn to have me quietly put away somewhere. And people will listen to what I have to say about him. I'm looking forward to that part.'

'I see.' The realization that his association with the tall Mollanian was soon to end, that he had to return to the circumscribed realities of life on Earth, caused Hargate an unexpectedly fierce pang of regret. 'I was kind of hoping I wouldn't have to go back to Earth – this star-hopping game suits me fine.'

'I know it does, Denny. You've got the imagination and the spirit for it, and if there was any kind of justice in this universe you'd be . . . you'd be . . .' Lorrest turned away and stared out through the window, blinking rapidly.

'Christ, he's off again,' Hargate said disgustedly, horrified to find that his own vision was dissolving in a painful blur. 'How old are you supposed to be, anyway?'

'Old enough to vote.'

'Then stop acting like a big nancy – it's bloody embarrassing.'

'I'll do my best, sire,' Lorrest looked owlishly at Hargate for a moment, then his shoulders came up, his face darkened and he had embarked on one of his excruciating whole-body laughs. Hargate felt his own chest give a sympathetic squeeze and within a few seconds he had lost control and was honking and snorting through his nose as an ungovernable tide of laughter went through him, relieving the stresses that had been building since the previous evening. The sight of Lorrest's contorted, plum-coloured features defeated his every attempt to calm down, and he knew that his own nasal bleatings were having a similar effect on the Mollanian. On the verge of panic over the idea that his lung function might cease altogether, Hargate wheeled himself to another part of the long cabin, shaking his head and cackling, and waited for the return of sanity. It was the first time in his adult life that he had experienced that kind of laughter – nobody on Earth had ever created the necessary climate of camaraderie – and the incident, trivial though it was, magnified his regret at losing Lorrest. He tried to locate a source of hope.

'If things are going to be different on Earth when you have forced Mollan into open contact,' he said, 'maybe you'll go back there.'

'I'd like to – I *intend* to – but there'll be a lot of court procedure on Mollan.' Lorrest looked uncomfortable. 'It could be quite a few years.'

'Enough said.' Refusing to yield to self-pity, Hargate went to the front of the cabin with the intention of sating his hunger for strange horizons while he still had the opportunity. Almost as if his movement had affected the aircraft's balance, the nose of the machine dipped under automatic control and it began boring down into lower layers of the atmosphere. Within five minutes they were on the ground at the point from which they had departed on the previous day and Lorrest, who was rapidly regaining the use of his left arm, had unloaded Hargate and his chair. They left the wooded area, crossed the stream and proceeded up the gentle rise in the direction of the invisible node.

'Have you made up your mind?' Lorrest said, effortlessly propelling the chair on the incline.

'It had better be Cotter's Edge – that's where it all started.' Hargate suddenly realized he felt something akin to claustrophobia at the prospect of returning to his former existence. 'Besides, from Valparaiso the Moon would be upside down. It wouldn't look right.'

Lorrest halted the chair a few paces from the node, came round to the front and extended his hand. 'We'd better take the chance to say good-bye. There'll be Bureau men waiting for me at the other end, and things may be a little difficult.'

'Sure.' Hargate was in the act of reaching for the offered hand when – with a silent, mind-numbing shock – his reality changed.

Standing behind Lorrest, where a second earlier there had been emptiness, was a towering figure in a gold-belted tunic of silver brocade. His head was leonine and massive, with the unmodified Mollanian cranium, and in one hand he held what appeared to be a radiation weapon. Hargate recognized Warden Vekrynn on the instant and his mind was invaded by darkness.

Lorrest spun on his heel and froze as Vekrynn made a stabbing gesture with the pistol.

'That's the way – both of you stay perfectly still,' Vekrynn ordered, using English for Hargate's benefit. 'These paralysis weapons are basically harmless, but I'm told it's quite painful when the effects begin to wear off.'

Still trying to adjust to the startling change in the situation, Hargate glanced up at Lorrest. Their eyes locked briefly and Lorrest gave a barely perceptible shake of the head. Ambiguous though the signal could have been, Hargate fully understood the message. *If he finds out we've seen the sixth copy of his Notes, he'll kill us on the spot.*

'And you couldn't bear to inflict pain, could you?' Lorrest's tone was relaxed, almost amiable.

'I can bear it when I have to,' Vekrynn said comfortably. 'Especially when I'm dealing with a man who has recently committed murder.'

'Did Gretana tell you that?' For the first time Lorrest began to show concern. 'Didn't she mention that the Terran was on the point of killing her?'

'Perhaps it slipped her mind. Her memory has been at fault several times recently.'

'I wasn't able to subvert Gretana, if that's what you're implying,' Lorrest said. 'You've got nothing against her.'

Vekrynn shrugged, sunlight rippling on his bright tunic. 'I'm more interested in you right now, Lorrest tye Thralen. What are you doing here?'

'I came to find Denny, and since then we've been sleeping and eating mostly.' Lorrest nodded towards the remains of the previous day's meal, visible a short distance down the slope. 'It seemed quite a good place to hide out until . . . until a certain astronomical event had taken place.'

'Really?' Vekrynn's eyes narrowed as he studied Lorrest's face then he began to smile. 'You have a knack for getting things wrong – especially about Ceres and the Moon. There isn't going to be any collision.'

Lorrest shifted uneasily. 'That's what you think.'

'Did you really believe I wouldn't be able to find Ceres?' Vekrynn's smile broadened into a jubilant grin. 'I'll admit it was a costly operation, but not all that difficult. It was simply a matter of pouring in men and equipment, saturating a smallish volume of space. I'm pleased to inform you – in fact, I'm *delighted* to inform you – that I have knocked out every screen placed on

214

Ceres by 2H and have made it clearly visible. We're already using thruster rays against it. There is a tremendous amount of kinetic energy to overcome there, but Ceres is being deflected enough to miss the Moon. The Terrans are going to wonder what's been going on, of course, but that's a . . .'

'You're a liar,' Lorrest shouted, his lean face hardening with anger.

'Why should I lie?' A tremor of excitement was now evident in Vekrynn's voice. 'Face up to the fact that you have failed, Lorrest tye Thralen. All I have to do now to tidy up this little matter is dispose of you and that.' On the final word Vekrynn's pistol pointed at Hargate and swung back to cover Lorrest.

From the lowly vantage point of his wheelchair, Hargate had been viewing the exchange as a confrontation between two Olympian giants, but Vekrynn's gesture with the weapon was a reminder that he too was vitally concerned. He had no way of knowing if the Warden had psychologically prepared himself for a straightforward act of murder, but even if the plan was to paralyse them and dump them in a remote desert or snowfield, his immediate personal prospects were bleak. The weapon Vekrynn was holding may have been classed as harmless, but Hargate suspected that only held good for targets in normal health. In recent months he had been experiencing growing difficulty in breathing and coughing, and he was almost certain that any serious interference with his nerve functions would be lethal.

He gazed up at the two Mollanians, seeing them with preternatural clarity, while the fear that his life had ended pulsed behind his eyes. Lorrest, in spite of the terrible setback in his schemes, was playing his part with great skill. He looked sullen, disconsolate and beaten – perfectly concealing his knowledge that in a short time the machine his organization had planted in the Oceans of Storms would activate itself, and that Ceres would be drawn back on to its collision course. Hargate suddenly became aware that something in Lorrest's physical appearance had changed. He had not seen the Mollanian make any kind of movement with his hands, but now a rectangle of white card was projecting from his breast pocket.

Wondering if Vekrynn might sense any significance in the card, Hargate examined the Warden's resplendent figure and saw with some surprise that he was perspiring and that the close-waved blond hair was slightly in disarray.

*Why, he's just a man, after all*, he thought. *A man who invented a new kind of crime.* Abnormally keyed-up though he was, Hargate was unprepared for the firestorm of sheer hatred that blazed through his mind, robbing him of both his humanity and the power of sequential thought. A dozen voices seemed to yammer inside him at once, shrieking, advising, threatening, cajoling . . . *Enemy of my people, I need you to die . . . and all the days of Methuselah were nine hundred and sixty-nine years . . . Lorrest is too much the idealist to do what should be done . . . and Lamech lived after he begat Noah five hundred and ninety-five years . . . not only do I need you to die, enemy of my people, I personally need to smear your brain into the shit of your gut . . .*

'I don't think there is any point in prolonging this,' Vekrynn announced, a new note of finality entering his voice. He raised his pistol with obvious intent.

Hargate, all his attention concentrated on Vekrynn, received only a blurred impression of Lorrest diving towards the Warden, hands outstretched. Vekrynn fired the pistol in the same instant and the card projecting from Lorrest's pocket pulsed once with a fierce blue aura. An

216

intangible *something* hit Hargate, like the beating of rubber hammers over his entire body, stopping his breath. He heard Vekrynn give a startled grunt. Lorrest snatched the pistol from his hand and with a powerful twist of his wrists snapped it into two pieces. Vekrynn swayed like a teetering statue, but otherwise appeared unable to move.

Lorrest stared at him, his eyes baleful as he flung the ruined weapon to the ground. 'What's the classic line at this point, Vekrynn? It looks like the tables are turned?'

Hargate scarcely heard the words over the tumultuous pounding of his heart. The reflected backlash from Vekrynn's paralysis gun had been devastating in its effect. He was breathing rapidly, yet was in real danger of asphyxiating due to the fact that his lungs were unable to expand. His attempt to attract Lorrest's attention produced only harsh clicking sounds as the air he so desperately craved refused to penetrate any further than his throat.

'I'm warning you,' Vekrynn whispered, his voice hoarse and distorted with the strain of speaking. 'What you have done to me is . . .'

'What I've done to you is nothing to what I ought to do,' Lorrest interrupted savagely, advancing on the immobile figure of the Warden. 'I should kill you, Vekrynn. The only thing stopping me is that I don't want to be like you.'

'An animal can never be like a man.' Vekrynn, his face pale with strain, took a halting step towards Lorrest.

'Lie down before you fall.' As he spoke Lorrest put out his right hand, seemingly with the intention of pushing Vekrynn off his feet, but the thrust was never completed. As his fingers touched the material of Vekrynn's tunic there was a *splat* of unleashed energy and Lorrest dropped exactly where he had been standing, like a puppet whose string had been released. Vekrynn reeled grotesquely in a circle while he fought to remain upright.

Hargate, still waging his own inner battle, saw that

217

Lorrest was fully conscious, but apparently unable to move. He was emitting regular groaning sounds with each breath.

'Another fool,' Vekrynn commented, beginning a slow flexing of his fingers. 'What do they think I am?'

*I know what you are, enemy of my people*, Hargate thought, his brain stirring into action as air finally began to make its way into his lungs, removing the immediate threat of death. It occurred to him that he had been lucky to receive only a fraction of the reflected discharge – anything like the amount stopped by Vekrynn would have shut down his nervous system for ever. He moved his arms, satisfying himself that they were sufficiently functional for what he had to do, and – scarcely able to believe what was happening to him – came to a terrible decision.

Grasping the wheels of his chair, he rolled himself closer to Vekrynn. Smiling his lop-sided smile, deliberately relaxing his eyes into a squint, he looked up at the Mollanian and extended one hand.

'Please listen to me, sir,' he said. 'This isn't my fight. None of this had anything to do with me. Please take me back to Earth and I'll make it worth your while.'

Vekrynn managed a small step back, his mouth working with revulsion. 'What do you think you're talking about?'

'I'm talking about the Moon.' Hargate glanced at the crumpled figure of Lorrest and gave a nasal snigger. 'There's a machine there, in the Oceanus Procellarum. I believe Lorrest called it a cone field generator. It will activate itself in a few minutes before Ceres is due to go by – and you know what that means, don't you?'

'Don't believe him,' Lorrest ground out, his neck corded with the effort of speaking. 'It's a trick.'

'Trick? Trick?' The Warden shuffled slightly, almost losing his balance, and looked down at Hargate. 'If what you are saying is true, there isn't any time for me to . . .'

218

'It *is* true and there is *time*,' Hargate cut in. 'They located a node there – that's why the spot was chosen – and I can tell you exactly where it is. You've got time to go there and . . .'

'*Denny!*' Lorrest twitched convulsively. 'You can't do this!'

'Keep it shut,' Hargate said with a contemptuous wave. 'Why should I get done over you? I want to go home.'

'That can easily be arranged,' Vekrynn said urgently. 'You claim you know the position of the machine and the node?'

'You bet! I can give you its lunar coordinates, or I can even work out the Mollanian equation for you.'

'I doubt very much that you could – it will be enough if you simply tell me its position.'

'Not so fast, man.' Hargate renewed his grin. 'Do we have a deal?'

'Most certainly – as soon as you demonstrate that you can fulfil your side of the bargain.'

'Okay.' Ignoring Lorrest's desperate efforts to shout him down, Hargate summoned from his memory the precise coordinates given to him earlier and slowly called out the figures. Vekrynn nodded repeatedly as he absorbed the information.

'I'm grateful to you,' he said, gazing intently at Hargate as though seeing him for the first time. 'Now we must hurry. Can you reach the top of this hummock unaided?'

'I believe so.' With Hargate struggling to overcome some loss of strength and feeling in his arms, and the Mollanian progressing by ludicrously small steps, they reached the crest at approximately the same time. The Warden's broad face was drawn and liberally streaked with perspiration, evidence of the tremendous physical effort he was making in order to move at all. Bending his arms with agonized slowness, he fumbled with one of the square links of his golden belt, causing it to spring open like a locket. Inside was a small piece of what looked like dark red glass which Vekrynn touched briefly before closing the link again.

'Dome field generator,' he explained. 'We must take air with us.'

'With *us*? I don't want to go to the Moon.'

'But it's so close to your final destination,' Vekrynn replied reasonably. 'A very small detour.'

'Does this mean you don't trust me?'

'Of course not! I trust you every bit as much as you trust me.' Vekrynn extended his left hand for Hargate to clasp it and, eyes narrowing with the exertion, gradually raised his right hand in preparation for the tracing of a mnemo-curve.

*The Moon!* Hargate had expected to feel terror, but instead a deep searching sadness diffused through him as he considered what he had to do, the obligation he had accepted on behalf of every man, woman and child now living on his home world, and with the mute authority of all those who had gone before. *Bring me my bow of burning gold, bring me my wheelchair of fire . . .*

The transfer took place.

In spite of his foreknowledge of where he was going and the fact that he had seen a thousand pictures of the Moon's surface, Hargate gasped aloud as the sky went black. His previous jumps between habitable worlds, dramatic though they were, had not equalled the emotional shock of seeing a carpet of living turf instantaneously replaced by the ancient and sterile dust of the Oceanus Procellarum. The plain stretched without interruption to the horizon, with the few distant mountain peaks that were visible rising from beyond the curve of the lifeless world. A blindingly brilliant sun hung almost at the zenith, drenching everything with a harsh vertical light, and closer to the horizon Earth was visible as a blue-white hemisphere.

Taking his bearings from familiar star groupings, Hargate swung his gaze around the plane of the ecliptic and almost immediately found what he was seeking. Low down in the sky was an object that had no right to be there, a celestial trespasser. The asteroid Ceres was visible as a first-magnitude star. In Hargate's imagination he could see it growing brighter by the second as it bored its way in at inconceivable velocity from beyond the orbit of Mars. He glanced at his watch and his eyes dilated as he saw that the collision time quoted to him by Lorrest was closer than he had realized. In a scant eighteen minutes a ball of rock seven hundred kilometres in diameter was going to impact with the force of millions of H-bombs, and he – Denny Hargate – was sitting at the precise centre of what would become a continent-sized crater.

'Where is the machine?' Vekrynn shouted, tottering away from Hargate. 'I don't see the machine.'

Wrenching his thoughts away from visions of hell, Hargate shielded his eyes and scanned his surroundings. The first thing he noticed was that there were numerous footprints in the dust beneath his chair. They formed an irregular swathe leading to an area, perhaps fifty paces away, where the surface had been extensively disturbed, apparently by excavation.

*Lorrest didn't tell me they'd buried the machine*, he thought. *So much the better*.

'Over there,' he called out. 'It seems to be under the ground.'

Vekrynn turned in the direction indicated, broke into a hobbling run and promptly pitched forward. The semi-paralysis that still affected his mobility prevented him from breaking the fall with his hands, even though it

221

seemed to Hargate that he had gone down in a dreamlike slow motion. Vekrynn lay prone in the dust for a moment, then struggled to his feet and resumed his progress at a more prudent speed. It took Hargate several seconds to appreciate that the lesser gravity of the Moon was actually making walking more difficult for the Mollanian in his present condition.

He switched on the wheelchair's power and moved the drive control. As he had expected, the chair surged forward, its partially rested batteries more than adequate for propulsion when the whole assemblage had only a sixth of its weight on Earth. For the time being, he was in the novel situation of being more mobile than his adversary.

'It's all working out my way, Vekrynn, you bastard,' he whispered vindictively, reaching into the hiding place between his right hip and the back of his chair. 'Perhaps there *is* some justice in this universe – perhaps there's just a trace.'

Vekrynn, having finally reached the site of the excavation, studied the broken ground for a short time and looked up with evident surprise as Hargate brought his chair to a halt close by. 'What did they think they were achieving?' he said. 'I may not be able to deactivate this type of machine from here, but I can do it from there.' He nodded in the direction of Ceres.

Hargate glanced at the oncoming asteroid and was positive he could now discern an increase in its brightness. 'How?'

'That region of space is filled with Bureau engineers and equipment. I can contact my men from here and in less than a minute have this site vaporized to a depth of a thousand metres. That will take care of any number of cone field generators.'

'I daresay.' Hargate frowned thoughtfully. 'I suppose it will also take care of us if we don't transfer out of here.'

'Your grasp of the situation is excellent,' Vekrynn said, beginning to smile. 'The Ceres operation is being directed from a small space habitat centred on a drifting node little more than a light second from here. That will be my vantage point for the final minutes of this affair.'

'Suits me fine – Let's go.'

'I'm afraid your understanding of the situation isn't quite as good as I thought.' Vekrynn turned and began to shuffle towards the point at which they had arrived, exercising great care with his balance. 'I'm not taking you with me.'

'You can't leave me here,' Hargate said in a kind of startled whinny, going after the retreating figure. 'The stuff they pour in here is bound to kill me.'

'Wrong again!' Vekrynn did not look back, but his voice carried clearly. 'When I transfer away from this dismal spot my dome field and the air it contains will go with me. No, I don't think you need worry about being vaporized.'

Hargate swore loudly and increased his speed. 'Let's drop all the phoney Agatha Christie politeness, Vekrynn. I'm not letting you go anywhere.'

The Mollanian continued his ungainly progress, still without looking back.

'Listen to me, Vekrynn, you great bag of dung,' Hargate shouted, acutely aware that Ceres was no longer a star-like point of light. Within a very short time it had begun to exhibit a visible disc – testimony to its frightening speed.

Vekrynn kept on lurching forward, seemingly oblivious to everything in his determination to reach the nodal point.

'Lorrest put one over on you,' Hargate said gently. 'We found the sixth copy of your Notebook. We know you, Vekrynn.'

The Warden stopped abruptly, a huge clockwork figure

whose mechanism had jammed. Hargate steered to the right and went in a semi-circle which enabled him to halt directly in front of the Mollanian. In the relentless vertical light Vekrynn's face was no longer human, the eye sockets reduced to blind black cavities. He remained motionless for a few seconds, then started forward with increased urgency.

'I told you I wasn't letting you go anywhere.' Hargate reached down behind his right hip, brought out his most treasured possession – the complex, glittering shape of the Mollanian travel trainer – and held it aloft like a talisman.

'Look at this, Vekrynn,' he gloated. 'Look at the curve, Vekrynn – it's the one you just used to get to this place. I've *got* you.'

Vekrynn uttered a single word in Mollanian and swayed directly towards Hargate. Remembering the effect on Lorrest of one brief contact with the Warden's tunic, Hargate hastily selected maximum speed and swung the chair out of Vekrynn's path. Vekrynn changed direction and came after him.

There followed a nightmarish sequence in which the Mollanian, in spite of repeated falls, pursued him in a snaking course throughout the vicinity of the nodal point. A minute and then another minute went by, and Hargate made two unnerving discoveries – that his batteries were growing perceptibly weaker, and that Vekrynn was learning to cope better with the lunar gravity. Instead of simply trying to overtake the wheelchair, he began launching himself at Hargate in a series of sprawling dives which carried him several metres through the air and which at times brought him dangerously close. Hargate had to assist the chair's slowly fading drive with his hands in order to evade the hurtling giant, and he began to panic as he realized that were he to topple over Vekrynn would be upon him before he could hope to move again.

He was profoundly relieved therefore when the bizarre hunt came to an unexpected end. Vekrynn, his face and clothing caked with grey dust, struggled into a crouching position, but instead of turning towards Hargate he remained doubled over, staring at the sky. Hargate followed the direction of his gaze and quailed as he saw that Ceres, closer now to the horizon, had become an irregular patch of brilliance whose intensity changed every few seconds. The asteroid was tumbling in its course, bearing down on them, winking like a malign eye. As he watched in frozen fascination, a bluish glow sprang into existence off to his left at the site of the buried machine, and he knew that the awesome rendezvous had become inevitable.

Vekrynn gave a tremulous sob, straightened up and – turning his back on Hargate – floundered towards the nodal point with the dragging gait of a man wading in deep water. Hargate rolled after him, getting as close as he dared. On reaching the node Vekrynn stumbled to a halt and raised his right hand. Circling round to the front, Hargate saw that the Mollanian's eyes were closed and his lips were moving silently.

'It's no use, Vekrynn!' Hargate grasped the bright shape of the training device in one hand and began running his fingers along its curvatures. 'You can't concentrate. You can't get away from me. You're in the middle of a third-order whirlpool and you're going to stay in it.'

He began to chant the terms of the equation which had brought him to the Ocean of Storms, using them like an incantation which gave him the power over Vekrynn's mind and body. The new phase of the duel between the two men lasted more than a minute, then Vekrynn sagged on to his knees, and covered his face with his hands.

'Why are you doing this?' he breathed, his voice barely audible. 'I can't die, I can't die, I can't die.'

'You're not about to,' Hargate said peacefully. 'Provided you do exactly as I say.'

Vekrynn was silent for a moment. 'I can't *die*.'

'Right. I want you to switch on your communicator – the one you were going to use to call your engineers – and I want you to put it on the ground where it can see and hear us.'

Vekrynn removed a bracelet from his wrist with unsteady fingers and set it in the dust in front of him.

'I want proof it's working,' Hargate snapped. 'I want a response.'

Vekrynn mumbled a few words in Mollanian. There was a brief silence and three or four voices answered simultaneously. By a technology that Hargate could not even visualize, the fidelity of the reproduction was almost perfect.

'That seems good enough,' he said. 'I'm sure you know what to do next.'

Vekrynn remained silent, head bowed, face again hidden in his hands.

Hargate numbered off sixty seconds before saying, 'Vekrynn, you must tell us what is in the preface to the sixth copy of your book. And I want it in English.'

When there was no response he counted a further sixty seconds and said, 'Vekrynn, I think you ought to take another look at Ceres – it's becoming quite a spectacle.'

He glanced over his shoulder as he spoke and was appalled by the gross changes in the asteroid's appearance. It had swollen sufficiently for its rotation to be visible as a continual alteration of its shape. It appeared to be alive, quivering and bristling with menace, and the knowledge that the colossal energy it contained would atomize the plain on which he was sitting for hundreds of kilometres in every direction filled Hargate with a near-superstitious dread. The amount of overkill was irrelevant

– but the sheer magnitude of the impending destruction had a desolating effect on his soul. *We're not much*, he thought. *We don't amount to . . .*

'Confession?' Vekrynn suddenly blurted. '*Confession!* 'Since when has total dedication to the Preservationist goal been a crime?'

Turning in the direction of the voice, Hargate saw that Vekrynn had risen to his feet. Instinctively he started to roll his chair backwards, but checked himself when he saw that the Mollanian was no longer aware of his existence. Vekrynn had begun to brush the lunar dust from his tunic with slow and uncoordinated movements, and had turned his face to the sky, possibly in the direction of his home world.

'The Government of Mollan can only guide our social evolution by means of one instrument – and the instrument is *knowledge*. Surely the greatest gift the Bureau of Wardens can bring to the people of Mollan is *knowledge*. It is my intention, my ambition, to give you sociological data in its ultimate form – the detailed chart of a technological culture from its earliest beginnings to its self-inflicted end.' Vekrynn paused and drew himself up to his full height.

'I am a patriot, and if I am guilty of any wrong it is that of personal pride – I longed to perform the greatest possible service for my people. It is true that when I found the planet Earth in my youth the life expectancy of its inhabitants was close to the human norm, but what is the value of a life spent in that insane chaos? Who could *want* to endure centuries of such an existence?

'For a culture trying to evolve in that turmoil of third-order forces there could be only one outcome, one inevitable fate. Better by far to accelerate the whole process . . . to have done with it . . . and to salvage something of permanent value . . .' Vekrynn's tone became uncertain and he lapsed into silence.

'You're not finished yet,' Hargate prompted. 'And time is running out.'

Vekrynn stared briefly at the ominous patch of light which pulsed and pounded low above the horizon. A visible tremor coursed through his body.

'The torpedoes were upper atmosphere coasters of the type used on Mollan during the Second Epoch to seed the biosphere with longevity agents. But in the case of Earth . . .'

'Go on,' Hargate said, a black chill filtering downwards from his brain, numbing his whole body.

'In the case of Earth they contained a thymosin degrading agent which – over a period of several centuries – had the effect of reducing human life expectancy to . . . to seven decades.' Vekrynn paused, and when he spoke again his voice was stronger. 'My life's work, my *Analytical Notes on the Evolution of One Human Civilization*, will soon be completed and will be of incalculable value to all Mollanians. That is my personal statement, my justification, my *boast*.'

Hargate gave a deep involuntary sigh which, even to his own ears, sounded like the relinquishment of life. He had expected Vekrynn's words, the naked confession of a crime that was beyond comprehension, to engulf him in a plasma of hatred and fury – but there was only a melancholic detachment, a sense of resignation. *I guess it hardly matters*, he thought. *It's just as easy this way, and the end result will be the same.*

'I trust you are satisfied,' Vekrynn said loudly and with a hint of manic jubilation. 'I am ready now to face my peers, to accept their judgement.'

'I dare say you are.' Hargate backed his chair off a short distance and raised the Mollanian travel trainer from his lap. 'But that's not the way it's going to be.'

'What are you saying?'

'I'm saying that you – as well as being a mass-murderer – are a liar, Vekrynn. I'm no psychoanalyst, but I know you don't really care a shit about preserving the Mollanian culture. You are pathologically afraid of dying, and that's the real reason for everything you've done. Your Notebook is symbolic immortality. You've cast yourself in the role of God – overseeing all that happens on Earth, from beginning to end, from Genesis to Revelations – and gods aren't supposed to die. Are they, Vekrynn?'

Hargate turned his gaze towards the sky and looked at the face of Ceres. It was bloated, poisoned, grinning, visibly swelling. He began to speak faster.

'I'm also saying that you will answer for your crimes right here – not on Mollan. I know that your people don't believe in the death penalty – but I do. You are looking at your judge, Vekrynn, and I'm sentencing you to death.'

'No! This can't . . ' Vekrynn swayed once in a complete circle, like a monolith that was being undermined. 'You don't want to die.'

'That's right,' Hargate said, summoning up his lop-sided grin. 'But I'm a vindictive little bastard.'

He tensed himself for flight, fearing that desperation might enable Vekrynn to overcome his slow-fading paralysis, but the Mollanian stood perfectly still, transfixed, mumbling. His eyes were locked on the fell apparition that had begun to dominate the lower sky.

Holding the pliant metal of the travel trainer before his face, whispering its mathematical spell, Hargate engaged the drive of his chair and slowly circled around the nodal point to a position from which he could see both Vekrynn and the hurtling mass of Ceres. The asteroid now occupied an area many times larger than that of the Moon as seen from Earth, and its tumbling motion was clearly apparent, giving it an intimidating solidity not associated with celestial objects. It was easy for Hargate, staring at the expanding asteroid, to appreciate that the energy bound up in it would be enough to set the Moon spinning wildly on its axis, to bring about the gravitational destruction of an entire world.

*It can't be long now*, he mused. *Two minutes, three at the most – then everything will be the way it was before I was born.*

He considered the prospect with a kind of wan disbelief, and his consciousness ricocheted away into the past. Again he felt the handgrips of the duralloy crutches become buttery with sweat, again he heard the purposeful drone of insects and rustle of dry grasses. The yellow hillside shimmered before his eyes and the plume of field maples beckoned at its crest against a wind-busy sky. He was going again to Cotter's Edge, to the secret place, and there he was going to meet . . .

'Gretana!' He called her name involuntarily as the slim, auburn-haired figure – looking exactly as she had done when he was twelve years old – materialized at the nodal point close to Vekrynn, as though he had conjured her by the sheer force of his nostalgic longing. She glanced once at Vekrynn, who was still lost in communion his with blind executioner, then came running towards Hargate. Boosted by the weakness of the lunar gravity, she covered the intervening ground in two precarious steps, lost her balance and pitched on to her knees at Hargate's side, gripping the arm of his chair for support. The miracle of her presence swamped his senses.

'You've got to let Vekrynn go,' she pleaded, green eyes seizing on his. 'You've done enough, Denny – hundreds of people at the habitat heard what he said.'

'That isn't enough,' he said dully, wondering how he could deny her anything. 'Not for Vekrynn.'

'But you don't want to be a killer.'

'You're wrong, Gretana.' He reached out and touched

230

the face that had haunted most of his days, then a new kind of fear geysered through his mind. 'For God's sake, get out of here! Get away from this place!'

Almost smiling, she touched the gleaming sculpture of the travel trainer. 'How can I, Denny? You're holding me here.'

Hargate sobbed once in his anguish as he collapsed the artifact into the neutral configuration.

He tried to beg Gretana to run for the nodal point and save herself, but the words died in his throat as he looked beyond her and saw the monstrous, glowering countenance of Ceres now filling an eighth of the sky.

For a moment he tried to resist as Gretana swung herself round to the back of the chair and began pushing him in the direction of Vekrynn and the node, then he realized she was not going to let go and that his suicidal perversity was threatening her life. He urged the chair forward, and Ceres swelled hugely, rushing to meet them, completely outlining the motionless figure of Vekrynn.

Hargate felt Gretana's left hand close on his. Obeying her unspoken command, he snatched for Vekrynn's hand, but a shrilling, gibbering voice told him it was already too late . . . *because the whole sky was a convexity of falling rock . . .*

Within twenty seconds of skording to the Bureau's nearby habitat, Gretana had positioned the wheelchair at one of the solid-image projectors which were providing the Mollanian engineers with a magnified view of the Moon.

But by that time Ceres had already kissed the surface of the Sea of Storms, and had half-exploded, half-blossomed into a spray of whirling fragments which were racing on divergent courses towards the outer darkness of the solar system.

And, although it was not immediately apparent, the

Moon had been jolted out of its aeons-old quiescence, and had begun to spin. Destructive stresses were sundering ancient geological strata as they sped towards the Moon's core.

Hargate watched the spectacle in silence, rediscovering the meanings of words like awe and blasphemy and pride, then he looked up at Gretana. 'Do you think Lorrest is right?' he said. 'Is this the start of a new age?'

'I don't see how anybody can hold it back,' she murmured. 'Not now. Not on Earth. Not on Mollan.'

'In that case maybe I'd like to go back to Earth, after all,' Hargate said reflectively. 'Just for a while.'

# EPILOGUE

It was late afternoon in mid-winter, and a hard clear darkness had moved in over Carsewell and the neighbouring borough of Star City.

Gretana paused on the steps of the Mollanian Embassy to button up the collar of her overcoat, her gaze drifting across the electrically-jewelled architecture of the diplomatic and trade buildings of more than thirty worlds. They were arranged in sweeping crescents around a park containing the low hill which had once been known locally as Cotter's Edge. In some respects it would have been more convenient to have Star City close to Washington, DC, but new priorities had dictated that it be built around a major east coast node. Gretana found the ambience of the scene reassuring and, as always, she was prompted to look for a moment at the sky.

The stars were only faintly visible through the wash of urban radiance, but the swarms of irregular moonlets that formed the horizon-to-horizon band across the heavens shone with undimmed lustre. Dissolution of the old Moon had been accelerated by enlightened UN policies – all companies to whom mining franchises were awarded ¹ ad to assist in equalizing the orbital distribution of the lu. 'ar mass. As a result, even a Mollanian with Gretana's perceptiveness could sense no real disturbance in the matrix of third-order forces. It was now possible for embryos to grow in peace, for babes to be born in peace.

She turned up her collar against the cold and was about to go down the remaining steps when she saw a figure in a grey one-piece heatsaver ascending towards her. For an instant she thought he was an exceptionally tall Terran, then – with a tingling shock of recognition – she noticed the lean, beard-shadowed face and the sculpted black hair. She stopped abruptly, taken unawares by a conflict of emotions.

'Gretana!' Lorrest's face registered surprise and pleasure. 'I was hoping to get here before you left. How are you?'

'That's an Earth-style greeting,' she said, with greater coolness than she had intended. 'You know a Mollanian is always in peak condition. You're supposed to say "Fair Seaons".'

'I thought you might have gone native by this time.' He gave her a candid stare, his expression changing to one of seriousness. 'Gretana, I've just arrived on Earth, and I've got to get this out of the way first – do you know the murder charge against me was dropped? My cerebric deposition showed I acted only to save you.'

She avoided his gaze. 'I heard that. It was just that actually *seeing* the . . . Can't we forget all about it?'

'Please do. That's what I had to do to live with myself, and it wasn't easy. I've been doing four decades of rather boring community service on Mollan for my other misdeeds – and there weren't too many distractions.'

'I knew you'd been sentenced.'

Lorrest shrugged. 'I was lucky enough. It would have been ten times as long if Vekrynn's case hadn't set off all the changes back there.'

'I haven't been back to Mollan even once,' Gretana said. 'With one thing and another, I haven't even considered it.'

'Very cosmopolitan,' Lorrest said, looking impressed. 'What sort of work do you do?'

'Emigration counselling mostly. Now that we're pumping longevity agents into the biosphere the population problem is going to get worse for a while. The birth rate is dropping like a stone, as you would expect, and most of the people born here within the last forty years have the ability to skord out – but there's a lot of work to do.'

'I can imagine,' Lorrest said. 'It's going to be funny to see these people spreading out to other worlds.'

'Funny?' Gretana thought about the way in which the Terrans had been moving out into space for only a few decades, and the demands they had already begun to make, starting with the Earth-type world Vekrynn had found far inside the Attatorian sector. 'They're already a bit restless with sector system.'

'That's all right – all systems must adapt to change.'

'Yes, but nobody knows how it's going to end.'

'That's good, too.'

'This isn't a good place to talk,' Gretana said, shivering slightly. 'The cafeteria here has quite acceptable Eyrej dewberry juice, if you've got time.'

'You remembered my favourite!' Lorrest gave an exaggerated leer. 'Does that mean . . .?'

'It means I've got a good memory,' she cut in, indicating the way to the cafeteria at the rear of the building, and wondering why it was that Lorrest was able to disturb her composure with the most casual remark. When they were seated in a booth, with beakers of hot amber-coloured juice before them, she resolved to take a less passive part in the conversation, to give Lorrest less chance to be disconcerting.

'I see,' she said, glancing at him over the rim of her beaker, 'that you haven't had reversal surgery.'

Lorrest toyed with his glass. 'I was offered it, but I said no, mainly because I knew I'd be coming back to Earth, and I really want to *work* with these people. Anyway, things are really changing on Mollan – you can quite often see a Terran on a city street and hardly anybody stares at him. How about you?'

'I had the offer, too, but by then I'd proved to myself that the Lucent Ideal is a parochial concept.' Gretana stared down at the vapour patterns swirling on the surface of her drink. 'Besides, I didn't want a certain character calling me Big-head.'

'I doubt if he'd have been as polite as that.' Lorrest's face became solemn, childishly wistful. 'I've got to find out about Denny. How long did . . .?'

'He lived almost another three years.'

'Did you stay with him?'

'Yes. In fact, we got married. When he came out with the suggestion I was so astonished that I said yes before I realized what was happening.' Gretana tried to smile. 'You should have heard the proposal – he ended up by saying he wouldn't be able to consummate the marriage, only he didn't put it as delicately as that, but it shouldn't matter to somebody from a race of undersexed beanpoles.'

'Perfect,' Lorrest said, his eyes growing thoughtful. 'You know, the worst thing about having to stand trial was that they wouldn't let me come back to see Denny. I was pretty mad at him when we parted company. I had no idea . . .'

'He understood.'

'I'm really glad. I suppose he kept on trying to skord?'

'For a while, then he pretended it wasn't worth the effort when I was around all the time to do it for him. It's hard to believe, but we visited more than eighty worlds. Even at the very end – when he couldn't move his arms and needed servo assistance to breathe – we made a trip every few days, always to a planet he'd never been on before.'

'His personal mathematics.'

'Yes.'

'I can believe it.' Lorrest pushed his drink away, almost untouched. 'I've got to go, Gretana. I've got myself a brand-new job, designing educational imprints in the Hamito-Semitic languages group, and I haven't even reported in yet. I wanted to see you first.'

'I'm pleased that you did,' Gretana said, watching Lorrest get to his feet. 'Will we be seeing each other?'

'Do you want to?'

Gretana sighed impatiently. 'Would I have asked?'

'Relax,' Lorrest said, his shoulders giving a preliminary heave. 'I just wanted to hear you say it.'

Watching him hurry away through the peachy twilight of the cafeteria, Gretana realized he was struggling to suppress one of his laughs and she found herself unable to stop smiling. She finished her drink at a leisurely pace and went out through the building and down the bowed steps of the Embassy's main entrance.

The darkness of the park was split into many wedge-shaped sections by the glowing paths which converged on the floodlit nodal point at its centre. Because of the high density of the traffic between Star City and the other worlds in the new Federation, it had been necessary to clear away the maples and other vegetation that had once screened the node. Gretana gazed at the spot for a moment, newly-awakened memories causing her to wish that at least one tree could have been preserved, then she recalled that Denny Hargate had never had any use for symbolism.

*Concentrate on the real thing while you have the chance,* he would have said.

She nodded once, no longer smiling, and walked away in the direction of the future.

*Observe!*

*The planet falls away beneath us, then its sun, then the other stars in that part of an undistinguished galaxy. Now we see the star clouds shrinking, condensing into a spiral of light, and other island universes crowd into our field of view.*

*Let us consider important questions.*

*Have we – whose lifespans compare to those of Molla-nians as those of Terrans do to their mayflies – learned anything from the example of Denny Hargate?*

*Have we pofited from the association?*

*If not, let us hope that we will fare better on the million worlds we must visit before childhood ends.*

*Let us hope!*

## THE WORLD'S GREATEST SCIENCE FICTION AUTHORS
## NOW AVAILABLE IN GRANADA PAPERBACKS

**Ursula K LeGuin**

| | | |
|---|---|---|
| The Dispossessed | £1.50 | ☐ |
| The Lathe of Heaven | £1.25 | ☐ |
| City of Illusions | £1.25 | ☐ |
| Malafrena | £1.50 | ☐ |
| Threshold | £1.25 | ☐ |

*Short Stories*

| | | |
|---|---|---|
| Orsinian Tales | £1.50 | ☐ |
| The Wind's Twelve Quarters (Volume 1) | £1.25 | ☐ |
| The Wind's Twelve Quarters (Volume 2) | £1.25 | ☐ |

**Ursula K LeGuin and Others**

| | | |
|---|---|---|
| The Eye of the Heron | £1.25 | ☐ |

**Ian Watson**

| | | |
|---|---|---|
| The Very Slow Time Machine | £1.25 | ☐ |
| God's World | £1.50 | ☐ |

SF481

All these books are available at your local bookshop or newsagent, and can be ordered direct from the publisher.

*To order direct from the publisher just tick the titles you want and fill in the form below:*

Name _____

Address _____

_____

Send to:
**Granada Cash Sales**
**PO Box 11, Falmouth, Cornwall TR10 9EN**

Please enclose remittance to the value of the cover price plus:

**UK** 45p for the first book, 20p for the second book plus 14p per copy for each additional book ordered to a maximum charge of £1.63.

**BFPO and Eire** 45p for the first book, 20p for the second book plus 14p per copy for the next 7 books, thereafter 8p per book.

**Overseas** 75p for the first book and 21p for each additional book.

Granada Publishing reserve the right to show new retail prices on covers, which may differ from those previously advertised in the text or elsewhere.